A DESTINED TO FAIL NOVEL

HAYDEN HALL

Copyright © 2023 by Hayden Hall

All rights reserved.

No part of this publication may be reproduced, stored or transmitted in any form or by any means, electronic, mechanical, photocopying, recording, scanning, or otherwise without written permission from the publisher. It is illegal to copy this book, post it to a website, or distribute it by any other means without permission.

This novel is entirely a work of fiction. The names, characters and incidents portrayed in it are the work of the author's imagination. Any resemblance to actual persons, living or dead, events or localities is entirely coincidental.

Edited by Sabrina Hutchinson

Cover by Cate Ashwood

Photo by Edgar Marx (xramragde)

Written by Hayden Hall

www.haydenhallwrites.com

ISBN: 979-8-3778-9831-3

CONTENTS

Preface	V
Prologue	1
1. Levi	17
2. Parrish	37
3. Levi	60
4. Parrish	71
5. Levi	91
6. Parrish	103
7. Levi	116
8. Parrish	128
9. Levi	139
10. Parrish	165
11. Levi	177
12. Parrish	188
13. Parrish	209
14. Levi	222

15.	Parrish	235
16.	Levi	247
17.	Parrish	262
Epilogue		274
Acknowledgments		283
More Stories From Hayden Hall		285
About Hayden Hall		287

PREFACE

Thank you for choosing to read *Destructive Relations*. Before you proceed, please be aware that this story features stepbrothers falling in love, mature content, foul language, and all the fun things you already expect from Hayden Hall. However, *Destructive Relations* also features light BDSM (specifically, bondage and some dom/sub dynamic between the protagonists). If you're cool with that, read on.

PROLOGUE

My ears rang while she spoke.

At some point in this whole fucking mess, her voice morphed into a high-pitched buzz that filled my head. Her lips kept moving. Sharp lips. Lots of red lipstick. The skin creased around her eyes and the corners of her mouth as she said that she was sorry it came to this.

I stopped listening a while ago.

Right around the time she said: "I think it's best for everyone if you move out."

Her husband of seven years crossed his arms over his chest like a club bouncer and gave a grave nod.

I didn't look at him. It amused me to imagine him hyping himself up for the role, taking deep breaths to make his chest appear larger, and frowning at the mirror in search of that unique look of fatherly disappointment.

Not that Harold Bartlet was my father. But he sure liked playing the role. "Now, Parrish, you can't speak like that to your mother," was his favorite of *disappointed dad* phrases. That was because he couldn't meddle too much. I wasn't his son to school. He had his own offshoot upstairs; the best boy ever created, incapable of doing the wrong thing.

Margaret preferred saying things like: "Don't you dare use that tone with me, young man," even as I pushed into my twenty-third miserable year.

"Parrish?" Margaret's voice was deep and warm, whereas Harold spoke in a nasal, metallic rasp. This was her calling me back to the present moment. "Parrish, are you even listening to what I'm saying?"

"Yeah," I said, voice oddly dull. "Got it."

Fuck me if I did, I thought. She could have been telling me that the Martians invaded our planet and were heading straight for River Bend to crown her as their queen. How long did it take a person to monologue about throwing their son out of their house before they felt their conscience was clear?

"Then you understand why we don't have a choice in this matter," she said, not quite asking, but still expecting a reply.

"I totally understand," I said with a sarcastic compassion. "Your hands are tied, Marge."

My sarcasm translated. Harold's arms dropped by his sides and Margaret's face hardened. "Don't be like that.

Why are you always like that?" She slurred these words all at once, somehow.

This, at last, made me grin. *I win*, I thought. It was petty for sure, but you had to give the newly homeless guy a break.

I'd stopped arguing with Harold and Marge a while ago. When I realized annoying them subtly was so much more enjoyable than shouting the roof off the house, I changed my tactics. Now, they had no idea what to do with me.

It hurt Marge on that artificial level where she was expected to be hurting. You know? A weeping mother who didn't deserve a troublemaker of a son who only ever disgraced the family.

Family this, family that. It was always about our family. What a dumb joke. We had never been a family despite their desperate attempts. Harold had known that all along. That was why he couldn't scold me as often as he would have liked. Oh, there had been an odd occasion now and again when he grabbed me by my arm and dragged me where nobody could hear us, then told me things. Empty threats. Poorly disguised desperate pleas for the sake of my mother.

And then, there was Natalie. My little sister. She'd fallen for the story they'd told her. Abandoned by our actual father before she ever got to know him, Natalie had welcomed two new residents into our house. She was just happy to have a bigger family, even if they never could be our family. We had been doing well on our own. We didn't need our estranged father or his new, hot wife. The three of us had been enough. Or so I'd thought.

And finally, there was Levi.

Our little stepbrother. Not that he was so little anymore. At eighteen years old, his impression of a spoiled youngest child was no longer excusable. He still lived the geeky, carefree life like he had when he was only eleven. Bubbly, happy to be a part of the family, glad to have a substitute mommy, Levi was a fleeting annoyance in the periphery of my awareness. He was that scream of morning sunshine that woke you up when you were hungover. He was Vivaldi's *Spring* played at full blast as an alarm sound. He was Willy Wonka's on-screen introduction; and not the original one, but the cringe-inducing 'the Earth says hello' Johnny Depp one.

For a while there in the beginning, Levi had looked up to me the way Natalie had some years earlier. He'd looked at me like he had expected some profound life lessons an older brother could impart. Fuck him. He wasn't my anything. Never could be.

I had made sure quickly enough that Levi stopped harboring hopes he could ever be close to me. I had been sixteen when that nerdy eleven-year-old moved into our home and took the spare bedroom next to mine. Suddenly, he and I shared the bathroom that separated our rooms, and that rubbed me wrong, among all the other things he did. Harold took a heavy step forward and placed his hand on Margaret's shoulder. "Your mother and I are willing to overlook the damage to the car."

"How gracious," I said.

His mustache trembled. "You should be grateful, Parrish. Or would you rather we send you a bill?"

"Send where? I don't have an address," I said.

Margaret whimpered. *Give me a break*, I thought. *You're sorry that you'll have to explain this to people.* "Where's Parrish? Haven't seen him in a while." I could already hear Layla, Margaret's hairdresser, asking.

"Careful, Parrish," Harold continued, dropping his voice a little. He gave a nervous glance at Margaret, like he wasn't sure how far he was allowed to push me. After all, I was Margaret's son and her responsibility. "You're pushing it."

I leaned back on the dark green sofa. The dim lamp-lights made the entire room feel somber and a little stale. I never saw any warmth here. Not in the living room, not in the entire house.

"You will listen to Harold, young man," Margaret snapped. "This man has been nothing but kind to you for seven years and you've spat in his face whenever he offered you a hand of friendship."

Jeez. Could you be more dramatic? I nodded instead of saying that. "Okay. Then, *kindly*, could I get the fuck out of here now?"

"You can thank him for his patience with you," Margaret said, her voice dropping lower with every word. "The repairs will cost us a fortune. We'll have to spend our savings for Cabo, won't we, Harry? And you can't even apologize? Do you have nothing to say for yourself? Nothing to tell us?"

Would you believe me if I told you I swerved when a hedgehog scurried into the middle of the street? I thought. She hadn't believed me once since Harold dragged his perfect son into his house and made an example out of him. I was done trying.

I blinked in mock thought. "You know, now that I think about it...*No*."

Margaret pursed her lips at the same time Harold sighed. She glared at me with the restrained anger only a mother could feel. It didn't matter if we talked of a good mother who'd gotten a bad deal with her child or a crappy one who fussed over the appearances far more than she worried about her kids. Good thing I wasn't a kid anymore. And her eyes sparked with rage. And her lips quivered. "Get out," she spat.

I clapped my hands and hopped onto my feet.

Tears did well in her eyes, but I had a hard fucking time distinguishing hers from a crocodile's. "Bye," I singsonged as I headed up the stairs. I had shit to pack.

As I nearly reached the upper floor landing, I spotted her. Natalie. Standing in the doorway of her room. Though she was twenty years old now, she looked infinitely smaller in the pale night light coming from the open door. Her big eyes twinkled. "Parrish?" she whispered.

My throat constricted. "Hey," I managed to squeeze out.

"W-what happened?" she asked.

"Nothing," I said. "Everything's fine. Don't worry." I did my best impression of a soothing voice. I was shit at it. Especially with Natalie, who had been my world since Dad walked out on us.

"Don't lie," she said softly. "I heard Mom's voice."

I shrugged, holding onto the banister at the top of the stairs. "What did you hear?"

"She's upset," Natalie said.

I made a step toward her, my hand falling off the banister and hanging by my side. "I'm going to leave for some time," I said. My skill at talking softly about sensitive topics wasn't something I honed a lot. I was direct. Always. "I don't know how long."

"They're throwing you out?" Natalie asked, voice cracking. She made a jerky move, but paused like I was contaminated. Perhaps she knew that showing emotions wasn't my strength, so she spared me.

"Pretty much," I said.

"They can't," she protested.

"They can. And should. I overstayed my welcome," I said. "Twenty-three, remember?"

"I'm twenty and I'm still here," she pointed out.

"It's different," I said.

She understood my meaning. Natalie was someone we all loved no matter what. That was the only good thing I could say regarding Harold and Levi. Whatever their faults, they loved my little sister.

"I might have scratched the car a bit," I said with a sinister grin. "And got Officer Cooper to drag my ass here, threatening Marge that he'd jail me next time."

Natalie's eyes widened.

I didn't elaborate. It was funny in a dark and twisted way. I bumped the car against a lamppost while Cooper watched from the coffee shop where he'd been waiting for his caramel latte. He ran out and crossed the street, spilling hot coffee over his fingers. When he reached me, he set the cup on the hood of Marge's car, and had to wipe his sticky, burnt hand against his pristine uniform. That was probably what angered him the most. Not the fact that he'd been bringing me to Marge and Harold's door for the past seven years on numerous occasions. Misunderstandings, most of them, of course. What teenager with abandonment issues hadn't set trash on fire? Or bombarded the mayor's house with toilet paper and eggs? Or stolen a stop sign from an intersection? Or snuck into the police station and slipped a fart balloon under this very officer's cushion? Little things that brighten your life, right?

"Parrish, why?" Natalie asked, voice cracking again.

I spread my arms and pulled her in for what was supposed to be a comforting hug. "It's all good, Sis. I'll still see you all the time." I said that knowing there was no way I could make that promise. "You'll see. It's gonna be better than ever."

That was when Natalie cried. I couldn't be sure, but my guess was that she knew my words meant nothing. I was saying these things just to soften the blow. She probably knew they were as good as lies.

Natalie hugged me tightly, fingers clawing into my back, and sobbed quietly against my chest. At long last, when silence enveloped the entire house, she sniffed once again and pulled back. "Promise to call all the time, Parrish."

"I promise," I said right away. "All the time, you'll see."

"I'm not kidding," she said. "If you try pushing me away, too, I'll find you and kick your ass."

"I don't expect any less," I said. And, when I had nothing else to say, I added: "I should start packing."

"What? In the middle of the night?" she asked.

It was barely midnight, but that wasn't the point. "I wanna be out before they wake up."

"Goddammit, Parrish," she said softly with such bitter regret that it tickled my eyes.

I shrugged in defense. "I'm sorry."

Natalie nodded, mouthed that she loved me, and smiled when I mouthed it back. We'd had that thing going on for ages. I had always been awkward around speaking the exact words. Natalie had been the first to mouth the words instead.

I would never forget the delight on her face when I returned the gesture.

She shut the door and I walked down the hallway, past Levi's room and into mine. His was in the middle of the upper floor's plan. Down the hallway was my room.

I barged into the room, then stormed into our shared bathroom to gather my shit.

Not a minute later, the other bathroom door creaked open. "Parrish?" he whispered.

"Mm." With him, I had the least amount of patience. Less every day. Lately — well, for the last couple of years, really, but I pretended I hadn't noticed until a few months ago — Levi had been changing. Something about his behavior was always shifting.

He was still that bubbly person he'd always been. But he had also gotten moody with me. Not that I paid much attention, but it was hard to miss when your roommate was sulking for no fucking reason.

But, the truth was, I cared so little about Levi Bartlet that I never bothered to find out what caused these mood shifts around me.

"What's going on? Is Natalie crying?" Levi asked.

I rolled my eyes. Couldn't he see I was trying to ignore him? Why the hell did he have to go and make himself appear good by worrying about Natalie? "She's fine," I said.

"Oh," he muttered as he leaned against the doorframe. His blond hair appeared silver in the moonlight that poured through the small window looking over the backyard. "It's just, I thought I heard some noises from downstairs."

I walked out of our bathroom and headed for my closet. Levi followed behind me and watched as I began throwing my things out on the floor. "Nope," I said. "You must have dreamed it."

"I wasn't sleeping," he said harshly. "Don't treat me like a child."

"Don't be one, then," I said, not even looking at him. Within seconds, my T-shirts cluttered the floor around me, pants falling on top of them. I couldn't pack all my shit, but I didn't want to leave some behind either. Not that there was a tradition of Levi inheriting my worn out stuff, but I still didn't want to risk him destroying my style. This was the guy that could make ripped skinny jeans lame.

"What are you doing?" he asked.

"Minding my business," I said matter-of-factly.

"Parrish," he said, firmer.

I spun my head to face him as he stood up. "What do you want?"

"I want you to tell me what the hell is going on," he insisted.

"Marge and Harry will tell you tomorrow. It's not my fucking job to keep you posted." I turned away from him and found my duffel. Quickly, I started filling it with my clothes.

Levi crossed the short distance between us before I was completely aware of him and touched my shoulder. My defensive instincts, mixed with my anger at the turn of the evening's events, got the better of me. I grabbed his wrist, twisted his arm up behind his back, and pressed him face-first against the closed side of the closet.

Levi grunted as I released him.

"Don't fucking touch me," I growled, though it didn't come out as stern as I'd meant it.

"You're such an asshole," Levi said.

"Then be happy you're rid of me," I replied, stuffing my clothes into the duffel and realizing I would need a suitcase as well.

Levi rubbed his wrist where I'd twisted it. "I was just asking, for fuck's sake."

"And I answered," I said. I dropped my duffel on the floor, zipped it up, and straightened. When I faced Levi again, his big, green eyes were wide and catching the moonlight. His lips parted and he inhaled. I couldn't tell if that was fear I saw on his face or something completely different.

"Are you leaving?" he asked.

"Jesus Fucking Christ," I snapped. "Can't you see I don't want to talk to you?"

"I can," he said calmly. "Are you leaving?" The corners of his mouth stiffened.

I groaned. "Yes. I'm leaving. Happy?"

The rest of his face hardened now.

I frowned in disbelief. He didn't look overjoyed at all. Quite the opposite in fact; Levi looked like he was trying to keep his sadness in check.

Releasing a deep breath of air, I spun away and scanned the rest of my room.

I spotted my medium sized suitcase at the top of the closet, reached for it, and felt a sigh of relief leave my lungs. I could pack all of my clothes, at least.

When I dropped the suitcase on the floor and looked up, Levi was closing the door and leaning against it. His arms were crossed at his chest. His blond hair was unruly and growing in every direction. He wore a pissed off expression on his face.

I promptly ignored his entire existence and headed for the dresser where my underwear and socks were stacked in two drawers. Filling up my suitcase, I was aware of Levi's gaze on the back of my head.

Fine. Alright. I was loud. I was the reason he couldn't sleep right now. But did he really have to stand behind my back and stare at me? I could practically feel him breathing down my neck.

"Listen," I said as I turned my head to look at him, voice tight. "Not sure if you've noticed, but I'm having a crisis and my life's splitting apart. Would you mind giving me some privacy?" The politeness failed to translate and sarcasm was all I managed.

Levi rolled his eyes. "*Will you* stop being a child?" he asked, putting his hands on his hips and stepping up to me. I dropped what I was doing and stood up, staring down at him. I was a head taller, so towering over my little stepbrother was as effortless as annoying my mother. "Yeah, you heard that right," Levi spat. "I'm trying to be here for you, for once in our fucking lives. And you're being a brat."

"Ooh," I said, amusement spiking in my chest. "You really want to talk to me about brats?" I cocked a corner of my lips and took a step forward, practically forcing him to take a step back. "You? The cover model of *Brats Quarterly*? The president of the Spoiled Rotten Club?" I let out a mirthless laugh, taking another step forward and trapping Levi on course toward the closed closet door. "You want to talk about that, huh?" He bumped back against the door, eyes wide with something that wasn't quite fear, but it wasn't annoyance either. I couldn't read him. "Can't you see?" I asked, touching his chest with mine for the briefest of moments as I lifted my hands and pressed them against the door on either side of his head. "I don't give a fuck about you, Levi," I said slowly and with terrible darkness in my voice. "I only see you when you annoy me. Sadly, you annoy me very often, but I have learned to live with it. You are nothing to me. I don't need your help. I don't want your sympathy. You and I only know each other because your dad and my mom like fucking each other and get along reasonably well. That doesn't make you my friend, let alone my brother." I was slowly leaning in. Levi's short breaths were coming out in quick bursts. I could feel them on my face as my nose came a fraction of an inch away from his. "You're free to be their little puppy all you want, Levi. Do the tricks, get the treats, have a fucking blast." The tip of my nose brushed against his and I felt his chest rise against mine when he sucked in a breath of air. "I wonder how long you'll be in their favor without me to make you look good in comparison." Every word that left my lips traveled straight into his mouth. He glared at me, but didn't dare move. "And when I walk out this door, you'll be the thing you've been to me all along. *Nothing.*"

As I emphasized the last venomous word, my body pushed into his. It hadn't even been intentional. And it was definitely without any meaning. But the moment our bodies touched, every alarm went off inside of me. Levi, blushing, breathless, and wide-eyed, let out the softest of whimpers. It happened at the exact same moment my thigh slid against his crotch and I realized he was hard.

I froze. My heart pounded and my body revolted against the first onslaught of thoughts. Except, it wasn't revolting at all. I was heaving breaths of air and staring into his wide eyes, seeing my own fright reflect in them. He throbbed against my leg, wincing and clenching his jaw. He wasn't moving. He wasn't even breathing. And all the while, my heartbeat was flooding my ears, pulsing in my neck, until I got my feet to work.

Jesus Christ Almighty, I thought as I stepped back. *Abort, abort, abort!* I narrowed my eyes as panic soared through me. *Did I do that?* I wondered.

I swallowed and pulled myself together enough to know that the only thing I could do was ignore. I had to ignore Levi; I had to ignore his hard on; I had to ignore the million reasons for his reaction to what I had said. But the hardest thing of all to ignore was the tightening in my pants at this devious, horrible idea of what would have happened had I not stepped back.

Maybe I was completely wrong. Maybe it was one of those spontaneous erections people got at funerals or whatever. But I didn't believe in coincidences. And I was definitely not getting myself tangled in this sick and twisted mess. I could only pretend; pretend I didn't notice and pretend it didn't make my pulse spike out of nowhere. I could pretend that it didn't make me shiver with an irresistible fascination for the mixture of eroticism and fetish.

"Now, if you'll be so kind," I said in the same, tight voice, pretending all the way. "Get out of my room while I pack and leave."

Levi, panic filling his eyes, gave a jerky nod and scurried away, slouching and sort of leaning forward like he was trying to conceal the very thing we were both fully aware of.

I needed a few minutes to cool off once the doors on both sides of the shared bathroom were closed and Levi was as far away from me as I could hope, in the middle of the night, in the house we would no longer share.

When I finally started packing again, my fingers were trembling.

In my life, I have been chased by cops and stray dogs. I had been in fist fights which had left me with a bloody grin on my face every time. I had been mugged at gunpoint when I was only seventeen.

But I had never been as scared as I was right now.

Scared of whatever storm began to rage inside my rib cage.

Terrified of the rising tide of a feeling so unfamiliar that I hardly dared to look at it, let alone believe it might be real.

I was petrified of what had gone through both our bodies just a few minutes ago, and oddly enough, relieved now more than ever to be thrown out of the house. At least, I had a really good fucking excuse to run away from him.

Chapter One

LEVI

I RUBBED MY HANDS together and twisted in the uncomfortable plastic seat of the arrivals terminal. Dad was late.

He was super late.

And no word from him at all.

I'd left a voice message when he didn't pick up, so I figured he was probably still driving and couldn't answer the phone.

The flight had left me exhausted. It had a four hour delay, which messed up Dad's schedule for the day. And I had barely slept last night already, but that was nothing new. I couldn't get any shut-eye in the plane either, with all the noise in the economy class.

I sat still, breathing in, breathing out. He would come, sooner or later. Maybe the change in my arrival had thrown his estimates off and he was now speeding. I hoped not.

I didn't want to cause any trouble.

I shut my eyes, thinking how that statement was the story of my life. Never impose, never cause trouble, never complain. Whatever inconvenience might arise, I kept my head cool. I looked on the bright side. I tried to be happy.

Recently, that had been increasingly hard to manage. Finding joy was easy when problems weren't a real factor. And when shit hit the fan and I couldn't cope, I could always escape into my sketchbook and let the world pass me by for a few hours.

Good luck doing that at the fucking airport, I thought and sighed.

My phone rang some time later. How much later? I had no clue. I had stopped checking the time. Now, I quickly pulled it out of my pocket and checked the screen. Dad.

"Hey," I answered. "You alright?" I kept my voice cheerful. God forbid I hinted at my dissatisfaction and made him awkward, or worse, guilty.

"Did he find you?" Dad asked.

I stretched my lips into a confused smile. "Did who find me?"

"Dammit," Dad muttered. "We've been trying to reach him. Listen, on your way here, you boys need to stop at *Oak Grove Vineyard* and pick up my order. It makes no sense for Margaret to drive down when you're on the way up, anyway."

"Dad, what are you talking about?" I asked.

Dad fell silent for a few heartbeats. "Oh," he said.

"What's going on?" I asked, panic rising sneakily in my tightening chest.

"I'm so sorry, Levi," he said, sounding genuine. "I completely forgot. I thought I'd already told you, but it must have slipped my mind. I hurt my back this morning. I'm not picking you up."

"What?" I chuckled in disbelief. "What am I supposed to do?" I didn't have any money for an Uber. Hell, I barely had enough cash on me to grab a bagel.

"That's just it," Dad said. And, at the exact same time, someone cleared their throat near me. Their body shifted in the periphery of my vision. Strong arms with many tattoos along the bronze skin he'd gotten from his estranged father drew my attention, his hands in the pockets of his sweatpants.

My heart sank and I almost let out a whimper.

"Parrish is driving up today," Dad said. I didn't miss the metallic anger around my stepbrother's name on Dad's lips. "Margaret arranged..." But his voice faded away as I lifted my gaze at Parrish, his dark eyes examining me intently.

"We going or what?" he asked coolly.

"He's here," I said into the phone. "See you soon, Dad."

"Don't forget about the wine. I'm sending you the details now..."

I hung up.

Terror erupted through my chest as I stared at the face I hadn't seen in five years. "Parrish," I whispered.

"It's a two hour drive," he said with all the grimness I remembered more than well enough. "If you want to hitch a ride, you better get your shit and start walking."

He spun the other way on his heels and marched toward the exit. And I — the inconvenience that I was — hurried to gather up my backpack, duffel, and my massive suitcase, then scurried on after him. "Yeah, shit, I'm coming," I mumbled.

My heart pounded in my chest as the reality sank in. Of course Parrish was coming home for Natalie's wedding. As far as I knew, Natalie was the only one who had had any contact with him in the past five years. Well, aside from me looking him up online every once in a while. But nobody knew about that.

Parrish rushed across the busy parking lot. There was a smell of dust in the late afternoon air. The sun was still burning hot, though it wasn't nearly as bright as it had been some hours earlier. The hues of the world were turning dark gold and orange.

My stepbrother popped the trunk of his car open and moved to the driver's side. He got in and sat behind the wheel, leaving me to load my own luggage. He only had one duffel in there, while I had my entire life packed neatly and carefully, waiting for me to figure out what I would do with it.

Once I was done, I got inside the car, fastened my seatbelt, and stared ahead. The initial shock began to wear off. Annoyance replaced it. This was one of those rare occasions where I couldn't keep my head completely cool and focus on the bright side. There was nothing bright about this.

Somebody could have given me a fucking heads up or something. I didn't appreciate being surprised by the last person I ever wanted to see. Not after how we had parted ways. The last time I'd seen Parrish, he had sent me to another room so he could pack in private. That had happened moments after he'd spilled some nasty truths to my face. Truths I'd only heard in the back of my consciousness because I had been too horny from his proximity.

Jesus, I shouldn't think about that night, I reminded myself.

Five goddamn years had passed since I'd last seen him and he was still as unmoved by me as he had been then.

And though he stared well ahead, his attention not even near me, I couldn't help but keep my gaze on him for a heartbeat longer.

Parrish Turner wasn't someone who often posted photos on his social media profiles. He had one blurry, night-time photo as his profile picture across all his accounts and he got tagged by friends on occasion. The last I'd seen of him was a poolside photo in which Parrish had been looking over his shoulder at the camera.

It did him no justice.

Parrish was a six-foot-three, black-haired, black-bearded, brown-eyed statue of physical strength and simmering annoyance he wasn't bothering to conceal.

His arms were a lot more interesting than they had been the last time I'd seen him. Tattoos covered his bronze skin. Snakes, birds, fish, faces; his arms were a sculpted canvas for several pieces of art, all forming one huge masterpiece.

I bit my lip and decided not to think about this anymore. Parrish was infuriatingly good looking; always had been. Even at sixteen, when I'd first met him, Parrish Turner had been a stunning sight; dark circles around his eyes had never gone away, his dark hair always curly and short, his eyes never trusting. I'd been too young to look at him like that. Long before I'd learned its name, I'd always had that uneasy feeling around him.

Too bad he'd never noticed me.

And too fucking bad he was my stepbrother.

To say there had never been any brotherly love between us was an understatement. He'd been out to make me feel like shit since day one and I hadn't been much better. It was only that, as years had gone by, I felt more than annoyance.

Parrish got us out of the parking lot and onto the highway. The AC pumped cool air into the car and a radio announcer talked nonsense from the speakers, but the volume was low enough that I didn't feel like I had to listen. It was also just loud enough that it drowned out the deafening silence that would otherwise make me want to bite my nails.

It was the only reason I managed to go ten minutes without speaking.

"I didn't expect to see you," I said.

"I didn't expect to be asked a fucking favor," Parrish said sourly.

It rubbed me the wrong way. "I wasn't the one asking," I protested.

"And yet, you're the one I'm driving," he said resignedly and sighed.

I scoffed and dug my fingernails into my knees. There had never been a time when I wasn't squirming and uncomfortable around Parrish Turner. "You could have said no. They would have found someone else."

Just as I glanced at him, Parrish pulled on a sinister grin. "If you must know, I prefer a detour than getting to River Bend any sooner than I absolutely must. Of the two evils, being your chauffeur is better than sitting on the porch with Harry and Marge."

I winced. Though I was never expected to call Margaret anything other than Margaret, she was his mother. But Parrish had stopped calling her mom a long time ago. And it always felt weird. "Why are you even going this early, then?" I asked without thinking. Of course, I knew the answer as soon as the words were out of my mouth.

"Natalie," Parrish said softly. "She wants me there."

I said nothing. There was nothing I could say to that. For five years, Parrish had cut all contact with us. He'd reached out to Natalie and she, in her peacemaker role, always found the nicest ways to present the news of him to the rest of us. I'd always doubted that "Parrish sends his love," but I had never told Natalie that. Of all of us, she had probably been the one hurt the most by Parrish's exile.

I glanced at him in secret. He either didn't notice or didn't care. It was all the same to me.

The T-shirt he wore was a billowy piece of olive green cloth, stylishly torn, sleeveless, and with loose, elliptical holes for arms that did a poor job of covering up his rib cage. With Parrish's right hand on the wheel, this T-shirt was the bane of my existence while he drove. The entire right side of his tattooed rib cage was on display for me to stare at and drool over.

I shut my eyes, letting his bare skin only exist in my imagination. But even so, whenever I inhaled, I discovered bergamot, nutmeg, and cedar scents, mixed with the faintest hint of sweet summer sweat, coming from my stepbrother's bare skin.

The last moment I had seen Parrish before he'd left River Bend played out before my closed eyes. The way he'd towered over me effortlessly. The way he'd brought his face down to mine. The way his breath smelled a little sweet from the wine he'd had that evening. And the way he could have snapped me like a twig if only I crossed him.

I'd lived in a strange sort of fear of Parrish for most of our time together. I had been intimidated by him before I'd had a reason and he had picked up on it. He had always known he could control me if only he spoke the right words in the right tone. But that night had been different. I had already been imagining some unspeakable things for a long while. And when he'd leaned in so close to my face that I could have kissed him with a moment of carelessness, it had been too much.

My entire body had caught fire.

My cock had stiffened so quickly I hadn't even realized it until Parrish pushed into me.

And then, it was too late. He'd blinked in surprise, whether because he had felt it or because he hadn't meant to push me that hard, and then the moment had been over.

In the years that followed, I pulled those events from my memory, and let them play out in all sorts of ways. My favorite, by far, was that of Parrish feeling my erection, then giving me that lazy smirk of his before placing his hand on my crotch. That one fantasy had given me plenty of happy endings when it had been too hard to concentrate on studying.

If you were actually studying instead of pleasuring yourself to the memory of your stepbrother, maybe you wouldn't be in this miserable mess right now, my voice of reason said.

I'd been miles away when I realized, with spiking fear, something was wrong. Parrish was slowing down, giving the right turn signal, and getting off the highway. "The hell?" I asked. "That's the wrong exit." *Shit*, I added internally.

Parrish didn't say anything.

"Do you know how long it's gonna take us to get back on the highway?" I asked and scoffed. "Unbelievable."

"We're not going to River Bend," he said flatly.

"We're not what?" I gaped, finally looking at him head on without having to hide it. Fuck, he was handsome. Also, possibly, in the middle of kidnapping me. "What do you mean?"

"We're staying a night at some motel or something," Parrish said, voice tired more than anything else.

I stared at him with a confused frown for a while longer. "Um...we're an hour away."

He shrugged. "I'm falling asleep at the wheel," he blatantly lied.

"I'll drive," I said.

"I'm not trusting you with my car." For the briefest of moments, I thought I noticed the right corner of his lips tick up.

"Another lie," I said.

Parrish rolled his eyes. "Fine. I mean to milk this detour for as long as possible, even if it's for just a night."

I'd already guessed as much. "You could have asked," I muttered.

"What good would that do?" Parrish asked, frowning at me.

"Sure. Because my opinion doesn't matter." I narrowed my eyes at him.

"Jesus, Levi, you're really just picking a fight, aren't you? So, what if I asked first? Option one, you agree and we do the thing we're doing. Option two, you say no, and we end up fighting, and we do the thing we're already doing." He shrugged. "You weren't going to get it your way no matter what."

I scoffed at that last part. "It's not about getting my way."

"Of course it is," Parrish said sourly. "That's what things were always about with you."

Now, he crossed the line. "Screw you, Parrish," I snapped. "It's been five years. I'm not that kid anymore. And no, this isn't me admitting that I was a spoiled child like you're suggesting. But even if I was, I'm not anymore."

He glanced at me for the briefest of moments. "Yeah. Your tantrum really shows growth."

A groan broke out of me as I sank back into my seat. Screw him. Screw all of this. He had always strong-armed me any way he liked. And I had always let him. At first, because he had been older and bigger; but later, because I would have done fucking anything just to get a bit of his attention. Even if it meant disagreeing with him for the sake of disagreeing, until he had no choice but to literally twist my arm and bring his face up close to mine.

Yeah, I was fucked up. Nothing new there. I'd been aware of how messed up my desires were since the moment they had emerged. And I would never forget the moment it had happened. A June day much like today, and a pool party behind our house. I hadn't been invited. Parrish and his cronies were hanging out there.

Parrish had always been generous with displaying his skin. He was one of those guys who shed off their shirts at the first hint of warm sunshine. A polar opposite of me and my squeamishness. But that day, he'd also been wet. He'd gotten out of the pool on the side of our backyard porch, where I'd been eating stolen cookies. The weight of the water that had soaked his shorts pulled them an inch lower than he usually wore them and I saw a clear line between his suntan and his natural, lighter brown skin. That had been the moment everything changed for me. Realizations snapped in my brain rapidly. I discovered I was gay. I discovered there had always been a reason I was uncomfortable around Parrish. I discovered there was nothing that was sacred to me. I discovered that I was doomed to lust after my stepbrother until I either killed my ability to feel anything or destroyed my family.

And Parrish hadn't even realized I was there.

As the years went by, my desires shifted and morphed. Hell, I might as well say 'twisted'. Either because Parrish could never be nice to me or because I was inherently fucked up, my desires from mere proximity with him had turned into a desperate need to be strong armed by him.

The fact that his arm was now so sculpted and decorated with ink didn't help these desires at all.

"Somebody needs to let Dad and Margaret know," I murmured, accepting my defeat. Really, the fact that he was doing this without even consulting me should have annoyed me more. Instead, it ever so slightly turned me on.

"Not it," he said.

"Don't be a child," I protested.

"I'm not. See, I don't care if they worry about where we got stuck or what happened. You do. And, since you're the only one in this car who cares, you should probably do the 'letting them know' bit." That sinister smirk on his face was both scary and alluring. Though I was irritated by the fact that he was somehow right, I couldn't focus on my irritation from the blazing heat of his aura. *Christ, he has a fuckable aura.*

I pushed that thought away as soon as it crossed my mind. Still, my heart murmured as I typed out a message to Dad, letting him know Parrish and I "need some rest. Besides, we should really catch up after so long." The last bit was a risky argument. It played into the old desire of our parents to make Parrish and me into real brothers. But those desires had died a slow death over the years in which Parrish had been more and more of a cause for their headaches.

Dad texted back to remind me about the wine and I said we'd pick it up in the morning. He didn't reply.

"That one looks good enough," Parrish said after a long silence.

I glanced ahead. It was a crappy roadside motel, no better or worse than any other roadside motel I'd ever seen. A large googie style sign, the sort you'd see in California and Nevada a lot more, but with its neon lights broken, said MOTEL so you really couldn't miss it. The units appeared as sturdy as cardboard and checking for cleanliness wasn't advisable if you didn't want to run away screaming.

Parrish got off the road and parked the car, then hopped out of it like we'd just arrived at a luxury resort and he had a spa day to kick off. He really didn't want to be home if this sort of place made him happy. But who was I to judge? The chance to sleep another night before facing the inevitable made me happy, too.

I followed my stranger of a stepbrother out, the backpack hanging from my left shoulder, duffel over my right. Quietly, we reached the reception desk, which we found thanks to a large, red sign that said ECEPTION. We filled in the rest.

"One room's enough," Parrish replied, pulling me out of my thoughts. "Separate beds."

I swallowed. *Still too close*. But I wasn't going to say anything. *If you can't afford your own room, keep your mouth shut.*

Parrish paid upfront with cash and took the key. He walked by me, leaving a trail of bergamot, cedar, and nutmeg for me to follow. Damn him for smelling that good. He had no right.

Without speaking a word to me or even acknowledging me with a look, Parrish walked down the asphalt parking lot, looking at the numbers nailed above the doors, until he found ours. "Here we are. Lucky thirteen," Parrish said in that husky voice that made needles prick my skin.

I raised an eyebrow. "Thirteen? Yeah, that checks out," I murmured. To my surprise, Parrish cocked one corner of his lips up in a half-grin.

He unlocked the door and walked in, leaving it open for me.

The stuffy air inside wasn't as bad as I'd expected. A faint note of dust pinched my nostrils as I stepped inside. The peeling wallpaper, the paneling covering the lower half of each wall, bed spreads, carpet, bed frames, nightstands, doors, and curtains were all different shades of brown and beige that attacked my eyeballs.

Parrish didn't seem to notice or care. He leaned down over one of the beds, pushed his fists into the mattress, and let his weight test it. "Good," he muttered, then met my gaze. His brown eyes were colder than they physically should have been. You don't expect the rich color of chestnut and fall to bring the temperature down in a room, but Parrish's gaze certainly did that.

He tossed the key to me and I scrambled to catch it. I locked us inside.

"Dibs on the shower," Parrish said, already turning away from me.

"Sure," I sighed. It wasn't like I'd flown across the entire goddamn country, then waited at the airport for hours, huh? But it wasn't worth picking a fight over. Especially so when I glanced at Parrish again and found him facing away from me, reaching for the edge of his sleeveless T-shirt.

My skin prickled and my mouth dried. A red alert sounded in my head and every rational cell in my body knew it was time to look away. Sadly, I had very few rational cells left in me.

Parrish grasped the bottom of his T-shirt, his muscles rippled and flexed. The strong contours of his shoulders and upper back were revealed as he pulled the fabric up and over his head. His back was a sight to behold, a testament to the strength and beauty of the human form. Each muscle was defined, toned, and gave a sense of power and control. It was clear that Parrish had worked hard to sculpt his body to raw perfection.

I felt a rush of attraction toward him as he threw his T-shirt onto the bed and swayed his shoulders, stepping toward the bathroom. The pull was stronger than I'd anticipated, and once again, I remembered why it was a bad idea to share the room.

Just one night, Levi, I whispered to myself.

Besides, it wasn't important in the least. It was just his physique and the allure of the thing you could never, ever have. Not only was the object of my hidden desires off limits for obvious reasons of our parents being freaking married, but it also hardly knew I existed. Parrish had always looked at me like he'd forgotten all about me until the moment I was in his line of vision. There had always been that slight surprise at seeing me, today more than ever. I'd seen it every time his gaze touched me.

I huffed and spun away just as Parrish shut the bathroom door and the sound of water splashing against the tiles — they were probably also brown — reached me.

My face heated as I made myself forget about this entire thing. I shouldn't have been watching in the first place. I'd done this to myself. Again. Like I had back when we'd still lived together, shared the pool, saw each other on the way in and out of the shower, and so on. I'd discovered these odd and rising feelings, these waves of attraction wrapped in a blanket of anxiety and animosity, slowly over time. It had always been Parrish, one way or another. It had always been his brooding, pissed-off pout that squeezed my chest and clenched my heart and left me short of breath.

The water stopped abruptly and Parrish walked out of the bathroom some minutes later.

I looked over at Parrish and felt my pulse rise. His dark hair was wet and still just as curly and unruly. His torso was rippling with muscles. His chest was strong and broad, tapering down to a narrow waist, and abs toned until he entirely appeared to be chiseled from marble. And his smooth, bronze skin was inked into a messy perfection. Words, images, hieroglyphs; it was a storm of meanings that together were completely meaningless. The canvas of a sculpted body, shaped through hard work and dedication, with a pissed off expression that almost never changed.

Then I saw them. His black boxer-briefs, balled into one fist. And, unless Parrish always carried a spare pair of underwear in the pocket of his sweatpants, I could tell with great certainty that he was going commando for the night.

He was decent enough if you didn't look too closely at where the fabric of his light gray sweatpants creased. I didn't look that closely simply because it was too hot inside already.

Parrish threw his underwear in the corner of the bed, next to his T-shirt, and lay down. "So, what's your deal?" he asked, his voice smoky deep.

I slowly filled my lungs with air to calm my nerves. "My deal?"

"Did you, like, graduate?" Parrish asked, folding his hands behind his head.

For an instant, I was distracted by his sprawling body, set out on display and designed to make me drool. "I've, uh, got a few exams left."

"A bit late in the game, huh?" His voice was uninterested. That fucker.

When I didn't answer, he continued. "Natalie mentioned you were studying statistics or whatever."

"Data science," I corrected.

"I've always wondered," he said, lifting his gaze to the wooden paneling on the ceiling. "Is it really a science if they have to put the word in the name? Like, you don't say biology science."

A snort escaped me. That was my mistake. I'd let his silly joke bring my guard down.

He pointed an intent gaze right to my eyes. He watched me as I stared back, then looked down, then squirmed like my skin was too tight for me. And, when I finished the entire exhibition of blatantly hiding my obvious guilt, Parrish snorted. "You're not going to graduate, are you?"

I swallowed, though it was hard. My throat constricted with fear. "Why do you care?" I asked and shook my head jerkily. "Do you realize this is the most you've spoken to me in, like, a decade?"

His eyebrows flattened and he thought about it. "You're right. I don't care."

"Then get your nose out of my business," I huffed and unzipped my duffel, then rummaged for clean clothes. I pulled some out at random and headed to the bathroom to shower off the stink of travel.

When I returned, the lights were out and the sun had already dipped below the horizon. A subdued glow was still coming through the thick curtains, but it was mostly dark inside.

Parrish was breathing peacefully on his bed, so I tiptoed to my side of the room and slipped under the thin cover.

I lay in bed, wide awake, my mind a maelstrom of thoughts and emotions. The secret I had been keeping weighed heavily on my conscience, and I couldn't shake the feeling of guilt and shame. Minutes turned to hours and the truth ate away at my soul.

As I lay there, I couldn't help but be distracted by Parrish sleeping just three feet away from me. I couldn't help but let my gaze wander over his peaceful face and the way his chest rose and fell with each breath. My attraction to him was undeniable, and I couldn't help but feel a twinge of longing and desire.

I tried to push the thoughts out of my mind, focusing on the sound of his breathing and the way the moonlight filtered through the empty spaces between the curtains, casting a soft glow on his skin. I tried to find solace in the peacefulness of the moment, but my mind wouldn't stop racing. I felt trapped in my own thoughts and emotions, unable to escape the weight of so many terrible truths.

As the night wore on, I found myself feeling more and more awake, more and more troubled by my secret, and more and more distracted by this feeling for Parrish. He existed in this realm of impossible things; the fantasy of him that I had kept with me since the first forbidden thought of him had crossed my mind was still present. Perhaps not stronger, but no weaker than it had been when Parrish had left.

He could see through me. A stranger who'd never cared to look at me twice could see I was hiding something.

How the hell was I even hoping that my own father would believe me? Sure, it was easy over the phone. "Yup, passed another one. Oh yeah, aced it. Professor told the entire class to take notes from my project." But when I had to look him in the eyes and keep the lie going, he would see right through me.

He would see that I'd dropped out four months ago.

And, if I wasn't very, very careful, he might catch me blushing at the thought of my stepbrother.

Chapter Two

PARRISH

The uninterested elderly gentleman at the reception desk wasn't impressed by my question regarding breakfast. He was, however, generous enough to fill up two mugs of coffee free of charge while I procured our breakfast at the vending machine.

I stuffed my pockets with two chocolate croissants that were probably old and thanked the receptionist. I carried our coffees to number thirteen, where Levi was fiddling with his phone, wearing a white T-shirt and a pair of dark red briefs, his legs mostly hidden under the thin cover. Not that I was looking.

Levi was hard not to notice, though. The moment I had spotted him at the airport, words seeped back into my subconscious mind. I had lost my ability to articulate. I had reverted to the prehistoric form of communication, grunting and growling in discomfort at the blinding allure of someone I shouldn't even consider attractive.

Whenever my gaze landed on him, I had to remind myself of who he was. See, when I left home five years ago, Levi had been a scrawny eighteen-year-old Margaret and Harold held up as an example of what a son should be. And me, at twenty-three, without a degree and unable to hold a job for longer than three months, standing in stark contrast next to him.

I couldn't really say the grudge had completely faded away.

Still, he looked completely different. Gone were the bones pushing out of the skin on his tiny frame, replaced by layers of trimmed muscle in his arms and legs and presumably the rest of his body. Sure, he was wiry, but he had some physique. Gone was the regular haircut he could get in our crappy, tiny town, and it was replaced with stylishly floppy hair, parted in the middle. Pale golden locks framed his face like arches, his green eyes dazzling, if only tired, under black eyebrows.

It was hard to believe he was the same person as the kid I'd last seen five years ago. But I reminded myself that this was still him; the guy who'd made himself comfortable in my home when his father wooed my mother. The son Margaret had always wanted. The boy she could talk about nonstop in her knitting club and during her town festival planning committee meetings. The boy Harold could brag about down at Barry's Brew where my name had never been uttered.

Yeah, this was still the same little shithead I'd had to suffer living with for seven years of my life. Except for one huge point of difference. For the past five years, a single memory of Levi Bartlet had forced all my other memories of him into fading by comparison. The night I got thrown out. The proximity of our bodies as I spewed the nastiest things I could find right into his pretty face. The moment when I discovered he could absorb all my anger without flinching. And the moment his cock throbbed against my thigh.

"Your coffee," I growled without any intention of softening my words.

The space between Levi's black eyebrows wrinkled. "Black?" he asked as he took the mug.

"It's all I got," I said, reaching into my pocket and pulling out a small package containing one awful croissant. I handed it to Levi slowly. Really, there was no need to stand so close to him. I could have tossed the bag instead, but I didn't. I watched his long face and slender fingers as he reached over and took the other end of the bag. He licked his lips and lifted his gaze to mine.

"Thanks," he said, tugging the croissant out of my hand.

The tension between us dissipated as soon as the package left my hand and I stepped back. Something about him sitting there, his head approximately at the level of my waist, made me wonder if he still had nasty thoughts about me. Maybe he was struggling, just like me, to keep them at bay. Though I labeled mine as nothing more than dangerous curiosity.

There was something off about him. That delicate, slightly upturned nose with somewhat flared nostrils failed to give him the playful and innocent look he'd had in the past. His wide mouth with Cupid's bow no longer gave him the air of openness that had made him so dear to every goddamn inhabitant back home, especially Margaret.

Even his eyes weren't quite as bright as they had been and the color resembled moss more than spring grass. For every bit of him that looked infinitely better now that he'd grown up, other features came across as tired and worn out. And, as fucked up as it might sound, the tiredness suited him. The circles around his eyes were a little darker than the rest of his pale skin.

I liked it.

Levi was carrying some burden. I'd called him out on it, but he hadn't taken the bait. He hadn't given me a chance to dazzle him with my skill of deduction. As he'd reminded me last night, it was none of my business. Perhaps it would make my life easier if Harold and Margaret were busy fussing over Levi these weeks and whatever demons haunted him. Still, I had a nagging feeling that I would be embroiled into any mess, even if only to show that I was still not up to their standard.

A guy needed to create his own distractions. And Levi, with whatever hauntings weighed him down, and with his pretty lips and an old weakness for my thigh against his crotch, seemed like he might do. I could already see these two weeks flying by as I tortured him for shits and giggles.

I sat at the edge of my mattress, though the space between our beds was so small that extending my legs meant I was brushing my toes against Levi's bed. In silence, Levi slurped his hot coffee, then set the mug on the nightstand, and threw the tired white cover off his legs.

Like a predator cat pinpointing its prey, I gazed at his entire body. His skin was paler than mine by quite a few shades, even if he'd caught a bit of an early tan over the sunny weeks wherever it was that he had studied. Portland, was it? The hair on his legs appeared soft and thin, almost transparent. He'd never grown any real hair, not on his legs and not on his face. The faintest of shadows on his chin and above his lips was the best he could do.

That was the look that often made me glance twice. Guys I got together with fit into that twinky mold and it was divine irony that my infuriating stepbrother should grow into one of them too.

And it was a whole different level of weird that, since the last time I'd seen him, the thought of Levi equaled the thought of something so dangerously attractive that I was almost willing to gamble the world for a chance to feel the same high again. The high of every red flag rising, every alarm screaming at once, and my body bolting in fright from its own desire.

Levi stood up as I glanced away. There should have been nothing there for me to look at. He had a bulgy crotch in those little briefs, like every guy who'd ever put a pair of briefs on. Nothing original and definitely not something I couldn't find under a rock. And yet, looking away hurt.

This was someone I could and should never look at.

Swiftly, he found his jeans and yanked them up his legs, put his sneakers on, and checked the contents of his backpack. "I'm ready," he announced.

I nodded wordlessly and drained the rest of the coffee out of my mug, then got up. Unlike Levi, there was nothing for me to pack. This morning, after waking up, I had rummaged through my bag in the car and changed into clean clothes, including underwear. Now, I got up and strolled out of the room. "Come along, then."

Levi did as he was told. He was that kinda guy.

We hit the road early enough, the sun peeking well over the horizon. The highway stretched out before us, a ribbon of asphalt winding its way through the countryside. I pressed down on the accelerator, the engine roaring as I picked up speed. The wind rushed past me through my open window, whipping through my hair and filling me with a sense of freedom and adventure. But my heart was heavy, as I knew I was headed home. Or the place I'd called home a long time ago.

Halfway there, we made a little detour to a vineyard Harold insisted we stopped at. They'd prepared several crates of wine, all paid for and only waiting to be picked up. And then, we were driving again.

Some time later, I exited the highway and took the road that led to Harold and Margaret's town of River Bend. The streets of the town were lined with old-fashioned lampposts, and the houses were quaint and well-kept. Truly, time had stopped in River Bend.

I'd never had any love for the place. My heart belonged to New York, where nobody ever ran into me twice. It belonged to my tattoo shop and the people who worked with me. The only person I truly loved in this town was the reason I returned. My sister.

"Home sweet home," I muttered sourly.

"Right," Levi huffed out.

I glanced at him. Somehow, I still expected the bubbly, agreeable boy that he had been to reclaim that body of his at the return home, but the glum expression was intact. His eyes were puffy with tiredness, dark circles framing them. His light hair was messier today than it had been yesterday when I'd picked him up.

"Didn't sleep well?" I asked for no reason at all and regretted it as soon as the words were over my lips. *Why do you care?* He'd ask.

He shook his head.

Well, that was not the reaction I expected, so I nodded in return. It wasn't a total ceasefire, but it was better than if he went for me with sharpened claws.

Margaret would prepare him a nice chicken broth and tuck him in as soon as she felt a hint that he was tired, no doubt. Then, she'd feed him her homemade cookies and force hot tea of her own blend down his throat.

We passed the center of the town and followed the main road. Large, lavish houses, with their sprawling front lawns adorned it. Each grabbed every bit of privacy it could by letting the hedges grow tall. Margaret and Harold's yard was no different, except the house was smaller.

Someone had already opened the gate, so I followed the path to the garage. "Journey's end, I guess," I said with an air of fatalism that surprised even myself. It wasn't a chopping block we were heading for, but it wasn't far off.

From the garage, a narrower path led toward the house.

The house was neocolonial, with a symmetrical shape and clean lines. It was painted in a timeless white color, with a red brick chimney adding a touch of elegance. The front porch was pretty cute, with white columns and a wraparound deck that had more seating arrangements in the back. The front door was a classic, six-panel wooden door, with a brass knocker and keyhole. The windows were tall and narrow, with white frames and shutters that let in plenty of natural light. The roof was peaked and made of dark shingles, with a central dormer window breaking up the expanse of the roof line.

Margaret had always known how to seem refined. And that was where the problem lay; Margaret had always cared more about appearances.

Though smaller than most houses on the road, Margaret and Harold's house used most of its space for common areas. There were only three bedrooms on the upper floor, a master bedroom downstairs, a small study nobody ever used, and plenty of space dedicated to the dining room, kitchen, and living room.

We got out of the car and Levi followed behind me, his suitcase thundering against the cobblestone path. The scent of early summer was in the air and I almost — *almost* — felt a certain kind of longing for my childhood.

God have mercy on my soul, I thought sourly as I pushed open the front door and glanced around. In front of me, the staircase led up to the bedrooms, bathrooms, and the study. To my right was the large dining room with breakfast already served and mostly eaten. Leading from it to the back of the house was a hallway, connecting it to the kitchen. Straight ahead, next to the staircase, was another hallway, leading out to the backyard. And to my left was the spacious living room which I had last seen on the evening of my exile.

"They're here," Margaret shrieked for Harold as she paced quickly from the back of the house. "My boys."

I was shocked to be included. And even more so when Marge spread her arms wide and pulled both of us into a hug.

Of all the heart-wrenching thoughts I'd had about how this might go down, being hugged after five years of near perfect radio silence had never crossed my mind.

"My sweet babies returned home," she said, almost sobbing. "Ah, one last time we're all together."

I snatched the opportunity to pull out of her steely grip, a storm of emotions raging through me, and grinned. "She's only getting married," I said of my sister. It wasn't like she'd leave town or something. The way she'd told me, she was literally just moving across town to Jarred's — and, let's not forget, Jarred's parents' — house.

"Still," Margaret said. "Things won't be the same."

I wanted to say they hadn't been the same for the last five years. Twelve, if you were really nit-picking. But I kept my mouth shut. Two weeks ahead gave us ample opportunity to fight. I didn't need to light the fuse on the first day.

Margaret was all emotional and I could let her have that moment. Sooner or later, one of us would say something to rub the other one the wrong way and all hell would break loose. I, for one, didn't come here in search of redemption. And, if my mixed feelings around Levi were any indicator, I might dig the hole for myself even deeper by the time I leave.

"Oh, you must be exhausted, my darlings," she said in her deep, motherly voice. "Come, come." She snatched Levi's hand and yanked him after her, waving at me to follow. "How was the ride, love?" she asked neither of us in particular as she led the way to the backyard porch.

I muttered something like 'It was great.' Levi followed Margaret through the hallway where Harold greeted him with delight while I stood a little further behind. Another voice sounded and my heart inflated a little. My sister, Natalie, was with them. She was, by far, the only person in this entire house I not only genuinely liked, but sincerely loved. Three years my junior, she had always tried to find some common ground and strove for this untouchable idea of family and unity.

My sweet Natalie, finally getting a chance to build a family of her own. Truly, had it not been for her wedding, I wouldn't have returned. Even for a visit. There was nothing here for me but bad memories. And a weird one that made my heart murmur.

Margaret and Harold had attempted, early on, to turn Levi and me into model brothers for the whole town to see how well we got along. It hadn't worked and the blame was always pinned on me. Not that I cared. Besides, five years between us made all the difference; he'd been eleven and I had been sixteen. There had never been a chance of me babysitting a sniveling brat where someone might spot me. So, Natalie had taken that role.

Once the greeting chatter had settled with Levi, I crossed the short distance and emerged outside. In the same heartbeat, Natalie jumped up and threw herself at me. "Parrish," she squealed.

She visited me in New York once or twice a year. And every time I'd done my absolute best to show her the time of her life. And every time, she begged me to visit home and finally bury the hatchet. It took a proposal and a wedding to make it happen.

"How's my little sister doing?" I asked as I squeezed her tightly in my arms. She smelled like a spring breeze in a forest with a sweet finish.

"Gah, I couldn't be happier that you're here," she said and stepped back to let Harold greet me. She still held onto my hand for a few heartbeats longer.

I didn't know what to expect from Harold. He'd usually followed Margaret's lead. And he'd been happy to see the back of me five years ago. But now, the man stood up and extended his arm for a handshake.

When I took it, he placed his other hand on my shoulder and looked into my eyes. "Welcome home," he said in that raspy, metallic voice. "It's good to see you."

My tongue was tied. Again, it had never crossed my mind I might receive a lukewarm welcome or more. At best, I'd hoped for indifference. And indifference I knew how to take. "Thanks," I said, mouth dry.

There was, to an extent, a sense of 'water under the bridge' to this whole affair.

"The wine is in the car," I added when I realized I'd run out of things to say.

"Good," Harold said as he pulled back and sat down with a grunt. Apparently, his back hurt or something. I hadn't been paying attention after Natalie had asked me to pick Levi up. The mention of his name had been enough to make my ears ring.

I sat down with the rest of them, feeling the tension walk out the door with a confused frown on its face. Was it not supposed to sit with us for the next two weeks?

"Would you like some lemonade, darling?" Margaret asked and it took me a moment to see she meant me. Normally, she would call me by my name and I would return the favor. Well, I wasn't calling her mom again if she brought the Moon down to Earth.

"Uh, sure," I said, suddenly realizing how desperately I wanted a glass. The air outside was stuffy and hot. It wasn't going to be one of those mild summers from my childhood. And the pool looked pretty damn inviting.

Marge poured me a tall glass of lemonade, ice clinking in the pitcher as she smiled. The smile didn't exactly touch her eyes, but they weren't shark-like either. I couldn't decide what it was she felt in this moment. "How have you been?"

I let the silence linger for a short while longer, pondering over her intentions. When I couldn't figure them out,

I finally exhaled with relief. "Great, actually. The last few years treated me well."

"Oh?" Harold generously contributed.

"I'm not kidding," I said, throwing one leg over the other and leaning back. I shot a mischievous look at Natalie, who knew everything about my life. "I'm finally comfortable, you know? Got my own shop, got a mortgage for my own place. Not to brag, but I've never been better." A smile crept to my face before I could wipe it off, so I let it spill. Never before had they wondered how I was doing. And, even if it was just out of politeness, it felt good to talk about my success.

"The tattoo shop?" Marge asked, her voice ever so slightly tight. She glanced at my arms. Oddly enough, when I'd come out to her, she'd been supportive as hell. But when I asked her to sign off on me getting my first tattoo, she had a tantrum and nearly disowned me. She concealed her disgust well this time.

"Yep," I said. "I've got four employees on payroll, a couple contractors, and an apprentice. I'm actually thinking of expanding if I could find the time."

Marge and Harry conceded a round of approving nods. But, I guess listening to my success was as good an opening as any, so Harry leaned in. "Levi here is about to graduate. Did he tell you? He never brags."

I swallowed a snort. "Really?" I feigned interest.

"Uh-huh," Levi said. "It's not a big deal."

"Come, come. We can celebrate this new chapter of your life over the weekend," Marge said.

I wanted to laugh out loud, but somehow I'd kept it down. Weren't we already here to celebrate Natalie's new chapter in life? "I can't wait," I said straight to Levi's reddening face. He was as tiny as a breadcrumb on that white, wooden chair, leaning back and slouching at the same time. His mossy eyes stared at the edge of the table like it was telling him the secrets of eternal life. Or of passing grades, which he would probably prefer right now.

"I think I'm going to shower the travel stink off myself and get some shuteye," I said, looking for an acceptable excuse to leave the conversation. I winked at Natalie when nobody else was looking and she grinned. I mouthed a quick 'I love you' and she did the same. Five years later, and I still choked on those words whenever I needed to say them aloud. Luckily for me, I didn't have the necessity that often. My flings were mostly one-time-only arrangements and Natalie and I had our own language. Who else was I going to inform of my feelings?

"Oh, be careful not to wake Lauren," Marge said.

Levi was the first to frown. Natalie bit her lip. Harry looked like a flying saucer appeared in the sky and occupied his attention. The tension that had left the porch earlier was barging back in, lifting its index finger, and shouting 'And one more thing.'

"Aunt Lauren's here?" I asked.

In the past, every six or so months, Lauren would either dump a man or be dumped by one, and she would return to River Bend to cry it out. And when Lauren was in River Bend, someone had to sacrifice their room for weeks on end. Most often it had been Natalie, who would volunteer, and who split her time between a friend's house for sleepovers and my bed or Levi's. But Natalie was a twenty-five-year-old woman about to get married. She needed her beauty sleep and all the space she could get.

"Of course she is. Our baby girl is getting married. Lauren wouldn't miss it for the world," Marge insisted in her deep voice.

"Ah, I see. So, where is she crashing?" I asked. "Not between the two of you, huh?" I shot a hopeful glance at Harry and Marge.

"Nonsense," Marge said, almost laughing. "She's in your old room. After you left, she all but claimed it."

After I was thrown out, I wanted to correct her until I recognized that the source of my annoyance wasn't the semantics, but the lack of a bed.

"Okay," I said slowly, dragging out the last syllable. "And where am I supposed to sleep? Not between the two of you, huh?" I repeated my words. I was the only one who seemed to find that funny.

"With Levi, of course," Harry said.

"What?" Levi gasped at the same time I barked out a laugh.

"What will the pearl-clutchers say?" I joked, but no one listened. Levi was whispering a million nos into the empty space between us, while Marge shook her head at me for implying there was something improper about the two of us sharing the bed.

"Don't be silly, Parrish. You boys are brothers. Aren't you over your silly squabbles by now?" She sucked her teeth quickly in succession.

I winced at the thought of Levi being my brother. No one here knew about his physical reactions to my proximity. And, possibly, vile things I could summon and tell to his face.

"Why would you mind that, Levi?" Harold asked, positively bewildered.

Levi stopped and blinked, then smiled. Dimples emerged in his cheeks, but that smile was fake. "You're right. I don't mind."

"Seriously?" I asked. "Come on, guys. I can stay down at the inn."

"Good luck finding a room," Marge said. "Senator's relatives booked it months in advance."

I nearly rolled my eyes at how emphatically Marge said 'senator.' Natalie's father-in-law to be was a *state* senator, but Marge didn't care about the difference. She cared that she was going to be related to a senator.

"Fine," I said. "Shared room it is, then." I threw my hands up in surrender. After all, Levi was the one who would have the worse time.

Natalie's phone buzzed. "Oh, it's Jarred. I should go. His family is gathering at the inn and he'd like me to be there to greet some of his aunts." She waved her hand like it was unimportant while I frowned at such a ridiculous request.

Margaret hopped onto her feet and brushed her palms one off the other and saw Natalie out.

I rolled my eyes and sat down at last, but the party was over. Harold was getting up and muttering something to himself on his way inside. Levi, the last company I had on the porch, inhaled and held his breath, but he didn't look in my direction. "I think I should unpack...or something." He got up and scurried away.

With a deep breath, I took in the sight of the backyard. At the center of the yard stood a sparkling blue in-ground pool, surrounded by a wide deck made of smooth gray stone. The pool itself was large and rectangular, with a diving board at one end. It was meticulously maintained, with lush green grass and well-manicured bushes and flowers surrounding the deck. A few lounge chairs and tables were arranged around the pool.

It was only that I cared little for any of it. On paper, it had the perfection people dreamed of. In reality, it had a married couple yapping about the local doctor eloping with the mayor's daughter in the middle of the night, ruining everyone's time with silly gossip.

Slapping my knees as I got up, I made my way out of the house and headed for a walk in River Bend for some peace and quiet from the hectic house I was doomed to spend the next two weeks in.

Five years had gone by, but you couldn't tell that from the look of River Bend. Sitting by the Rushing Brook, the river by which the town was named, or having coffee in

Cora's Cafe, or grabbing a solo dinner at the brewery, everywhere I looked, I found memories.

There, I scratched the car on that fateful night.

Here, we set off firecrackers that had half the neighborhood running out and yelling.

It was late evening when I finally headed back to the house and everyone was slowly retiring by the time I got there. Slipping in as quietly as possible, exhausted from the day, I made my way upstairs and into Levi's room.

He was on his knees, rummaging through his massive suitcase and placing his things in the closet.

I clicked my tongue as I shut the door and leaned against it, crossing my arms and observing Levi. He wasn't reacting to my presence.

"You're not going back to Portland at all," I said, the final pieces of this puzzle finally falling into place.

Levi dropped the pair of jeans he'd been holding. "What?"

I was a tattoo artist in my profession and in my heart. That meant I had an eye for detail. And damn me if I hadn't noticed some delicate paradoxes in Levi's behavior. "Fuck, man," I said, amusement growing. Really, I was just proud of myself for getting it right. But, as it all began making sense in my head, I also realized that he was far from the perfect son Margaret and Harold had always pushed onto me to learn from. "You really screwed up, didn't you?"

"I don't know what you're talking about," he said. It was a weak refute, but it was more than the total silence I'd gotten last night.

I snorted. "Tell me if I'm right. You dropped out and nobody knows the truth. You were hiding it for a while, I think, but now that Natalie is getting married, it was as good an opportunity as any to come clean because you knew you had no other options. It's been eating away at you. I noticed you looked tired. Ah, it's keeping you awake at night, isn't it?"

Levi spun to face me, his cheeks red and upturned eyes wide open, glaring. "You're fucking crazy."

My eyebrows wiggled playfully. "That's why you're extra agreeable, right? You wanna soften mommy and daddy before you tell them." And that explained why he was okay sharing his bed with me. "Tell me I'm wrong."

His nostrils flared. "You're wrong."

"Too late," I said when he took a fraction of a second too long to spit it out.

His lips quivered.

I laughed. "Jesus. That's great news. Levi the dropout, huh? The perfect boy finally disappoints. See, I always knew you had it in you."

Levi's eyes narrowed.

"It was just a matter of time. And here we are. The end of the road." I sighed. "Gah, it feels as good as I always imagined."

The deep growl that escaped from his throat sent shivers down my spine. Before I could even process what was happening, Levi pressed both of his hands firmly against my chest and forcibly pushed me backwards until I was almost slammed up against the door. "Imagined?" he demanded. "You've spent all this time imagining me failing? What the fuck is wrong with you?"

I couldn't help but gape at him in shock. "Whoa, take it easy," I said, pressing my index fingers against his chest and pushing him away.

"You're pathetic if this is what you've been fantasizing about," he squeezed through his clenched teeth.

The next words poured out of my mouth venomously when the sting of his argument took root in my heart. "And what are you fantasizing about, Levi? My hand on your dick? Like that night I left?"

His face hardened with terror and he took an abrupt step back. "Shut up," he whispered. "Shut your mouth."

"You thought I didn't notice, huh?" I asked casually, but the truth was it took all my strength to conceal the trembling in my fingers. I shouldn't have said that. I definitely should have kept pretending that it had never happened. But my anger had gotten the better of me once again.

"Th-th-that..." he stammered. "You're a sick fuck."

"Me?" I laughed darkly for a moment. "Of the two of us, you're the one getting hard on family." That wasn't exactly true, but I wasn't here to write a factual history of Levi and myself. I was here to kick back and pass some time. Maybe settle a score or two.

His eyes shimmered. Was he going to cry? That took less effort than I'd imagined. "Shut the fuck up," he threatened, his voice drenched in a mixture of horror and desperation.

"How about no?" I retorted.

Levi stepped up to me, broadening his chest and rising on his toes to bring his face closer to mine. The sneer of hatred was unmistakable. I could play him like a violin.

"Why the fuck do you hate me so much?" he hissed. "What did I ever do to you?"

I opened my mouth to answer this question when a sudden realization blinded me. It had been a decade since I'd last thought of the reasons and the whys. Back then, still a teenager, it had been easy to fall into hatred.

You ruined my life when you moved in here. You ruined what little family I had left.

You were always loved more.

You made me look bad in comparison.

I lost my mom to you.

I was abandoned, yet again, when you joined this house.

There was no fucking way I was going to let any of these words cross my goddamn lips.

But Levi wasn't waiting for an answer. "You have treated me like shit since the day I arrived. And for what? Just because I existed? Because my dad married your mom? You can't be fucking serious. You do realize it wasn't me who fucking proposed, right? So stop fucking tormenting me. I've got more problems than you can imagine and dealing with a thirty-year-old brat isn't something I'm in the mood for."

I bared my teeth. "I'm twenty-eight." Of all the things, was that really the most important argument? I didn't have time to think it over.

Levi brought his face even closer to mine and hissed louder. "And don't you fucking dare mistake momentary lust of a teenager for something more. I don't even like you."

I grabbed his shoulders and spun us around, pinning him against the bedroom door and pulling on my most sinister smirk. This, at least, was something I could disprove as easily as breathing. Oh, I'd seen him looking my way every time he thought I wasn't paying attention. "Are you really sure about that?" I asked, my voice dropping seductively low. My chest pressed against his and Levi's eyes widened. "Because I have a good fucking reason to think you're lying, Levi."

I closed my hand around his face and stared into his eyes. He blinked, his body heating up so much that I could feel it. "Wh-what are you doing?" he whispered. Everything about him was tense, but one rub of my leg proved my point to both of us.

Levi's cock stiffened and throbbed through his skinny jeans and he let out a strangled whimper.

I grinned. "See? You don't have to like me to want me."

He did push me away, then, but not before I had already begun taking a step back and letting go of his face. And that made all the difference. It wasn't like I was going to do anything. But, when it was clear to Levi nothing would happen, he scrambled to make it look like his decision.

I chortled and walked over to our bed. "Good luck falling asleep with that," I said, glancing down at his crotch. His bulge was as visible as the redness in his cute face.

I slipped under the cover and faced away from Levi, who was panting softly by the door. In truth, I had no choice but to turn away. For all my nonchalant teasing,

I was a goddamn hypocrite. My cock ached and my breaths grew shallow.

Dammit.

Was it worth terrorizing him if it would only fan the desire I absolutely shouldn't even have? Was it worth annoying him into madness if I went mad with him?

But my temper often flared and I did things before thinking. And now, I had a painful erection and a hot twink to sleep next to and resist because I couldn't keep my fucking mouth shut.

Chapter Three

LEVI

Fuck. Me.

I stumbled into the bathroom, from where I could hear Aunt Lauren snore twice as loudly from my bedroom. The walls in this house were dangerously thin for the sort of talk I'd just had with Parrish. Luckily, Aunt Lauren was still fast asleep.

My fingers trembled as I let the water in the sink run and splashed my heated face.

He knew.

He knew everything.

All this time, he had known about my feelings. And he had never even bothered to address them. Of course not. Parrish Turner was and always had been a self-centered asshole.

But he doesn't owe you anything, a voice whispered into my ear. *They're your feelings. Yours to deal with.*

And so they were.

Mine to deal with and mine to be tortured by.

Even now, my heart was burning up in my chest under the weight of it all. For all their faults, Harold and Margaret were still my parents. Dropping out of college would break their hearts, but that seemed like a minor inconvenience next to the truth of my feelings for Parrish. It would absolutely destroy them.

And Parrish acted like it was nothing.

He had never seen me as anything more than a guest in his house. The fact that we were related by marriage, brothers in our parents eyes, meant nothing to him. Of course not. The guy had nothing sacred in this world.

But the saddest part? That was exactly what attracted me to him so much. The careless, ruthless actions and views of his. The fact that he would burn this house down to the ground just to make me blush in the sweetest pain I knew. The way he could spin me around his little finger.

I loved being on my knees, both figuratively and literally. And nobody had ever known how to make me feel that way better than Parrish. No guy I'd ever been with came close to what I imagined Parrish could do.

I was such a fucking loser. I compared everyone to the guy I'd never been with. And never would be with. Never *could* be with.

I avoided looking at the mirror. The sight of my face made me sick. The fact that I was still hard as fuck made me want to sob.

Once again, I splashed my face with icy cold water and realized I was only postponing the inevitable. I turned the water off, dried my face with a fluffy towel, and walked back into my room.

Parrish had, at some point, undressed all the way down to just his underwear. Of course he had. Fuck my life.

He was sprawled out on the left side of the bed, half covered and half on display.

My lips twisted downward and he noticed. "Don't even think I'll sacrifice an iota of my comfort to help your conscience," he said darkly. The fucker knew where my problem was. He knew I would have collapsed before him if he was anyone but my stepbrother. And he knew that I could never.

"Fuck. You." I took my pants off and found a pair of sweatpants in the wardrobe to wear in place of pajamas which I didn't have. These had to do.

And Parrish found that funny. The throat chuckle that he had mastered a long time ago sent shivers down my spine, but I ignored him.

I pulled my knees higher up as I covered myself when I got into bed. He turned on the side. It took me a full moment to parse through hormone-made fantasy and reality and realize he hadn't turned to spoon me or claim me, but away from me. And with him went the thin cover.

I yanked it back, kicking a groan out of Parrish. "Are you gonna be like that all night?" he asked.

"Don't steal the cover," I warned.

He growled. "Don't be a child."

"Don't be an ass," I said, mimicking his tone.

"There," he said. "A child. A spoiled brat." And, as if to himself, he added. "Just my fucking luck."

"Don't talk to me like that," I snapped as if I was offended. Really, it was a desperate attempt to conceal that when he called me a spoiled brat, it turned me on. *Everything he does turns me on.* And I hated it.

Parrish yanked the cover back, almost taking all of it. I only managed to grab one corner and tug it back. "If you want to be pampered, you should sleep with mommy and daddy."

I turned on my back at the same time he did, pulling the cover hard. My lower arm brushed against the side of his torso and my skin prickled. I pulled my arm away abruptly and yanked the cover so hard that it ran through his hands. Now, he lay on his back, a surprised smile on his face, body uncovered.

I did my best not to look. I failed.

The lamp on his nightstand was on, illuminating his darker skin. Further down, his black boxer-briefs packed something big.

I turned away from him quickly, panicking that he might steal all of the cover again and reveal that my cock was still as stiff. He would have a lot to say about that. "Just sleep," I rasped. "You can have half." I wiggled my arm around and freed half the cover.

As Parrish adjusted, his right arm pressed against my back. It was lucky I had my T-shirt on, even if it was getting soaked with panic-sweat that broke out over my whole body, because feeling his skin on mine would have made me do something unspeakable.

I shut my eyes and pretended to sleep, all the while listening to Parrish breathe in and out steadily.

Tonight was gonna be a long night. And then, two more weeks remained.

Long after Parrish's artificially steady breaths turned into natural, sleeping ones, I listened. I listened until mine matched his and our hearts beat in unison. I listened and told myself it was the most I would ever get from him. And I should be content with that.

I would never have the courage to reach out and take it, even if he offered it.

Even if he wasn't only messing around with me for the sake of making me feel like shit. How could I? It was like giving my soul to the devil. And for what? A blazing, passionate night of lust, of acting on all my primal instincts, or soothing all my desires. And Parrish would still be the same Parrish I had fallen for. And that Parrish would turn his back on me in a heartbeat.

Had we met in another life, would there ever have been a chance? Perhaps. But this was the life we'd met in, when our parents got engaged without bothering to introduce us to each other before that. And we'd been doomed ever since.

Maybe never having met him would have been better. That, too, was impossible to change. Because we had met and we had been forced onto one another.

My father brought me into this house, forced me to spend time with this gorgeous, older boy, and let us grow up together with all the mixed feelings and hormones running wild. Was it really a surprise I fell for him? This raw, fiery man that defied every order and had a talent to infuriate everyone while wearing that casual smirk of his. God, he was the reason for all my wet dreams. He was what ruined all the guys for me before they even stood a chance.

Did I even have to say I didn't sleep that night? I kept my eyes shut when he woke up to the light blazing through the window and burning our faces. He grunted and sat up. I could feel him turning his head around, scanning the room. Was he looking at me? Was he even noticing me beyond seeing a toy he could use to pass the time?

If only you'd use me right, my tortured heart whispered, but I rejected the premise immediately. I would never let that happen.

It was a few minutes later, when Parrish locked himself in the bathroom, that I opened my eyes again and slipped out of the room. It wasn't like I would get some sleep now that the house was waking up. So, I made my way downstairs, where all the doors and windows were open to let the house breathe. The first hint of the day's heat was already creeping in as breakfast was being set on the large table on the backyard porch.

Margaret spotted me first, as I rubbed my eyes and haunted the hallway to the kitchen. "Darling, you're up," she said and kissed my cheek. "Breakfast is in a few minutes. Where's Parrish?"

"Bathroom," I said, voice groggy not from sleep but from being quiet for nine hours. All night, I'd been staring at the ceiling and telling myself to stop thinking of his heated body inches away from mine.

Dad was sitting down with a large cushion supporting his back and a newspaper hiding his face. He let the upper half collapse and looked at me over the edge. "Morning," he said.

"Why aren't you using the tablet?" I asked. The three of us had pitched in a year and a half ago to buy him a tablet for his birthday. Really, it had been a present for Margaret, because Dad hoarded old newspapers in the shed and she had better ideas for how to use that space.

"It tires my eyes, that damned thing," Dad said. "It's the thought that matters," he added gently afterwards, not to seem too ungrateful.

I chuckled. "Next time, you're getting a tie."

"I think I should like that," Dad said, fixing his newspapers and growing quiet. Every so often, he gritted his teeth. He'd been doing that his entire life while reading the news and it never changed.

Natalie showed up like a ray of sunshine. She stretched at the door and singsonged a good morning to both of us. "Did you sleep well?" she asked me.

I choked on air. "Great," I wheezed.

"I told you it would be alright," Dad said.

Margaret brought out her freshly baked bagels, platters piled up with a million different jams from her pantry, an abundance of coffee and homemade orange juice.

Aunt Lauren appeared at the door and brightened when she saw me. Hints of a hangover still lingered in her eyes and her lips were reddened by wine. "There's our little valedictorian," she squealed when she saw me. Her hug was like iron shackles, but I attempted to find some comfort in it.

She settled herself on the chair next to me and began speaking about the troubles of her flight and car ride up here and how exhausted she was by the end that she slept through the entire day and most of the night. Then, she directed the chatter onto her ex, who was a very dreadful and rude man and she couldn't believe she ever loved him.

Natalie looked at me from the corner of her eyes and I found plenty of pity for my seating arrangement. But someone had to do the job of Aunt Lauren's audience and it was simply a bad deal of hand. It was still better than if I had to sit next to Parrish.

Just as he crossed my mind, he appeared at the door. As always, he wore a pair of knee-length shorts and beach slippers, a scowl and nothing more. His body was a canvas of art that nobody but me and Natalie had seen before.

All eyes went to him and an awkward silence fell onto the porch.

I squirmed. Seeing his chiseled abs never got easier. Not even after a whole night of imagining what it would taste like to lick them.

Margaret and Harold had made their opinions on tattoos clear a long time ago, but their silence was a sign that they wanted some peace in this household for once. And, on a side note, it was one more reason why I definitely wasn't supposed to drool at the table over Parrish, because that would destroy the harmony they so desperately tried to inject.

"Parrish," Aunt Lauren spoke first. "Dear me, you look fresh out of prison."

Parrish dragged on a smile that made him squint. "Auntie dear," he said heartily. "Is that a new lipstick? *Merlot* rouge by any chance?"

I choked on a laugh that I definitely didn't want him to receive from me.

"Parrish," Margaret scolded.

And Aunt Lauren's face turned *Merlot* rouge as she fumed.

"Enough," Dad said. "Let's have breakfast like a family."

Visibly pleased with himself, Parrish plopped down into a chair across from me and forced me to rethink my earlier stance on sitting next to him. That way, at least I wouldn't have to stare at his broad, sculpted chest and have that dark appeal of his glum aesthetic making me salivate.

We did have breakfast like a family. An oddly quiet, awkward one, but a family nonetheless. And the awkwardness softened with every person who got up from the table, leaving their dirty dishes for the last one getting up to wash. Until it was just Parrish and me and the singing birds that lived in the old pines and oaks of our backyard.

"I see you survived the night," he murmured, slapping some more jam on a piece of buttered toast.

"Don't start," I said and reached for my milky, sugary coffee.

"I'm not," he said.

"You are."

"I'm fucking not."

"Yes, you are. See? We're arguing already."

"Christ, we're like that *Monty Python* sketch," he said and crunched the toast under his pearly teeth. He grinned at me, but I didn't return the smile. "Fine," he said at last. "Be the joy killer. The destroyer of fun."

Anger flared in me. Getting mad at him was the closest and easiest substitute for the thing my entire body wanted to do. But since turning the table over and jumping onto his lap to dry-hump his brains out wasn't a viable option, I was stuck with anger. "You should know a thing or two about killing joy."

He examined his fingernails, chewing the toast loudly before he swallowed and spoke. "Me? How so? As far as I remember, I set up your fun pretty well. Not my fault if you couldn't pleasure yourself in the bathroom after..."

"Stop!"

His eyes widened in surprise, but he recovered quickly and stretched his lips lazily. "Gotcha," he said, shooting a finger-gun at me, then pushing himself up from the chair.

Once he strolled into the house, I let myself tremble. Was this what my life was going to be like every day for the next two weeks? Getting murdered by Dad and Margaret for dropping out and hiding it seemed like the lesser of two evils.

If Parrish was so intent on torturing me for my feelings, I wasn't going to last very long at all.

And the worst part? Every time he pushed my buttons, my resolve crumbled. One of these days, it might finally break.

Chapter Four

PARRISH

Inside, it was a mess. The preparations for the lunch at the Wilkinsons' place were in motion and Margaret was almost whipping everyone into place.

"Harold, your shirt needs ironing," she said. "See to it while I get ready."

Harold looked down at his shirt and wrinkled his brow, then nodded.

"Would it be a huge deal if I came late?" I asked Margaret.

She inhaled sharply, as if to say no, then considered it. I could see the cogs turning in her brain. Even though we were all friendly in the house, with nobody around, I had already let my mouth run off on me with Lauren this morning. Right now, Margaret was imagining all the possible opportunities I could get to embarrass us all in front of the all-important senator. "You're supposed to drive Levi."

"I'm sure he won't mind lounging around here a little longer," I said just as Levi hauled half the dishes from the porch into the kitchen.

"But why?" Margaret asked, not very convincingly. It obviously suited her.

I shrugged. "I'm not feeling all too social. Couldn't sleep. Change of bed, you know?" I listed random reasons. "Besides, it gives you two more time to get familiar with the senator, right? And the lunch won't be for another few hours."

"Right," Margaret said and thought a little more about it. "Why don't you boys take care of the dishes, then?" Margaret asked me.

"I can do it," Levi said quickly from the kitchen.

I rolled my eyes.

"Why shouldn't Parrish help you?" Margaret asked.

"Yeah, Levi," I said softly so only he could hear the undertones. I knew he could. "Let me help you with that. You don't have to do everything by yourself."

He glanced at me for the briefest of moments, then nodded hesitantly. Every leading son point he lost was precious to him now that he needed to tell the truth of his failure to the two people who only ever cared about things to boast about.

We all got busy with our own things. Aunt Lauren, Margaret, and Harold went upstairs to get ready, while Levi finished hauling in the dishes.

"Jeez, you're really trying to soften them," I said as I scooted over for Levi to unload the dishes into the sink. "I'll rinse."

Levi said nothing.

Last night had been full of close calls and dangerous encounters. I'd loosened my tongue with him and said things to get a reaction out of him, but it seemed he took them all very seriously.

We stood side by side at the sink and I saw him blatantly direct his gaze at my bare torso for a moment that lingered just a little too long.

With nothing better to do while waiting for the first of the soapy plates, I wiggled my hips and bumped into him with my ass. "Hurry up."

"Stop," he said, strangled.

"Stop what?" I bumped my ass against him again. "This? It's bothering you?"

Levi pursed his lips and focused on the plate he'd been scrubbing for way too long already.

"Cos that was nothing," I said idly, then leaned toward him. My lips hovered an inch away from his left ear. "Imagine if I began whispering to you seductively like this."

Levi tensed and jerked his head away. The very first thing he did was scan the space around us in case anyone saw me do this.

I chuckled.

"Don't linger for too long, boys," Margaret called a moment later. "You'll miss lunch."

In all honesty, my little whispering bit had been just a tad riskier than I had planned, but we were safe enough.

Then, like we couldn't hear her, she spoke to Harold. "They seem to be getting along."

"As brothers should," Harold said, making the hairs on my neck stiffen. "I told you they would."

"They grew out of it," she said excitedly, but kept her voice low as all three of them filed out.

I glanced at Levi for some clue to his reaction, but found reddening cheeks. Was he angry? Was he ashamed? I just made a joke out of it. "As brothers should," I imitated Harold's raspy voice. "Am I supposed to take you out to play catch, now?"

Levi let out a strangled sound that might have been a fake laugh, but I couldn't tell. "Shut up," he huffed.

I snorted. "They're so fucking delusional."

Levi smacked his lips and looked at me, soapy water dripping from his hands. "And you're so negative. Aren't you supposed to be happy? Isn't that the whole point of you not returning back here for five years?"

"I'm happy enough when I'm away," I said flatly.

"You sure don't seem like it," he accused. "In fact, you sound like a miserable ass. Nobody likes complainers, Parrish. And all you ever do is complain. What's up?"

I took a step toward him. Being almost a foot taller than Levi, it was easy to tower over him. And when I brought my face down, inches away from his crumbling defiant expression, he fell silent. Lips parted, eyes wide. "Of course I'm fucking complaining. Who wouldn't when they have to share the house with a spoiled brat and the people who made him that way?"

"No one fucking asked me about anything here," Levi snapped, dropping the plate into the soapy water and shaking his hands dry. "And if you mean to take all your anger out on me when I had the least say in how things went, then you're a bigger asshole than I thought." The venomous hiss stopped abruptly when I lifted my hands and placed them on each side of his face.

My expression softened just as his eyes widened. Gently, slowly, I leaned in and puckered my lips as I brought them down an inch away from his. I watched as he slowly closed his eyes and his head tilted a little to the right, my chest tightening as Levi licked his lips. Then, at the very last moment, I lifted my head a bit and blew a soft breath of air onto his cheek.

"What are you doing?" Levi huffed breathlessly just as I did so.

Tension lifted off my chest. I frowned and pulled back, releasing him as his eyes quickly shot open. "Blowing an eyelash off your cheek. Why? What did you think I was doing?"

Levi blinked twice in close succession, roses blooming in his cheeks. I couldn't tell whether he was embarrassed he'd fallen for it or angry that nothing had happened.

"Is it just me or is it getting hot in here?" I asked, fanning my face. "You sure you need that top? Or those shorts?"

Levi seemed to finally remember where he was and who he was with and snapped out of the trance he was in just as I grinned. He frowned and turned partially away from me, getting busy with the sink. "Stop that."

"Stop what?"

"You know what," he said, voice hoarse, almost exasperated.

I stepped up behind him and put my hands on the marble edge of the counter around the sink and positioned myself right up against his back, my crotch on his bubble butt. *Christ, he smells good*, I thought as a red alert went off in my head. I was supposed to be the one in control around here. Dropping my voice lower and pulling my self-control together, I reached over and closed my hands over his. "Let me show you how it's done."

"Fucking hell," Levi snapped, craning his neck where my breath tickled him. "Stop bullying me."

I pulled my hands back and put them around his waist. "How am I bullying you?"

He didn't answer.

"If anything, you should welcome it," I said as he turned to face me. I lifted my hand and feathered my thumb over his high cheekbone. "No one's gonna treat you the way I do, baby boy."

"Fuck," he wheezed and slapped my hand away just as his pupils dilated.

I let out a lazy chuckle. "I'm just fucking with you, Levi. Remove that stick from your ass. It makes you boring."

"I'm not your toy to pass the time," he said in the same, strangled voice.

I narrowed my eyes as my lips stretched into a dark smile. "But you really are." The words came out of my throat as a purr, all the while I was leaning in. I was one heartbeat away from saying *rawr* but Levi pushed me away. I snorted instead.

Despite his protests, Levi dropped his gaze along my torso and let it linger near my hips. Or rather, just below my waist.

My cock gave a sleepy throb, having gotten semi hard from pressing our bodies together. It was nothing I couldn't control. I wasn't *really* doing anything, right?

"You're enjoying this way too much," Levi said.

I shrugged and crossed my arms at my chest. "We're young in a big, empty house. And, we're *not* actually related. Where's the harm?"

Shit. He was easy to play with. I could see the thoughts spinning behind his eyes. Was he really contemplating it?

I took a step forward and he took a step back, but he was stopped by the kitchen counter and I closed the distance between us. My heart pounded in my throat as I looked into his mossy eyes. I brushed his cheek with mine as I brought my lips near his ear. "If no one hears you moan, did you even come?"

Levi pushed me back and I barked out a laugh. Then, he spun away from me, murmuring something about taking a shower and something about me being unbelievable.

I gave him a head start before I headed after him, though I had no idea what to do once I reached him. I just knew he was cutting the fun short way too soon. I heard the doors shut in haste. First the bedroom, then the bathroom.

I walked into his – our – bedroom quietly with every intention to knock on the bathroom door before he got into the shower.

But as I raised my fist to knock, I froze. Was he fucking crying?

I perked my ears to hear better. Goddammit, I shouldn't have done that. Because Levi wasn't crying at all. Those weren't sobs he was choking on. He was panting. It was the slapping that clued me in and my entire body tingled. His fist, his crotch, his choked breaths.

Levi was jerking off behind this door.

My cock got instantly hard and fear made my heart drum fast. What was I even afraid of? I'd been pushing him in this direction all day, but I'd never committed. As if leaving my real reasons in the dark somehow made it all mean nothing. It was so hard to think. It seemed like I could hear nothing but the increasing speed of his fist and the occasional whimpers that left his throat.

Fuck. Me.

My heart pumped blood hard, most of which went straight to my cock. It throbbed and ached until I placed a hand on it and shut my eyes. I could picture him even though I knew I shouldn't. I had to stop, but the images kept pouring out. I saw his pants and underwear tight around his knees, the bottom edge of his T-shirt was lifted and between his teeth to stifle his moans. His abs were flexing, his cock slick with precum and his fist was tight around it.

Fuck. I could almost taste the salty sweat on his brow as he ground toward his orgasm. I could feel his perfect, blond hair tangled between my fingers as I yanked a fistful and brought him to his knees. I could hear him choke after telling him he wasn't allowed to come yet.

I sucked in a deep breath of air and tore my feet off the carpet. I needed to get out of this room. I needed to stop listening. This all got way too real, way too fast. And I wasn't sure I was totally against the idea. Every time I'd fired a shot, it pierced my armor, too. Every time I whispered seductively, it made my cock twitch. And every time his big, green eyes widened, I felt a little proud of myself. But I kept telling myself I was merely joking. And I needed to keep that in mind.

I rushed down the stairs and finished the dishes in a desperate hope for some sort of distraction, but my pulsing cock let me have none.

My head pounded with my heartbeat. My fingers trembled until I took three deep breaths and stilled them. And the worst of all, my heart ached with longing to travel back in time and open the door instead of walking away. Obviously, I would never have done that, but the fantasy lived vividly in my head.

When I saw Levi next, it was half an hour later. He was freshly showered and, as usual, quiet.

"We should go," I rasped, some time later.

"Yeah," he replied.

And that was the last we spoke in a long while. The drive there was unbearably silent. Whenever I opened my mouth, three things happened at the same time: an image of Levi's fist working his slick cock filled my brain; an overly sexual remark loaded behind my teeth; my ability to string words together decreased.

I needed to remind myself to breathe slowly and *not fucking think about where Levi's cum went*. Because that mystery had been on my mind. Had he sprayed the tiles in the shower? Or had it all gone onto his stomach? And what did his stomach look like? Was it as trimmed as his arms? Or was it just flat? And why didn't he take his T-shirt off at any point around me?

As we approached our destination, I couldn't help but roll my eyes at its grandeur. The huge front yard was perfectly manicured — probably by a bunch of underpaid workers — with lush green grass and neatly trimmed hedges. A long, winding driveway led up to the front entrance, surrounded by blooming flower beds and tall trees that offered a shady canopy.

After leaving the car, we walked up the steps to the porch and were greeted by a large, ornate front door. On either side of the door were large, frosted glass panels that allowed light to filter into the entrance hall.

A man I could only imagine was the goddamn butler opened the door.

"Hiya," I said, horrifying the poor fellow with my informality. "Turner and Bartlet. The other half of them, at least." Levi snorted next to me, half a step behind.

"Follow me," the hook-nosed man with a deeply receding hairline and thinning white hair replied.

As we entered the mansion, I was slapped by the sense of opulence. The entrance hall was spacious and airy, with a high ceiling and a large, sweeping staircase that led to the upper floors.

The butler fellow walked on, leading us to the back of the house and into the backyard.

The property was surrounded by lush greenery and had a massive lawn, dotted with mature trees and even more goddamn flower beds. Another winding path led to a spacious gazebo at the center of the yard, with plenty of room for seating.

The gazebo was made of white wood and had a peaked roof with shingle tiles. It was adorned with beautiful floral arrangements and had elegant wooden railings that offered a stunning view of the surroundings. The sun was shining brightly and I could feel the warm breeze on my face as I approached.

In front of the gazebo was a long wooden table, set for a large group of people. It was surrounded by chairs and was decorated with a white tablecloth, gleaming silverware, and crystal glasses. The table was surrounded by beautifully tended gardens, with tall trees offering a sense of privacy and serenity.

And there they were; the Wilkinsons, the Turners, and a Bartlet, rubbing elbows and chortling.

"Jesus Christ," I muttered to Levi, not because I was suddenly consumed with a burning desire to bond but because he was the closest thing with ears around me. Besides, I finally had something else but his self-pleasuring to talk about. "I think I'm going to gag."

"Shut up," Levi muttered under his breath.

I pulled my gaze back to examine him. His face was stony and expressionless, except for the curly corners of his lips that trembled for a heartbeat. He was trying not to laugh. "I hope they don't slap us with a wad of cash for being late."

The butler sniffed.

Levi bit his lower lip hard, refusing to look at me. There was a glint in his eyes that encouraged me more. "I bet there's gold particles in the champagne."

"Mr. Turner and Mr. Bartlet," the butler announced.

"Should I tip him?" I asked Levi, who suddenly slapped my elbow.

The butler looked down the length of his nose and right at me, sniffed, and walked back into the house. Why wasn't I surprised?

I looked at Levi and gestured with my head. "Come on." My gaze dropped to where he was balling his fists nervously and, for just one moment, I was ever so slightly sorry that he was walking on needles. From one disappointment to another, I understood what it felt like.

You'll get over it, I thought before I remembered I had absolutely no reason to make any of this easier for him. I'd only ever been slightly disappointing to Margaret before Levi had joined our home. The comparison had pushed me into oblivion.

We walked up to the crowd of people. The senator, a stout man in his early sixties, with more salt than pepper in his hair and neatly trimmed beard, and his wife stood with Margaret and Harold, while Aunt Lauren doted on an expensive port and Natalie in the gazebo.

"There you are, boys. We were starting to worry," Harold said in my general direction.

I was held back by listening to your son masturbate in the bathroom. I smiled politely. "I'm sorry, we got lost on the way here."

"Lost? What do you mean lost?" Harold asked.

I pressed two fingers against my temple in the universal gesture for *duh*. "Right? I should have just followed the sight of the castle on top of the hill."

Margaret cut in quickly to save them from further embarrassment. "Senator, Mrs. Wilkinson, let me introduce my sons. This is Levi Bartlet. He studies information technology and data science in Portland. Soon to graduate and, if you don't mind me bragging, we have no doubt he'll be at the top of his class. Isn't that right, darling? He's always been ever so smart, hasn't he, Harold? Valedictorian in high school. His career counselor told us there wasn't a career Levi wouldn't excel in. The world's his oyster, as they say. Isn't that so?" she asked no one in particular. "No doubt he'll be a leading expert in, well, information technology, I suppose. Don't you think so, Senator?" Margaret was almost teary-eyed as she spoke, though I didn't believe it. Besides, I was too busy trying not to laugh at the delusion of it all. She all but pinched Levi's cheek. "And this is Parrish."

I bit my lip so hard I nearly drew blood. It worked. The rapturing wave of laughter stayed inside of me. "Pleased to make your acquaintance," I said with a smile so fake it was criminal. When I looked at Levi, he was turning into a ripe Red Delicious. *Ready for plucking*, I thought idly, then pushed that idea away. Having heard the slapping of his fist against his groin just an hour earlier still made me feel all sorts of ways, none of which were particularly innocent.

"Parrish?" Margaret said tightly. "Senator Wilkinson asked you a question."

"Hm?" I was miles away. In fact, I was about two and a half miles southwest from here, still upstairs, listening to Levi's fist work its magic. Christ, why did he have to be so fucking sexy? Everyone was looking at me.

"What do you do?" the stout man asked with a fake smile that outranked mine.

"I have a tattoo shop in New York," I said simply.

Margaret squirmed. But not as much as Aunt Lauren with her glass of port.

"How interesting," Mrs. Wilkinson said and, oddly enough, sounded genuine. "Are those the samples of your own work?" she asked, gesturing at my arms.

I laughed. "On my right arm," I said. "See, I'm left handed." I turned my right arm for a short exhibition of my tattoos.

The next question everyone asked was: "What do they mean?" and I was already practicing not rolling my eyes. But Mrs. Wilkinson's eyes widened as she examined the art and nodded. "Fascinating. You truly have talent. Please, make yourselves comfortable. There are cold drinks over there."

I saw the cooler with beer and I rushed to close the short distance to grab myself one. Yes! That was just what I needed to get rid of this tension. Either that, or doubling down and taking my stepbrother to bed. Which I wasn't *really* going to do. Right?

Just as I opened my beer bottle, someone talking in haste grabbed everyone's attention.

I glanced back at the house where a man in his early thirties, blond and drop-dead handsome, made his way across the lawn. He waved at us, half-turning away to finish his conversation. "I don't care about your opinion," he said in a voice that was only mock-quiet for privacy. "No, I don't. You should have listened more carefully, then. No, no, no. I don't want to hear it. Are you even listening to me? Get those options today or I'll be looking for another assistant and I really don't have time for another task right now." He pursed his lips, nodding. He glanced at us and gave an apologetic smile as if to say the person on the other end was being silly. A frown quickly replaced that smile. "I want those options and I want them now. Get. It. Done." He hung up, pinched the bridge of his nose and exhaled. When he lifted his head again, he was all handsome smiles and polite words. "Welcome, friends. I'm terribly sorry to be late. Important business."

Jarred Wilkinson cracked a smile that outshone his father's and mine combined. Pearly white teeth reflected the sunlight blindingly as he extended his hand to greet the guests. He kissed Margaret, shook hands with Harold, and was indifferent to Levi and me.

Finally, he headed to the gazebo, introduced himself to Aunt Lauren, and kissed Natalie. "My love," he said. It sounded so forced and fake that it scratched my ear.

Everyone was slowly moving past the table and to the gazebo, but Levi and I were the slowest ones. "Is that guy for real?" I whispered.

Levi shot me a look that said he hadn't been paying attention. I had a nasty idea that he, too, was two and a half miles southwest, still in that bathroom.

For the rest of the day, I stewed in pleasantries. Senator was busy with his tablet, muttering about the news. Mrs. Wilkinson was doting on her son, and the man-baby himself seemed one 'no' away from throwing a tantrum. And if he wasn't making requests, he was bragging about stocks. As if the concept of stocks was his own idea.

Natalie, for what it was worth, seemed to have a good effect on him. When she was by his side, Jarred's smugness decreased. For the most part, but not completely. He still managed to sneak in a few patronizing comments about the way Natalie had done her hair.

I only realized my fists were clenched when my fingernails dug into my palms and sent pain to my brain. *I will not punch the groom*, I whispered my new mantra internally. *I will not punch him.*

I pressed the bottle against my mouth and pulled back a good swig of beer. From across the long dining table we sat around, a gaze ticked my attention. I looked to find a pair of mossy eyes with dark circles and thin, black eyebrows flat above them, staring at me. Levi was observing something until I saw him, then quickly looked away.

What's going on in that cute head of yours? I wondered and stretched my legs under the white-linen clad table. My foot bumped someone's. Levi shot me a glare.

Bingo, I thought. Now I was sure it wasn't senator Wilkinson's foot.

I kicked it playfully again, observing the way Levi's lips stiffened. I was willing to bet my tattoo shop that more of him was getting hard than just his expression.

I set my beer on the table, ignoring the chatter around me. I was lucky enough to sit next to Lauren, who pretty much refused to talk to me.

My right foot hooked under Levi's Achilles tendon and our gazes met. I wore a lopsided smile that bared my teeth a little and he wore that frightened expression that turned me on hard. He curved his eyebrows into a threatening frown, but I looked at him in a "Whatcha gonna do about it?" way.

As his gaze scanned the rest of the people around the table like they could suddenly see through tablecloths, I dragged the upper side of my foot along his calf. And while he wore denim knee-length shorts to appear polite but stay comfortable, I was the careless motherfucker who came here in regular cotton shorts and slippers. And I bet Levi was regretting not wearing his long jeans instead.

My bare foot caressed his smooth, tense calf as I relaxed back in my chair.

Flustered, Levi didn't pull his leg away. He could have done it a million times. Instead, he glanced at me, and sparks came to life when our gazes locked. But he looked away quickly, squirming in the chair.

You're fucking enjoying this, you dirty boy, I thought. But the thought was immediately disrupted when my heart throbbed hard and I realized I was, too. *Fuck, it feels good to touch him.* And the fact that he couldn't stop looking around, making sure nobody saw how horny I'd made him, made this a billion times better.

Levi swallowed so hard that it was almost audible all the way across the table. And then, old boy Wilkinson turned to him to inquire more about data science.

Levi blurted out an answer the best he could as my toe tickled the skin behind his knee. His eyes went glassy as his thoughts roamed away from data science and back to the sensations that soared through his body. I felt them, too. They filled me with energy and spite and desire.

For the nth time, I wondered if it was worth it. Teasing him into oblivion, but falling there right by his side.

At long last, when my big toe slipped under the bottom edge of his shorts, a hand grabbed my foot and jerked it so that I nearly lost balance in my chair.

It took all I had to stop myself from barking out a laugh. So, when it was free, I pulled my foot back and watched him with all the shameless smugness right there on my face.

It was after the elaborate lunch, when small groups emerged from our merry band, that I spotted Jarred talking to Lauren and Margaret in one corner. For a moment, I foolishly thought Jarred was trying to win them over, but then I approached the three and overheard the conversation.

"...bizarre, if you ask me. I would never have failed a client like that. No ma'am. I told him so, too. I told him I would be jumping out of the window if I were him." And then, as I plastered my face with a polite smile, Jarred all but vomited the word "stocks" all over my shoes. I heard it so many times that the word itself sounded meaningless. *Stocks, stocks, stocks. Socks. Ducks. Dicks. Ricks. Hicks. Hiccups. Cups. A few too many.* I blinked and pulled myself back into the present moment.

"Sorry, but what do you do, again?" I asked in a moment of silence.

Jarred didn't get my joke. No one ever did. "Trading, dude. I'm the new wolf of Wall Street. If you like profits,

I'm your guy." He immediately overstepped his boundaries and placed one scowl-inducing hand on my shoulder. "I'm not even kidding. I'll gladly do it for Natalie's family. I'll keep my commission at the minimum for you, my man."

I said nothing.

Jarred wasn't bothered. "The only question is, do you like winning?"

"Not particularly," I said and pushed his hand off my shoulder.

He didn't seem to notice. Or, if he did, he was quick to recover. He continued to amaze the Turner sisters with his tales of shorting overpriced stocks and making a killing. My head hurt just from the little I had listened to.

It was a long while later, when I killed the engine in Margaret and Harold's garage and got out of the car, that I finally found the words I could say to him. "I'm sorry I keep calling you spoiled. In my defense, I'd never met anyone as spoiled as that man-child Natalie is about to marry."

Levi sucked his teeth. "As much as I hate it, I have to agree with you for once. What the hell does she see in him?"

That bothered me a lot, too. What *did* she see in that guy? He was an absolute asshole. "Not to be crass, but..." I raised my eyebrows and shrugged.

Levi snorted. "If anything, that was small dick energy."

I laughed shortly. "You'd know, wouldn't you?"

"Did you just call me a size queen?" Levi asked in a way that I couldn't be sure if he was serious or joking.

I sauntered up next to him and threw my elbow up to rest on his shoulder. "If it talks like a duck and walks like a duck," I said.

He didn't push it away. "Let's just go inside," he whispered breathlessly.

Chapter Five
Levi

I punched the pillow under my head.

Though this was only the second night of sharing my bed with Parrish, there existed a routine. It was simple. I lay on the right side, facing the wardrobe and the desk under the window. Parrish had the left side and the nightstand. He didn't cross into my half and I didn't cross into his. And when I couldn't sleep from the crushing anxiety of having to face Dad's disappointment one day soon or because of the infernal heat of Parrish's body, I kept from sighing or talking, so that Parrish could sleep.

"Could you not?" Parrish growled. In reply to me directing my frustrations at the pillow.

"It's uncomfortable," I grumbled.

"Pretend it isn't," he suggested.

"Go fuck yourself," I returned without venom.

He sighed like he was giving up the fight. "Fine. Let me help."

Before I knew what was up, it was already too late. A strong, heated arm wrapped around me; his bare skin touched the parts of mine where my short-sleeved sleeping tee didn't cover me.

Every cell in my body strained to memorize what his touch felt like. And every ounce of energy went into speaking. "What are you doing?"

"Cuddling you to sleep," he said matter-of-factly. "So that I can sleep, too."

"What? That's not what..." I blurted.

"Shh," he said soothingly. Everything about it was so fake and designed to push my buttons that I couldn't even be outraged, but had to admire his resolve. His open palm pressed against the middle of my chest and he gave a little rub-rub. Then, he lifted his hand and began rubbing the soft spot of my ear with his fingers. "There, there. Would you like a little lullaby?"

"Parrish, stop," I growled, but a moan left my nose as soon as my words were out. *Fuck*.

He snickered. "You didn't mind it at the Wilkinsons' mansion."

I inhaled through my rapidly constricting throat. "What was I supposed to do? They were looking."

"Nobody was looking," Parrish said, using the back of his index finger to caress my cheek. Every hair on my body rose. And fuck if I didn't want to believe he was genuine. He wasn't. Of course he wasn't. But it was getting harder to tell.

Had I been born with the ability to have one hour to do whatever I wanted to do without any consequences, I would have used that hour now. I would have turned on my back, taken his hand in mine, and brought it down to where it could do the most good. And I would spread my legs for him and take him in and cry out with all the lust that I had gathered and never spent over the years.

Sadly, I was born without such a thing. It took everything I had in me to speak these words, but I had no choice. "I swear to God, Parrish, if you don't stop, I will kick you in the ribs."

He snorted against the hackled hairs on my neck one last time, then turned to lie on his back. "You know that saddest part of sleeping in the same bed?"

I didn't ask. I didn't need to. He was going to enlighten me regardless.

"When a guy just wants to let loose and can't because there's a prude lying next to him," he said. Obviously, he was leading me on.

And I fucking rose to the bait. "There's the bathroom. Let loose all you like," I growled.

He chuckled. "You know all about that, don't you?"

My breath hitched and my burning cheeks almost set fire to the pillow. I swallowed a pained whimper as embarrassment pulled me deep into the mattress. If only it would suffocate me. "What?" I croaked.

"Letting loose in the bathroom and all that," Parrish said idly.

He knew? How the fuck did he know every dirty secret I had? How? "What are you...?"

"Chill, little bro," he grunted and smacked his lips like he was starting to doze off. "It's only natural. Guys gotta do what guys gotta do. Nighty-night."

But I knew exactly what he was saying. He was calling me a hypocrite. And I was one, for fuck's sake. Whether his 'advances' were real or fake, it didn't matter. I was the one who'd shot them down, no matter how much it pained me, only to lock myself up and fantasize about an alternate universe in which I'd surrendered myself to him. I fantasized about being on my knees for Parrish, and him forcing me to keep quiet, filling my mouth with his undoubtedly thick, long cock until tears streamed down my cheeks.

It had taken me less than five minutes to bring myself to my climax today. He only needed to exist and I crumbled to pieces.

I wasn't going to survive this family visit. I wasn't going to get through this without making a horrible, unforgivable mistake. And that mistake started fucking snoring in unison with Aunt Lauren in the room next door.

I rolled my eyes and shut them to no avail. I couldn't blame him, though. I wasn't going to sleep either way.

I stopped pretending to be asleep when the first golden rays glimmered in the eastern sky my window looked to. They fought back the darkness of the night but did nothing to lighten up my heart. It gave a pained knock in my chest, letting me know it was still beating.

I breathed in and out softly and waited for more light outside to let me know I could get up. It happened, in time. The glow grew stronger and the rays of sunshine fell in through the window, lighting up Parrish's face. All his features seemed softer and gentler when he was asleep. There was nothing devious about this beautiful man when his brain wasn't working and when I wasn't a tool he used for amusement.

But a tool I was. And I didn't even hate it. Not truly. It was exactly what I had grown up fantasizing about. Just there, six feet away from me, there was my desk. As a child, back when I had still harbored some dreams and had imagination, I had spent countless hours learning to sketch just so I could put Parrish's gorgeous face and handsome body on paper. And even now, tucked in the corner of my desk, my backpack held two sketchbooks. One was for my idle sketches and the other was a sketchbook I had never brought myself to throw away. And because I couldn't throw it away, I couldn't let it out of my sight, either. Because it was filled with my imaginings of what Parrish looked like when he fucked.

Yeah. I had a hundred drawings of my stepbrother, each earning me a faster ticket to hell than the one before.

Would Parrish toy with me the way he did if he knew? Would he dare fan the embers that could start a wildfire? Or would he finally quit this shit and stop messing with me? Because he wasn't serious. I knew that. He didn't mean any of that shit. He just wanted to shock and torment me, blind to the fact that it made my desire run deeper every time.

I turned my head to look at him. His eyes were closed softly and he breathed through his nose. He slept on his stomach, the cover tangled under and between his legs, both of his arms underneath his pillow cradling his head. And I watched him.

I watched his handsome face.

I watched his muscular back.

I watched the beautiful curve of his ass in his black boxer-briefs and his sculpted legs, rare but coarse hair covering them. He was such a contrast to everything I was. Like an Adonis, he was someone I had always aspired to be more like. But I had never managed to come close.

Damn you, I thought as I watched the peaceful expression on his face. *I had no idea I was better off when you didn't know I existed.* But how could he ever understand a statement like that? Parrish didn't fall for people. Parrish flirted, fucked, and left behind. I didn't need to know it for a fact to know it in my heart.

I got up when sounds came from downstairs.

As quietly as I could, I went to the bathroom, washed my face and brushed my teeth, then headed downstairs. The sawmill in Aunt Lauren's room shook the roof and the foundations of the house and I wondered if she heard as much noise from our room. Margaret was in the kitchen, getting fresh cookies out of the oven. "Morning," I said, rubbing my tired, stinging eyes.

"Good morning, sweetie-pie," Margaret said, all but pinching my cheeks, which she probably would have done for real had it not been for the big mittens on her hands. "Did you sleep well?"

"Great," I lied and scratched my nose. "Need some help in here?"

"Oh, no," Margaret said, taking the mittens off. "It's all done already." She sucked a breath of air. "Your father's out back," she pointed at the sliding glass door leading to the porch. "He wants to talk to you. Why don't you sit out there with him while I run to the farmer's market?"

"Farmer's market?" I asked.

"We buy everything locally," she said with pride.

I smiled and nodded. She had always been an early riser and she liked people noticing it.

Dad was reading the newspaper over a mug of coffee outside. The air was still cool and dew sparkled on the grassy lawn under the first proper rays of sunshine. "Morning," I greeted as I poured myself a mug of coffee from the large pot in the middle of the rather empty table. Breakfast wouldn't be ready for another hour or so.

"Levi," Dad said like he hadn't seen me in ages. He folded his paper and pushed his reading glasses above his eyebrows, so he appeared like he had two sets of eyes instead of one. Then came the mandatory "sleep well?" and an automatic "great."

"Margaret said you wanted to…talk?" I winced. My heart twisted in my chest as weight appeared on my shoulders out of nowhere. I hadn't even realized I had shed it earlier. And now, I expected him to ask the truth about my studies.

I wasn't ready to face this.

I wasn't even goddamn close.

Dad sighed and shook his head. His voice dropped low. "This isn't easy, Son, but…" he let it hang.

My stomach dropped. Cold sweat covered my palms and my heart began beating in my throat.

Dad shifted uncomfortably in his chair and leaned a little closer. I didn't move. I sat unnaturally still, hands placed down on the table. How did people normally sit? Where did they put their hands? Not straight in front of them?

He cleared his throat. "I wanted to ask you about Parrish."

Terror ripped my heart into pieces the moment my temporary confusion shattered. I opened my mouth, but my lips were curving down and my eyes stung. Could he see through me? How much did he know? What had he seen?

Someone must have noticed the way Parrish rubbed his foot against my leg yesterday. Did Dad see it with his own eyes?

I licked my lips. "What about him?"

Dad looked more uncomfortable than when he'd tried explaining to me where babies came from. And even more than when I'd come out to him and he realized that entire conversation had been for nothing and he had a whole different kind of birds and bees to teach me about.

This wasn't good.

Dad rubbed his hands together and in the silence I heard some chatter deep inside the house, then Margaret saying goodbye and leaving for the market.

"It's only that I — *we*, Margaret agrees with me to a dot — worry. About you. And Parrish. You. With Parrish." He stammered as he looked for words and my heart all but stopped beating.

I was as good as dead. "Why worried?" I asked, but my voice was hollow. He knew clear as day. He knew how much I wanted Parrish to come from behind me, wrap his arms around my body so I couldn't breathe, let alone move, and how badly I wanted him to fuck me until I cried.

But how did he know? I wanted to scream the question desperately.

"Margaret and I talked a great deal about this, Levi. I understand what it's like to have an older brother." He couldn't. He had a younger sister he'd lost contact with. And neither could I; I had a stepbrother I lusted after. "It can be tempting," Dad said and let the silence linger.

My heart felt like someone was literally grilling it, slapping it with a spatula, then flipping it. Holy fucking shit, I wasn't going to live through this conversation.

I swallowed the growing knot in my throat.

"It can be *appealing*," Dad added. "Ah...to wish to be...how should I put this?"

Every survival instinct in my body was flaring. I wanted to run far away and not stop running until my legs failed me.

"To be more like him, you know," Dad finished.

I blinked. "What?"

He shifted in his chair again, wincing at the ache in his back. "Let me be clear, Levi. Margaret and I are worried that you might start seeing Parrish as a role model. You should absolutely not. You were too young to understand. That boy's trouble. We tried and tried, but nothing worked. No punishment or incentive could correct his behavior. And we worry he might be a bad influence on you."

I frowned. "Are you serious, Dad?" I couldn't help the anger that rose in me like a riptide.

"Why shouldn't I be?" Dad asked defensively. "You see, we're trying, for Natalie's sake, to have some peace in here, but you must know as well as I do that Parrish is merely tolerating us all. He's nobody you should look up to, Levi. For God's sake, he fancies himself a business owner, when his business is about permanent damage to people's bodies. And don't think we haven't noticed you two snickering. We sure have. And Margaret is worried he might impress you with that swagger or whatever you want to call it."

"She's okay with this?" I asked, unable to believe it.

"Of course she is. She brought it up." Dad shook his head like he didn't understand what part confused me. "Listen," he said, his voice even lower now. "You'll understand in time, Levi. You are a good kid. You don't need distractions like that. Finish your studies. You only have a little longer to go. Your future is still ahead of you."

I let out a bitter laugh. "Are you for real, Dad?" My head shook vehemently before I could rein all this anger in. "This is so unfair. And misinformed, I'll have you know. Feel free to say so to Margaret, or I will as soon as she's back." I slammed my full mug of coffee against the table, spilling some onto the white cloth. "You two made him feel like crap until you threw him out. Yeah, he misbehaved. What teenager stuck in a boring small town doesn't?"

Dad pulled back, suddenly not so much in pain, but wincing at my tone. "You never did, Levi," he said, then shook his head. "What is this reaction? I thought you'd understand."

"Oh, I understand," I said. "And no, he's not my role model in any sense. You can rest assured, he isn't. Even if I wanted him to be, he wouldn't do it. Parrish might be self-centered, but that's only because he was forced to be independent. And you two are worse. You did that to him." My lips quivered with rage as I stood up. "Do you not realize what you made here? A lifetime of resentment from the very first day you and I moved in here. That's what. You've both put me on a pedestal and treated him like crap. The guy never stood a chance, for Christ's sake. Oh, but you liked to flaunt us as true brothers whenever someone asked, all the while doing your goddamn best to rub his face in the dirt. You're not fair, Dad. Neither of you are."

Dad's eyes widened and he paled rapidly with every word I said. "Levi, calm down. You're not thinking rationally about this."

"And don't you think I'm protecting him because I want to be more like him. I really f-f-freaking don't. But someone has to take his side once in a damn while." I hissed out the last part and turned away from Dad.

That was when I saw it.

His figure receding toward the stairs, storming around, and stomping up.

I turned to look at Dad as horror crossed my face. My heart fractured through the center. I couldn't believe this was real. Tears of rage and sadness for the injustice in this house welled in my eyes and I balled my fists to calm myself even a little.

Parrish had heard.

And nobody ever fucking cared how Parrish felt.

Chapter Six

PARRISH

"Out of my way," I barked, blind with rage, nearly trampling Lauren as she stumbled down the stairs. She was yet another thorn in my sorry ass.

I slammed the bedroom door so hard that dust spilled out of the walls. Well, I didn't care if I slammed them off the hinges.

Why did I let myself even hope things might have gotten a fraction better? Yeah, it was all for appearances, but even that had been better than this. Why couldn't we just keep all this bullshit under the rug?

I wanted to punch something, but everything in this goddamn room was Levi's and he deserved his shit punched the least. So, I paced. To the window and back to the door. Window. Door. Window. Door.

I could go away.

I still knew people in this shitty town, even if we weren't fast friends anymore. I could go to Toby's place. Except, Toby now lived with Grace, and I had missed their wedding, and they had a baby.

I wasn't good with babies.

One of us would need to leave the house.

And I wouldn't bet much that Toby would send his two-year-old to a motel while I crash at his place.

I took a deep breath and reminded myself why I was here. *Natalie*, I whispered internally. I was here for her. I was here to support her, even if I secretly believed Jarred wasn't worthy of her love.

Christ, everything was so messed up. And, in comparison, occasionally getting a little horny for my stepbrother seemed the least fucked up thing around here.

I balled my fists like a punching bag might appear in the middle of the room if I only wished really, really hard. It didn't.

But a different sort of punching bag knocked on my door. And my heart sank. I hadn't done right by him.

"Parrish?" Levi called meekly. "Can I come in?"

"It's your fucking room," I barked. What was he doing? Thinking I was crying and protecting my pride? It took more than that to make me cry.

The door creaked open and shut while I stared out the window, fury clouding my vision.

"I can leave you alone if you want," Levi said, some more strength creeping into his voice.

I turned around to face him. "To do what?" I asked.

Levi shrugged. "Dunno. Be alone. I sometimes like it."

"Everyone likes it, but that's not what I need," I said grimly.

"What do you need?" he asked.

Why the fuck do you care? "I don't know," I said instead. I didn't need allies, but I didn't have to turn him into an enemy by proxy. "Then again, I didn't know I needed your sorry ass to stand up for me until you did."

Annoyance flashed across his face. "Nothing sorry about my ass, you dick."

I grinned. That was more like it. I was sure he added that last bit just to cheer me up. Heavily, I treaded toward him and towered over him the way I always did.

He stood still and returned my intense gaze with one equal to it. His chin lifted defiantly, like the fact he was so much smaller than me didn't make a difference.

I inhaled through my nose and reached up with my hand. My thumb and index finger took his chin and I lifted his head a little higher. "Why did you say those things?" His face was such a harmonious thing; everything on it was just perfectly molded for my liking. The upturned nose and the arch the locks of hair made over his brow. The dazzling green of his eyes and the boyish curl of his lips. They trembled for a moment, his lips. He pressed them tighter together.

"Why would you protect me? He's right, you know? I'm pretty much a heartless bastard." My eyes flashed at the last two words.

But Levi didn't flinch. "I didn't lie," he said and pulled his head back, freeing his chin from my hold. "You're not my role model if that worries you."

"Good," I said.

"But they're not fair to you," he said firmly. "I know you blame me. I know you're tormenting me these days because of it."

I opened my mouth to speak, but he shook his head.

"No, it's alright," he blurted before I could say anything. "Maybe I deserve it. I'm not sure. But I am sure of this: they've done you dirty, Parrish. And I'm sorry."

I stepped back. Bickering was far easier than this, dammit.

"You're not the villain," he said. "You're a headache and you're a stubborn ass, but..."

"You don't know me," I rasped. He knew nothing about me. Not how hateful I could get or how vindictive. Not how cold I was to everyone who ever tried to get close to me or how nasty I could get when I needed to push them away.

"I don't need to know you to see that they are wrong," he said tiredly.

I scanned him. His face. His body. Every inch of him. I watched him like I had never seen him before; like I had never seen a human being. Then, when my mind came up short with anything meaningful to say, I whispered: "Maybe I'd like to be alone after all."

Levi nodded and turned on his heels. He walked out without another word and I watched his back sway as he opened the door. He shut it gently on his way out and the memory of his body, facing away from me, was burned for eternity in my mind.

And my heart murmured.

And my skin felt too tight for my body.

And I wondered if being horny had ever felt like this before.

I slipped out of the house when nobody was looking, got into my car, and drove away. At first, I headed out of River Bend. The winding road between the windswept hills, the sprawling pastures, and thick forests gave me something other than a mess to look at. There wasn't a mother and stepfather towering over me with poorly hidden hatred. There wasn't a sister who was making a terrible mistake. And there wasn't a stepbrother I wanted to fuck so badly that I could taste his sweet and salty cum on my tongue if I only let my guard down for an instant.

There was nothing but nature. Creatures living in harmony and a cycle of life and death. Predators and prey. Shepherds and their flocks. Green grass and rolling valleys and old trees.

But every road had an end. And this one was the connection to the highway. So, I pulled over and got out of the car, walked around, and sat on its hood to take in some sunshine. But I couldn't photosynthesize for too long, either, because my stomach rumbled with the lack of breakfast by lunchtime, and I decided to drive back.

I didn't go to their house. Not yet, at least. My first stop was the brewery. But, as I parked the car, my phone went off with another message from Natalie. "Still hurt? Let me come."

I sent her a single word back. *Brewery*. And waited in my car until I spotted her. I never liked sharing my feelings. Ever. And Natalie asking me if I was still hurt came dangerously close to talking about how I felt.

She gave me a long, heartfelt hug like she always would. Then, when she pulled back, she looked into my eyes.

"I'd rather not," I said before she could ask if I wanted to talk about it. There was nothing to talk about. I was, and always had been, a big disappointment. It was a label I normally managed to carry with outward pride, but this morning had hurt me in more ways than one. To warn Levi against me, after shoving me into his room and his bed, after forcing me to drive him from the airport, stung. The possibility that they might turn him against me, however ridiculous, made my blood boil.

I hadn't known how much I liked his attention until the moment I thought I was losing it for good.

I hadn't realized how much more there was between us, though never tangible or real, until the bastards tried to take it away.

"I'm starving," I said and dragged on a grin only I could.

Natalie threw her arm under my elbow and marched us into the brewery. We sat by the large window looking out at the street and the passersby who never failed to look in, spotting someone they knew — often Natalie herself — and waved with big smiles on their faces. River Bend was such a place that people knew people and they wore that with pride.

I was the outcast. Not just by their choice. Or, rather, not at all by their choice. I had volunteered. Growing a community in a small town in the middle of nowhere, where everyone felt like they got a dick enlargement the moment one of their own had become a state senator, was never the sort of life I wanted any part of.

I liked my anonymity. The intimacy of being one of the masses. The privacy of being a grain of sand on an endless beach.

The server brought our thick, juicy burgers, fries, and sauces, and set them before us. The beautifully made medium rares that made me drool nearly as much as Levi Bartlet's strangled moans behind the bathroom door.

"I feel like I've barely seen you," I said as I tasted the explosion of scents and flavors. "Wow, these people really improved their craft."

Natalie nodded, chewing carefully but with pleasure. "Everything improved. Everything's a craft now. They have artisans or everything you can imagine. Want a burger prepared by someone who'll faint if you order a well done? Come here. Want your coffee made by a hipster who can tell you the entire history of the exact bean used in your cup? His name's Earl and he's talking to that blond woman over there."

I laughed out loud. "You've really set your roots here."

Natalie shrugged. "Not everyone's desperate to leave."

"But you were. Once," I pointed out. The first time she'd visited me in New York, she'd stayed for two weeks. Almost enough to pretend that was the way of life. And she'd sworn to me it was how she wanted to live the rest of her life.

"Charmed by the big city," she said, a twinkle in her eye. It hadn't gone away. Even now, she seemed to think of it fondly. "But hey, that's not the real world."

"What do you mean?" I asked, shaking my head. I dipped one of the fries into mayo and took a good chunk between my teeth. Soft on the inside, crunchy on the outside, curly to perfection. "Fuck. These fries can have my babies."

Natalie laughed softly. "I mean, not everyone can just go away. Some people have to stay."

"Have to? Or want to? Nobody has to do anything, if you ask me," I said, narrowing my eyes to read her expression better.

"Have to, Parrish," Natalie insisted. "But it figures you'd say that. You always have been a roamer."

"A scoundrel," I said emphatically.

"A rogue," Natalie said, mimicking my tone.

"A bad motherfucker," I said in the end, a lot more somberly.

Natalie scoffed, her smile disappearing like it had never been there. "I hate it when you talk about yourself that way."

Guilt glimmered somewhere in me. Somewhere where I was still alive. Somewhere feelings existed. Perhaps I hadn't lost them all; perhaps I'd merely hidden them from myself. Perhaps everything was easier that way, because, when you didn't care, nobody could hurt you.

"So," I said carefully. "Jarred."

Natalie raised one eyebrow. "What about him?"

I chuckled to buy myself some time. "Not the guy I imagined my sister going for."

"Oh yeah? Who did you imagine?" she asked, her curiosity genuine.

I gave this a thought. "No one. No one specific, at least. I always thought you'd go on to become a pirate. I figured, you had to snap sooner or later, from all the peacemaking in the house."

"Oh, Parrish," Natalie said, laughing evenly. "If peacemakers were paid per commission, you would have made me a fortune."

"I wasn't that bad."

"You didn't like Jarred very much," Natalie pointed out, bringing us swiftly back to that topic.

I shrugged. "I'll give him a chance. If he treats you well."

Natalie licked her lips. The pause made me wince and lean in abruptly, but she waved her hands to stop me. "No, of course he treats me well. But...you know I'm not stupid, right? I know he's rough around the edges, but I can smooth those parts. Even if it means putting my career aspirations on hold, you know? He's a good man."

He was a good salesman and a good stockbroker, but I didn't believe there was much humanity to him. I believed his mother was too kind to him and his father too uninterested and Jarred needed to prove his worth to him while still being practically breastfed behind the curtains. And I had no respect for a guy like that.

"Besides, it's time to leave the nest. Again." Natalie laughed. She'd returned from college to live with Harry and Marge two years earlier, though she had never truly left. Even in college, she had been the one returning the most often and spending all her free days here if not with me in New York all those times. "I bet they're dying to have the house to themselves."

"Can't wait to see their faces when they realize it's not happening," I mused.

"What do you mean?" Natalie asked.

I slumped as the realization smacked me. "Shit. Forget I said that."

"No. Parrish? What do you know?" The mischief of my little sister blazed back to life as she leaned in to hear the juicy gossip.

I rubbed my eyes with the backs of my hands and groaned. "Swear to me you won't tell," I said.

"I swear," Natalie said solemnly, crossing her heart. "Not to a soul."

I sighed "Fine. Alright. But if you break this oath, know that I'll tee-pee the Wilkinsons' house like I did the mayor's."

"I knew that was you," Natalie said and squeezed her eyes in accusation.

"Wow, I'm on a roll here. Keep me talking and there won't be any beans left to spill," I said and chuckled.

"Don't even try confusing me, Parrish. I'm not a little girl anymore. You still didn't tell me what's up with Levi," she said.

"Ah, fine. Okay. So, you figured it's Levi." I raised my hands in surrender.

"Obviously. It's not you and it won't be me." She shook her head like she had stories to tell about wanting to leave Harry and Marge, but wasn't going to do that just now.

"Yeah, well, the Golden Boy isn't as golden as they think," I began.

"That's a little harsh," Natalie reprimanded.

I rolled my eyes at her. "He dropped out of college and he's been lying about it for some time. So, every time Margaret introduces him to your future in-laws as this genius who's about to conquer the world, just know there will be some explaining to do."

Natalie dry-washed her hands with worry. "Jesus. We have to be with him when he tells them."

"Tell me about it," I said. "I just *have to* see their faces when they get the news." And then, I added dreamily: "I hope Harry cries."

"Not because of that," Natalie said as she grabbed a napkin, balled it, and threw it at me. "They'll eat him alive and we can't let that happen."

"We?" I asked, incredulous.

She sucked her teeth. "You don't have to lie to me, Parrish. You care about him. And about time, too."

My heart tripped suddenly. "I don't," I rasped and grabbed my glass of water to wash down my surprise at her words. She had no clue how I felt. Hell, I had no clue.

"Obviously, you do. You just made me swear on the pain of having my father-in-law's house covered in toilet paper that I wouldn't betray him," she said and gave me her most infuriatingly knowing look.

I leaned back in my chair and crossed my arms in defeat, then mumbled: "I just don't want you to ruin the surprise for them."

"Liar," Natalie accused. "We'll help him, Parrish. We'll save his ass."

I winced. Even figuratively, Levi's ass was not something I wished to think about right now. "Fine," I agreed before I could properly think about it.

Natalie seemed pleased enough with the idea, but I wasn't so sure. Levi and I were on thin ice any way I looked at it. I'd been doing things to him for some time and going back to whatever normal meant for us, was hard to pull off. But I also owed him that much.

Except, I didn't want to give it up. Every time I put my hands on him, I wanted nothing more but to hear him welcome them.

But I'd trained him well enough to think it was all just a game. Hell, I, too, believed as much. But then he simply had to go and be a good person and ruin everything.

When he stood up for me, he made it all real.

And I didn't know what to do with it. I didn't know where right and wrong were and what should stay a kinky fantasy and what he deserved.

But one thing was for sure. If I could dampen Margaret and Harold's mood even once before leaving this godforsaken place, and help Levi even a smidgen like he had done for me, then I would do that singing from the top of my lungs.

Chapter Seven

LEVI

When I woke up, after a few miraculous hours of actual sleep, the other half of the bed was empty. The relief and disappointment washed over me simultaneously and in equal measures. I turned to lie on my back and extended my right arm across his side of the bed. It wasn't even warm. He'd left a while ago while I had still been asleep.

Really, I mostly hated the fact he was crammed into my space, but only because I could still cling to the reality of it. If I let my imagination run wild, the hatred for this setup melted away sooner than I could murmur 'Fuck me already'. That was why I needed to keep reminding myself what the real world was; and it was a shitty situation in which the only guy I could never, ever have was the guy I wanted the most.

I'd never been wild in bed. Guys I'd been with in the past were tame and none had ever scratched the itch that I'd carried in me for years. For some stupid, imaginary reason, I believed Parrish could do it.

You don't even know Parrish, my voice of reason sighed. It was sick of my nonsense.

That makes it all the better, I replied to myself, totally not going crazy. *The excitement is in the mystery, right?*

My voice of reason didn't respond. It was done with me.

After he'd gone out, I'd barely seen Parrish at all yesterday. Last night, he'd returned to the room quietly, slipped under the covers, and breathed soundlessly. Something had shifted between us, though I couldn't put my finger on it. Perhaps he'd just been too tired to start another battle, but I doubted that.

Even thinking about him overhearing Dad broke my heart. Nobody deserves to be treated like that. Single-handedly, Dad managed to wipe away most of my grudges and make me reconsider where I stood. Questions still filled my mind, but I knew one thing for sure; I wasn't going to sit idly by when Parrish was getting targeted just because he could be.

Both Dad and Margaret pretended like nothing had happened. But they had also pretended that the lack of Parrish at dinner was nothing unusual. As though he didn't exist at all. And that pill was too bitter for me to swallow when he had been the pillar of my obsessions for nearly as long as I'd known him. He could never stop existing to me.

I perked my ears for footsteps, but heard none. I was all alone for sure. With my heart pounding and my lungs barely expanding for air, I rolled onto my right side and closed my eyes. His bergamot scent was the strongest of the three distinct ones that followed him everywhere. It was all over his pillow. And now, as I buried my face into the pillow, it was filling me.

To know that something which has existed on Parrish Turner's bronze skin was now inside my body, did unspeakable things to me. I held my breath, savoring the fact we shared this, and felt the shame slowly rise.

Not only was I messed up enough to be attracted to someone who was part of the family, even if only on paper, but I was also a fucking loser.

I lay on my back again, frustration rising at the same speed my dick swelled and stiffened. Yesterday had been the first time I'd given in to temptation. When he'd joked about playing catch with me, the wanting for it crushed my soul. And when he called me a spoiled brat, I wanted nothing more than for Parrish to punish me somehow. And when I believed his offer to do exactly that was real, I couldn't hold it in any longer. It was either my fist or going down the path with no way back.

I shut my eyes. Playing catch had never been something I liked, but there I was, fantasizing about it. Fantasizing about Parrish playing the role of big brother, while also being his most seductive self and making me lust after him by doing little more than existing.

I wanted to cry out, to shout, to growl. I wanted to rip the T-shirt off my chest in anger that it had to be this way. It boiled in me, but I couldn't let it spill over. I had to keep the lid in place.

Three deep breaths didn't calm me down, but they made just enough difference that I could get out of the bed. My bedroom had a backyard view, so I paused by the window at the sound of splashing. Parrish.

He swam in the pool like a pro.

I practiced self-control for once and turned away. After changing into a fresh T-shirt, I went downstairs where Margaret was fussing over a tiny tear in Natalie's wedding dress.

"Judy said she'd see us today. She'll make time. Hurry, now, or we won't make it in time to the hair salon for the tests." She spotted me at the bottom of the stairs. "Darling," she said. "There are croissants and fresh coffee in the kitchen. You don't mind if we run, do you?"

"No, of course not," I murmured. In fact, I was relieved.

"Your father's next door. He'll be around if you need anything," Margaret said and pinched my cheek. "Oh, and remember, we're having people over this afternoon. Nothing big. Just a few neighbors, dipping in the pool, grilling some burgers." She kept shaking her hands around her head as she spoke to emphasize how not a big deal this all was. "Make sure you have your swimming trunks, alright? Tanya's bringing her son here. Did you know he came out as gay? Of course, Tanya already knew. We all suspected, mind you. He's a very dear young man. Anyway, dial up that charm of yours,

Pumpkin. I'm sure you'll get along with him just fine. And there's no one else his age who's coming, so you should entertain him. Ah, I'll leave him in your charge. You won't disappoint."

I gaped at the avalanche of information that left her lips at this early hour as Margaret headed out.

Natalie followed her, but paused and hugged me in passing. It lasted just a little longer than I was used to. She shot me a worried — or, rather, compassionate — look as she walked out.

I thought nothing of it, grabbed a plate, tossed a couple chocolate croissants on it, and poured myself a mug of coffee. Just a few yards ahead, I could see him, totally lost in his thoughts, swimming quickly like he had something to prove.

I walked before I even knew what I was doing. Step by step by step, I neared the pool, sipping my coffee and watching him. His elbows pulled out of the water in a steady rhythm and sharp movements. His hands sliced through the water as he sped up, reached the edge of the pool, and turned so skillfully you'd think he was a merman. His head turned left or right every third swing of his arms and he inhaled. But he wasn't splashing. His feet were almost completely submerged, propelling him with quick movement but never disturbing the surface of the water.

I walked around the pool toward the lounge that was positioned in the shade. I set my coffee on the stone pavement and picked up one of the croissants.

For a while longer, I busied myself with counting the strokes between his breaths. One, two, three and inhale.

One, two, three and inhale. The steadiness of the pattern soothed me enough that I forgot about the ruin that the rest of my life was.

The only thing I couldn't forget about was the worst sin of mine. And he was there, swimming consistently a few feet away from me.

When Parrish reached the side of the pool that was closer to me, he broke the pattern. He didn't turn elegantly like he had every time so far. Instead, his hands slapped the polished stone-tiled edge of the pool and his head emerged. Eyes closed, water pouring down his face; Parrish swung his head back, sending a splash of water through the air. It caught the sunlight that broke into a million flickers for one glimmering moment. His shoulders emerged, then his torso, until his waist leveled with the edge of the pool and his arms were straight, propping him up.

I held my breath purely because I forgot how to exhale.

His biceps and triceps were tense. His abs contorted as he lifted his left leg and set his foot on the edge of the pool. With the sheer strength of his body, he pulled himself up and stood tall. Water trickled down his bronze, decorated skin, beading in his beard and on his muscles. It dripped from his black swimming shorts that were sticking to his legs and crotch.

He saw me after shaking off the excess water from his curly hair that, when wet, looked completely black. He ran a hand over his beard and more water drizzled over the stone tiles.

I wondered what his beard would feel like on my tender skin. Would it burn my face after hours of making out? Would it tickle my stomach when he feathered it with kisses? Would my toes curl when I felt it on my ass all the while his tongue worked my hole?

I bit my lip quickly and let the pain cleanse my thoughts. My father was at our next door neighbor's house. His mother had just walked out of *our* house. These thoughts were a first class ticket to hell. And homelessness if our parents ever even suspected.

I wasn't ready to give up a comfy bed and a roof over my head.

Not even for a night with him? An hour? A hot goddamn minute? He's practically putting himself onto a silver platter for you all the fucking time.

He appeared next to me before I even had the time to pull myself out of my thoughts. He snatched one of the croissants off my plate and collapsed on the lounge that was located in the sun.

"Oi," I protested weakly, simply to have some sort of interaction with him.

"Where is everyone?" he asked and began enjoying my croissant immensely.

"Margaret took Natalie to fix an invisible rip on the wedding dress, Dad's hanging out next door, and Lauren is at the brewery, probably sampling everything from mead to mead makers." I rolled my eyes as if to appear casual, but the fact we were all alone pressed down on my chest like someone had placed a boulder there. He had been tormenting me nonstop since he'd picked me up from the airport and this was just another perfect opportunity.

But, instead of diving straight in, he munched on my croissant. "Some peace and quiet then."

As if. Parrish never let peace and quiet last for too long. Any moment now, he would probably hop over to my lounge and propose cuddling or whatever. Not that I was all too against that, I was desperately in two minds.

"There's this pool party," I began.

But Parrish cackled. "Good thing I got my swimming done for the day. I can slip away."

Horror washed over me as soon as I considered that. Though I hadn't given it any thought, I had simply assumed Parrish would be around. And to imagine the afternoon without him was like walking into one of the *Jigsaw* movies. "Don't abandon me, you knave," I said jokingly. It was after whatever the hell had happened yesterday that I felt freer to speak to him in more ways than purely bickering. "Margaret is setting me up with her hairdresser's son."

Parrish laughed out loud so hard I thought he was going to choke on my croissant. "You've got my attention. Bet she's planning the wedding already. Did she ask you which dates you prefer?"

I glared at him. "Stop it. It's horrible."

"I hope all three of you are very happy together," he said with a massive, sarcastic smile on his face. "You, your new beau, and Marge."

I snorted. "Hey, is Natalie...alright? It's just that she gave me this look."

Parrish choked and cleared his throat. "Yeah, uh, about that." He sat up in his lounge, feet on the stony ground. "I might have told her something yesterday and she might have guessed the rest correctly."

All my muscles tensed as I sat up. "Parrish, what did you do?" It could have been one of two things, and I didn't know which was worse. Correct that; I knew which was worse, but that didn't make the other one any better.

"I let it slip that you dropped out," Parrish admitted.

My heart turned to stone and sank fast into my stomach. "What?" I gasped.

"I'm sorry," Parrish said. "I wasn't thinking." He got up and crossed the short space between us.

"I can't believe you..." I frowned and got to my feet. "Actually, of course I fucking can. I knew you would," I spat out to his face. I started to pass him, but Parrish grabbed my wrist and held it tightly. His grip was so strong that I had no hope of breaking free.

And all my instincts told me to give in. *Surrender to him.*

"It's not like that. We were talking about something else and I said something," he explained. "But she figured it was about you." He yanked my arm closer and the rest of me followed until we baked in the sun, one foot of empty space between us, my wrist trapped in his hand by his waist. "She was worried it was something worse, I could tell. And we agreed to help you."

"I don't need help," I said with spite. "Not yours. Nobody's."

"You do," he said, jerking my arm closer until we nearly bumped into one another. He was so fucking close. And there it was, right on cue. My cock stirred and my pulse quickened. My breaths were shallower immediately as he brought his face closer to mine. "Whether you like it or not, we'll be there when you tell them. You fought for me. I can fight for you, too, dammit. It's the least I can do."

"It's not a bargain, Parrish," I said. "I didn't do it for you."

"Then I'm not doing it for you, either," he said. "But doing the right fucking thing for once."

I winced. He wasn't letting go of my wrist, but his grip loosened. His hand slipped a little lower and our fingers twined. I gazed up at him, utterly incapable of looking away.

I held my breath when he took my hand this way. I looked at his lips so I wouldn't have to face the intense gaze of his hazel eyes. "Don't," I whispered as quietly as a leaf rustling in the wind.

"Why not?" he asked, almost as quietly. "Give me one good reason to stop."

I don't want you to.
I don't want to hurt them like this.
We're family and it's wrong.

None of those were good reasons. Shit, none of them were even true. But the one that was true was the hardest one to say. So, I tensed my muscles like I was going to physically fight him. And I killed my emotions as best I could. And I lifted my gaze to meet his. "Because I don't believe you want it."

His eyebrows made the slightest twitch toward a frown.

"You toy with me and fool around and laugh. But you don't care what that does to me," I said, my voice trembling toward the end.

"What does it do to you?" he asked calmly, but the corners of his mouth stiffened.

I shook my head. "It's not important."

He jerked my hand closer, my fingers still trapped in his. "Tell me."

"No," I insisted. "What's important is that you dangle this opportunity all the fucking time, but you don't mean it. No matter how easy it is for me to believe it in the moment, I can't really trust you with my feelings."

His nose wrinkled and his frown deepened. Was he angry with me or himself? "And if I told you I meant it?"

I shook my head. "So what? You can make me say yes as easy as blinking," I said, finding my footing a little better. Every word I said fractured my heart, but I needed to plow through this. "You can pretend it's all innocent all you like, but we both know you're fully aware. You were aware since that night they threw you out of the house. You *knew* what happened to me then. And you know how to make it happen again. You know how to push me to the edge where I stare at the abyss and almost — *almost* — want to step over and let myself indulge. And if I do? What then? I fucking know you'd cackle and tell me it was a joke."

His fingers tightened around mine. "And if I promised I wouldn't?" It was almost a growl of frustration with me, with himself, with the whole damned world around us.

And I would have traded it. Now I knew for sure. Because, even with merely a hint that there was more to it than just messing with my head, I was ready. I would trade the world for one minute of his full, irresistible, lusty attention.

I jerked my hand free. It was the last cry of my strength leaving me.

But I didn't turn away from him.

I waited.

And Parrish used this heartbeat of time wisely.

He blinked.

He whispered my name.

He put his hands on my face and leaned in.

Time stopped as I frantically prepared myself for every last dream of mine to come true in the next instant. He was inches away from me and the chocolate on his breath was almost as alluring as the entire deal.

Here I was, ready to give my soul to the devil, just to be kissed by him once.

"Boys? Marge? Anybody home?" Dad called from inside the house and my blood froze.

Chapter Eight

PARRISH

"Shit!"

The word jumped off my lips and into Levi's slowly opening mouth.

I jerked my hands back and jumped into the pool without a second thought. Though it was the last thing I should have done to Levi, leaving him all flustered to deal with Harold, it was all I could do without dying on the spot. My body was too hot and it needed the chilly water to cool me down. My cock was hard and more than a little visible in my swimming shorts. And my frustration flared so quickly that I was ready to break something, so I needed to burn it off by swimming.

I only made one lap before I felt just cool enough to get out and feign a smile. "What's going on?" I called as I pushed myself out of the pool. By then, Levi was halfway across the yard. His cheeks were as red as strawberries and he shot me a glare that made me want to sink to the bottom of the pool. I didn't know why; either because I'd tried to fucking kiss him, or because I abandoned him a moment later.

Whatever the case, he shook his head at me to say he knew no more than I.

"Let's get this party started," Harold said, rubbing his hands, then quickly grabbing his hypochondriac back and adding a little limp to his stride. "Parrish, you'll have to get the grill from the shed. Mind my newspapers that are in there. I don't want grease all over them."

Fucking hell, the guy seriously collected old newspapers. "On it," I said.

Behind Harold, Bob and Susan walked in. "How lovely," Susan was saying. "Levi, young man," Bob bellowed. "It's so good to see you."

"Parrish? Is that really you?" Susan called.

I walked up to them and shook hands. "Ah, Marge always says how busy you are in the city running your own shop."

Annoyance flared in me like fireworks. "Does she? How nice." Right. Because it wasn't such a shame when she could brag to her neighbors that I had something of my own.

Levi was trapped in a conversation with Bob, who mistook data science for cryptocurrencies and Levi was explaining the difference while simultaneously looking at me in a way you'd think he was still a virgin *and* trying his best not to be. But he was close to drooling. And damn me if I wasn't, too.

I excused myself to get the grill out of the shed. It was a moment of relief I desperately needed. If only they came a minute later. Or five minutes sooner. But no. They had to interrupt the exact moment when every thought in my mind swirled around Levi and his sexy lips.

God, I wanted him.

I cleared the way in piles of newspapers in the shed and found the grill covered against dust particles. Though Harry hadn't upgraded since I had still been living here, this was pretty much the king of grills. So, with great care, I dragged it out to a sunny spot where people won't want to hang around too much. Everyone was running toward the shade already, though it wasn't even noon.

Good, I thought to myself as I uncovered the grill. *Leave me all alone*. My mind was set on avoiding everyone as much as possible, but not leaving Levi to the sharks by himself.

And the biggest shark of all arrived while I was wiping the grill with a wet cloth. Tanya's son, accompanied by Tanya herself. The boy was a frat bro and for one heartbeat I thought Margaret must have made a mistake about him. But then I saw him notice Levi. And I saw him notice Levi's cute haircut and piercing eyes, and Levi's kissable, fuckable lips. "Hello, gorgeous," I heard him say, taking Levi's hand in his and holding it for a moment too long.

The wet cloth in my fist saved me from cutting my nails into my palm, bone deep, when I closed my fist. Spots flared in my vision as I watched. The guy had 'fuckboy' written on his forehead. He also had a punching target drawn around his nose, if you looked through my eyes. Especially when he threw one big hand on Levi's shoulder and began talking.

"Haven't seen you in ages," he was saying. "Don't come around that much, you know? Got my own thing going."

My stomach hardened. You could say he was pretty in that all American way, with a slightly round face, blue eyes, sandy hair, dimples and all.

I took the grill brush to scrub the ash from the corners, then made my way back to the shed for the propane tank. Once I attached it and checked the amount of lava rocks, I lit the fire and turned it down. The rocks would heat up slowly from the flames beneath them while I stood by, arms crossed and a permanent scowl on my face warning people away.

Levi was facing away from me. I couldn't see any of his expressions, but his set shoulders and stiff neck told me everything I needed to know. How cheesy would it be if I walked up to them and said something like: "Is this guy bothering you?"

Plenty cheesy, I answered myself, and decided not to intervene. Fuck them. If Levi wanted to get out of that conversation, he very well could do that by himself. And I wasn't going to babysit him just because I kinda liked the idea of filling his mouth with my tongue. And more.

For a long while, I kept myself busy with everything I would need to man the grill, from burger and hot-dog buns, to meat, to cheese, to the vegetables Margaret had so neatly prepared and stored in the big fridge inside. I sorted all of these myself before I slapped the first round of meat on the heated rocks. The sizzling filled my ears and the first scent of grease hitting the rocks crawled into my nostrils. The only problem? I had no appetite. None.

Though a few of Harry's guests came by to say hi and pay tribute to the grill king — as was the custom for every suburban male ever — I didn't engage them in any prolonged conversation. "Those lava rocks?"

"Yep."

"Good stuff."

"Yep."

And so on.

A wave of admiration spread over the backyard when Margaret ushered Natalie out, like Rafiki lifting baby Simba for the whole kingdom to see.

My attention snapped from Natalie's entrance to Levi when he laughed. Something Brent had said made Levi laugh out loud and unimaginable fury rose in me. I'd been around the guy for days and hadn't heard him laugh once. But this little shithead just strolled in and got a laugh out of him?

Who are you angry with, asshole? A voice asked internally. *You're the one who never made him laugh.*

I pressed my lips tightly and flipped a grilled cheese on the vegetarian portion of the grill. It didn't matter. I wasn't a party clown whose job it was to make Levi laugh.

The grilling took place on a person-to-person basis. Since I'd claimed the spatula, individual hungry guests made requests, and I delivered. I wasn't there to entertain or chat. I was there to feign being a part of a happy family. And that was how my next few hours passed.

Levi was busy entertaining the guest of honor, making Margaret proud.

Harry was bragging about Levi's grades or whatnot.

Natalie was rolling her eyes at something Jarred was saying and I wondered if I could get my hand on some laxatives to slide into his next burger.

Just like I had wanted it, everyone left me alone.

At one point, Levi hopped off the lounge chair and said something to Brent, then headed toward the house. A moment later, Brent made his way toward me and I quickly dropped my pointy grilling fork. Everyone was better off if I wasn't holding it in the moments that would follow.

"Hey dude," Brent said in an obnoxiously husky voice.

"Dude," I growled.

"How's it hanging?" he asked, folding his arms one over the other, examining the contents on my grill.

I narrowed my eyes at him, but he didn't seem to notice. "Hungry?" I asked.

"Nah," he said. "After a swim, maybe."

I pointed the spatula away from us. "The pool's that way."

Brent laughed. "Right on, right on." He nodded, then grabbed the edge of his T-shirt and pulled it over his head.

Jesus Fuck, I thought as my stomach hollowed. I was a pretty fit guy with years of hard work that had gone into sculpting my body. But this guy...fuck. He seemed effortlessly hot. It sparked zero attraction in me, obviously, but I wasn't blind. Brent was also a gym rat with a pretty good idea on what a Greek god might look like today.

A curse loaded in my mouth, but I rolled my eyes. Why should I care if Levi saw him all muscled and fuckable? I shouldn't. It wasn't like anything really happened between us. Levi was his own person and I wasn't even sure I wanted him.

Liar, my conscience snapped at me.

That was when I lifted my gaze off the patty Rory Greenwell wanted well done and looked at the back door of the house. He wore a soft smile with only a hint of dimples and I drew a stark contrast between his and Brent's; Levi's dimples completed his innocent, boyish look. He'd swapped his regular shorts for a pair of swimming ones. They were red with black stripes on the outer sides.

Levi crossed half the backyard and slowed down, grabbing the bottom edge of his plain T-shirt. Clumsily, he yanked it up, flashing me with a bit of skin on his trimmed abs. They weren't too defined, but they were unmistakably there. Levi's narrow waist led up to his broader chest, as the T-shirt went over his head.

Fuck my life. My stepbrother was a hottie. Slender, for sure, but precisely the way I had imagined. And precisely the way I liked. The muscles he'd put on were there, unbearably to my liking, and so close that I felt the desire to lick him swell in me like a howling wind.

Brent noticed it, too, and marched up to Levi like a champion about to claim his trophy. He threw his arm over Levi's bare shoulders while Levi fixed his hair pointlessly. It would be wet soon. Why was he bothering? Unless it was a silly gesture of attraction.

He glanced at me and bit his lip. Was he feeling guilty? His fingers ran through his hair again and he looked away.

My hand jerked to a side and I knocked my half-empty bottle of beer over. I couldn't swear it was an accident, but I wasn't completely sure. "Shit," I grumbled, then called: "Hey, Levi. Grab me a cold one, will you?"

He looked at me immediately, while I cleaned the surface of the small table where all my shit was. I couldn't read the look he gave me, but all my movements slowed down as Levi spun away and marched into the house. His bare back begged for my lips and fingers. I yearned to touch him. Now. Right this fucking moment. To hell with everyone else.

He scurried back while Brent made his way toward the pool and nosedived. Levi paused a few feet away from me, then closed the distance at a much slower pace. He handed me the beer, which I took, closing half my hand over his.

He winced and bit his lip, but didn't pull his hand away.

Suddenly, everyone at this godforsaken party disappeared into nothingness. They didn't matter. Nothing around us mattered. The only thing I could see was the creeping blush on his cheeks from the touch. And I knew that, were I a few shades paler, my heated cheeks would do the same. My tongue tied at once and I wondered if I'd had too much to drink, then recounted I'd only had one and a half low alcohol beers.

What the hell are you doing to me?

I scanned him up close now, and had to bite my tongue when my gaze ran over his small, light brown nipples. His collarbones were pronounced above his smoothly sculpted chest and there were clear lines on the outer sides of his abs, leading into a V line that showed the way to his happy place.

I had a sudden urge to press my tongue against his small belly button.

"You're glowering," Levi said flatly, finally pulling his hand back and crossing his bare arms at his chest.

"It's my resting expression," I said.

"Oddly true, but could you tone down the death stare?" he asked, a corner of his lips curled up.

I glanced over his shoulder to where Brent was dragging himself out of the pool to sit on the edge, legs still in the water. "Your new boyfriend's waiting."

"Don't be a dick." Sparks burst from his eyes and I couldn't read his expression. When he inhaled, his chest rose, and I had to ball my fist in order to not press my hand against his bare torso.

"He sure is pretty," I muttered, taking a swig of beer to wash down the taste of my own bitterness.

"He's also as boring as they come and solely my responsibility because the only other person I want to be around has decided to brood by the grill and make me worry if the food is poisonous," Levi blurted flatly.

I couldn't help myself. A grunt-chuckle burst out of me. "Fair enough."

"Don't be jealous," Levi said bluntly.

I meant to protest his assumption, in vain, but didn't get a chance.

"And don't act like that moment didn't mean anything," he said, far softer than anything he'd said so far.

Did it, though? I had a long and complicated relationship with *meaning*. It made me feel all sorts of ways, not all of which were particularly good. It made me hate Brent, for one, though I didn't know the guy. And it made me possessive. But it also made me want to worship Levi for one endless night.

I nodded. "You're right. I'm sorry."

Levi's eyes widened.

"What?" I laughed. "I am capable of apologizing for my murder glares."

His ears perked and lips thinned as he fought back a smile. "We're good," he said.

As he took one step back, I snatched his wrist. Neither of us looked around in fear of being seen. I leaned in to whisper in his ear. "We need to talk about what happened earlier."

"Huh?" His voice was choked and I felt an instant spike in pride that I was able to do that to him. "Of course."

"When we're alone," I added softly.

Levi wheezed and whispered an 'okay' that sounded like it had taken him all his strength to produce.

Only then did I let him go. And for a long while after, I was still riding the thrill of this brief encounter. The adrenaline of risking it in front of everyone, even if only to plant the tiniest seed of suspicion; the great expectations of what tonight could bring; and the flustered look on Levi's pretty face. These things mattered to me, if nothing else did.

I flipped the burgers, grilled the sausages, melted the cheese, and fed the growing crowd. I even ignored Jarred when it took him two moments too long to remember who I was. And, shockingly, I found myself whistling a tune I couldn't recognize, while glancing around to see a golden lock of hair or a glazed, shining look sent my way from the prettiest boy in town.

Brent annoyed me, but I could live with it.

Because Levi was going to be all mine.

Chapter Nine

Levi

It was very late in the afternoon, as the golden sunshine aged and waned, that the guests mostly left. Tanya had gone away much earlier than Brent, who'd been trailing me the entire day. So, when he finally decided he'd had enough lounging, and was dry enough to make the walk home, he threw that big arm over my shoulders again.

I didn't need to look back to know that Parrish's scrubbing of the grill intensified as he glared at Brent, probably imagining it's his face he was scrubbing with that metal brush.

"It's still early to call it a day," Brent said.

"Are you going somewhere?" I asked politely, like Margaret would want.

"That's up to you," Brent said and I felt the weight of his arm on my shoulders. "Are you joining me?"

"Oh, I can't," I said. "But thanks."

"Why not?" Brent asked, seemingly not bothered. He even leaned a little closer and I finally couldn't handle it any longer.

I shrugged his arm off my shoulders and turned to look him in the eyes. "Don't get me wrong, you're really nice," I said to soften the blow. "But I'm not really in a place where I'm looking." Somehow, I'd marvelously managed not to lie.

Brent's expression slowly changed. "Looking?" he asked with contempt. "You do realize there's such a thing as 'no strings attached', right?"

"Yup," I said and nodded. I wasn't going to make my view of such an arrangement known to him. For one, I wasn't sure how I felt about it. A good test of my feelings was this: would I do it for Parrish? And the answer was almost always affirmative.

But that didn't concern Brent.

Brent simply scoffed and shook his head in disappointment. On his way into the house, he muttered something about losing the whole day.

"Do you want me to punch his face in?" the low growl sounded inches away from my ear.

"Jesus," I snapped and rubbed my ear where his breath tickled me. "You scared me."

"I'll take that as a yes," Parrish said and stiffened.

"No," I blurted and grabbed his tensing biceps as he made the first step after Brent. "Don't be an idiot," I said, although the resolve on my stepbrother's face made me feel all kinds of things. But it mostly made me feel breathless and a little feverish.

"Suit yourself," Parrish said tightly, his teeth bare. I could tell his jaw hurt from all the grinding as he watched Brent like a loyal Belgian Malinois. All he needed was a hackled tail.

As a new wave of heat and tingling flooded my body, I glanced at Parrish's bare torso, then marched away from him. He knew where to find me as soon as he wanted me, and I needed a moment to myself.

I shut the door behind me and paced around my room. Finally, everyone was gone. Finally, the house was getting quiet. Harold, Margaret, Natalie, Jarred, and Lauren were still downstairs, probably enjoying a few more rounds of drinks before retiring.

I looked out the window and found Parrish packing the grill away.

He was done.

He had nothing else to do.

He was on his way.

With a spike of panic that I could neither understand nor explain, I rushed into the bathroom for a long, thorough shower. But, when I dressed and walked out, he wasn't around.

I sat down, tapping my foot against my will and drumming my fingers against my knees. My pulse kept rising and my heart pounded in my ears so loudly that I almost failed to hear the door open. It was only when it shut that I jumped to my feet.

"Just me," Parrish said and crossed his strong arms on his chest. He'd changed into a different pair of shorts.

Nothing but shorts. I figured he had showered in the downstairs bathroom.

I reminded myself to breathe, then to relax. And in that effort, I stepped back and leaned against the edge of my desk. "Hey," I said softly.

"The last time I saw you, you were pressed against my closet door," he said, smirking like it was a memory he often pulled to the surface. "You've changed a lot since then. And I find myself..." He breathed as he searched for the right words. "Attracted to you."

His words rang in my ears and made my body vibrate with excitement. I tried to conceal it. "I've been working out," I said airily, moving away from the desk and a little toward him.

He sniffed. "Not like that." Parrish didn't break eye contact. He tilted his head to one side. "You've become serious. You know what problems are. You're not that carefree teenager, but an adult. A fuck up like me." There was something so sinister in his lazy smile that my heart throbbed. But that wasn't the only reaction in my body.

My underwear was becoming increasingly tight. "You're attracted to me because I'm less happy?" I asked, not entirely joking.

He sucked his teeth and made a big step toward me. "I didn't say that."

"Sounds like it." I pulled back toward the bathroom door. It wasn't fully intentional, but I quickly realized that my big thing was getting trapped between doors and Parrish.

"When Brent started drooling over you, it made me feel..." His voice was a low purr that sent shivers down my spine. "...like I need to protect you."

I blinked as he stepped closer, fulfilling my fantasy and resting his fists against the bathroom door on each side of my head.

"But also, like I don't want anyone else to play with you like I do." The smoky quality of his voice reached a new level of sexy.

I licked my lips. "Don't let them, then."

"I won't," he promised. His lips moved in fractions but no sounds came for a few seconds. "We'll burn in hell for this," he whispered. I'd stake my life that I heard a trace of humor in his voice.

I inhaled a breath of air and blinked up at him. His proximity did wonders to me. "Will you play with me, then?"

His eyes flashed with desire. "God yes. But it's a dangerous game, Levi."

I opened my mouth to tell him I was ready to throw everything away for one hot second of that dangerous game, but...

His hands suddenly dropped from the door.

Fumbling footsteps.

Turning of the doorknob.

The creak of hinges that, to my alerted senses, sounded like a horrible scream.

"Wrong room, Lauren," Parrish barked, stepping back just in time to make some decent distance between us.

I spun to where Aunt Lauren wobbled her head and blurted apologies.

She didn't even close the door as she stumbled on down the hallway. "She saw us," I hissed.

"She didn't," Parrish said, voice tight. "She's drunk. She's got no clue where she is."

It was a timely reminder, even if my entire body screamed with desperation. *Take me. Kiss me. Fuck me.*

Use me.

Break me.

In two heartbeats, he was by the door.

Wait, I wanted to say, fear rising rapidly that he was on his way out, changing his mind.

Except, he wasn't leaving.

I couldn't tell how much time passed after he'd turned away, but he was still there, by the door. And I was still leaning forward against the bathroom door, suffering with every fiber of my being.

Click. Parrish locked us in.

My ears rang.

I inhaled after I realized I'd stopped breathing.

His chest rose and fell as he breathed, standing still by the door. He pulled his shoulders back and straightened.

I couldn't tell why my heart beat this quickly. Was it the huge possibility that all my fantasies could come true? Was it the fright that we could get caught at any moment? Or — the worst option of all — was it the combination of the two?

He crossed his arms at his chest. The moment had passed. I was hanging in this limbo of uncertainty, torn apart by this self-destructive desire to be touched by my stepbrother. "So?" I managed through my constricted throat.

"So," he repeated softly and took a breath of air. He searched me with his knowing gaze, though I had no idea what he was looking for.

Parrish made one determined step toward me. "You can still say no, Levi."

His eyes were dark and fiery. His firm gaze was enough to make me want to fall onto my knees. I'd pretended to be a grown up for so long and all I'd gotten out of it were bigger problems. For once, I wanted someone as strong and independent as Parrish to take care of me.

"Why would I do that?" I asked. My voice sounded distant, detached from my body. I was fully focused on him and my own being became secondary.

As I leaned against the bathroom door, faintly hearing Aunt Lauren grunt and turn in the bed next door, Parrish walked up to me. "Because if you don't, it could destroy our lives."

I gave a soft laugh. "Do I look like I have anything else to lose?"

Parrish glanced up. "Roof over your head, at the very least."

"Stop trying to scare me," I said, pressing my hands against the door behind my back and pushing myself away from it. I stood an inch away from Parrish and stared up at him. "I'm not afraid anymore."

Parrish moved too swiftly for me to follow. His body pressed against me and I bumped against the bathroom door. Somewhere in the back of my consciousness, I was aware that the sound carried and that Aunt Lauren turned in the bed again. But that was so far in the periphery of my mind that it faded away before I knew it.

The heated, bare torso of my big stepbrother pressed hard against me, pinning me against the door. He placed his palms on each side of my head and stared down at me like he wanted to intimidate me. Like he still wanted me to change my mind.

"You keep towering over me," I murmured, barely capable of stringing words together.

One of his dark eyebrows arched. "And you keep getting hard every time I do."

He was right. Every shred of me was tense and what little vocabulary I had left was all gone now.

"Fuck, you're horny," he purred, pushing his crotch against my lower stomach, his bare leg touching my hard cock.

I whimpered softly and held my breath.

"You should know," he said. "I like it rough."

I gave a jerky nod.

"I *only* like it rough." He swallowed, his Adam's apple bobbing up and returning down. Instead of a reply, my cock throbbed once and Parrish purred out a laugh. "That's a good boy."

The half-smirk that I knew him for took a different meaning now. His right hand moved to my throat. He pushed me back until my head pressed against the door and gazed into my eyes. "If you really want it," he said, moving his leg just enough to tease my aching cock. "Then I have a few rules for you, Levi."

My eyes widened and I managed a little nod with his hand still holding my head pressed against the door. His lips hovered so near mine that I could almost lick him if I was just a little careless.

"One; you can say 'no' at any time, but this is your last chance to walk away with a clean conscience," he said.

I was no longer sure I owed any loyalty to this family. They'd deceived us in welcoming Parrish back, then asked me to stay away. Could I trust anything that left their mouths?

"And two; you are mine, Levi. Only I get to play with you. I don't like sharing." The low, quiet rumble of his voice filled my ears. His lips were so near mine that I could almost taste him. And I was desperate to do just that.

My lips parted, not to speak, but to take him in already. *Kiss me. Push your goddamn tongue down my throat. Make me yours already.*

"Is that okay with you?" he whispered.

I nodded.

"Say it, Levi," he commanded.

I nearly fell apart at the way he used my name against me. "It's okay. I agree," I blurted.

"How are you with protection?" he asked, pulling back from me.

Stop dragging it out, I wanted to shout. "Fine either way. I'm on PrEP."

"Me too," he said. "You do realize, if we do this, there's no going back." He came closer to me. "Things will change forever." That last bit, he said in a softer voice, leaning in and speaking virtually over my lips.

I shivered with the need to kiss him already, but it occurred to me that he hadn't only meant he liked fucking hard. He liked everything to be rough.

My heart skipped several beats when it sped to the maximum.

His other hand rested on my hip and every shred of doubt faded away. Parrish lost no time in finding both of my hands, grabbing my wrists, and lifting them above my head. Our hands bumped against the bathroom door and Parrish wrapped his right hand around both my wrists with room to spare. His other hand dragged down the side of my face and he took my chin between his thumb and finger. "Look at me," he said softly, voice deep and commanding.

I did. The dark circles around his eyes made him look sexy as hell. Everything about this was so unspeakably forbidden that doing it was all but inevitable.

"Now, close your eyes, sweet boy," he said.

I did. I would have done anything he asked of me.

My lips parted eagerly as I waited, eyes shut gently, and breath so shallow you couldn't tell I was breathing at all.

Kiss me, please, I thought and hoped against odds that he could read my mind.

Whether he could or he just simply had a great instinct for timing, I neither knew nor cared. I surrendered myself to the moment the heat of his breath washed over my lips. That instant before we touched seemed to last forever, though my heart only beat once in all the eternity between one moment and the next.

And when his lips touched mine, at long last, I stiffened my legs to stop myself from collapsing. The intensity with which he kissed me was so like him. Dangerous. Fiery. Destructive.

His hand tightened around my wrists like he needed to keep me in place. I wouldn't have squirmed if my life depended on it.

His lips parted wider as the feeling of anticipation boiled over and I pushed my tongue into his mouth. For every moment of this kiss — our first, most daring, most ruinous kiss — the storm of my emotions raged harder.

The desperate fear of doom we'd chosen splashed the stony shores. The thrill of finally tasting him rolled over the fear. The joy that he seemed to want me as much as I wanted him made a chuckle bubble somewhere deep inside of me.

Parrish pushed my tongue back with his and explored my mouth with insatiable hunger.

A whimper burst out of me and Parrish pulled back just enough to say: "Be quiet, Levi." It reminded me that two doors behind me lay someone who we both considered family.

God. Why did this taste so much better with that ingredient in the mix?

My smooth skin burned where his coarse beard touched it.

Parrish lowered his free hand all the way to my hip, where it slipped under my T-shirt. He kissed me deeper and harder, quicker and more intensely. He kissed me like there was no tomorrow. And really, if anyone found out about this, there wouldn't be.

But he lifted my T-shirt and the tender, smooth skin on my abs touched his heated, tattooed skin.

My knees nearly gave way.

But he was still holding my arms high above my head, kissing me from above, protecting me from falling down. He pushed into me harder, squeezing another moan out of the depths of my chest.

"Shh," he whispered into my parted lips and quickly silenced me again with his mouth on mine.

When he moved, it was abrupt and rough, just like he'd promised. His left hand lifted my T-shirt up and over my head, and all the way along my arms. He released my wrists to free me of the T-shirt, which he then dropped on the floor.

With all his weight, Parrish leaned into me. Our bare torsos clashed and our faces pressed together as he kissed me harder. His hips swayed back and forth; his crotch rubbed against mine with no mercy. His lips moved intently over mine, then on my chin, and along my jaw. He reached my ear, which he bit roughly and made me wiggle.

His left hand was still on my right hip, while his other arm reached around me, hand on the middle of my back. It was moving slowly down, tracing my spine, until his fingers touched the edge of my everyday cotton shorts.

Every fiber of my being was on edge. My cock hurt with how hard it was and my breaths hitched in my throat. I tried to inhale, mouth wide open, as Parrish bit my ear softly, then roughly, then softly again, his heated breath spilling over my ticklish, prickling skin.

He lowered his head so he could kiss my neck and the tingling spread through me at once. I wrapped my arms around his shoulders, fingernails digging into his muscled upper back. "Ah," I whispered shakily instead of moaning. The silence we'd artificially created was deafening and every tiny little sound seemed a thousand times louder than it really was.

Parrish slipped his right hand under the waistband of my shorts and briefs, cupping my ass and kneading it with intense steadiness. His lips returned to mine.

His other hand moved from my hip and to my crotch, where he felt the length of my cock over the fabric. I felt his smile spread against my lips. I was so hard that my cock was starting to push out of the edge of my tight briefs.

I could feel him pulse against my lower abdomen, his cock long and hard and comfortable in his shorts. "Need you," I whispered practically into his mouth. "Want you..."

"I'm here," he murmured over my lips. One rough move of his body spun us around. Now the whole room turned and Parrish made me walk backwards toward the bed, all the while squeezing my ass and dragging his hand along my length. He moved that hand lower, cupping my balls and all the fabric between them and his hand, before releasing me altogether. "Kneel, Levi," he said so quietly it was barely audible, but it filled the silent vacuum of the room much like a shout.

I collapsed onto my knees as soon as the command registered. My lips parted, knowing better what to do than my scattered mind.

As each second ticked away, I was less held together and more led by pure instinct and desire. No longer did I worry we might be overheard. The chatter from the back porch that came through my window even when it was closed might as well have belonged to perfect strangers.

I saw nothing wrong with what I was doing. And even less so as I rested my hands on his bare ankles, then dragged them all the way up along his muscular legs.

Parrish placed a hand on the back of my head. "Such a pretty boy," he purred only for me, almost mouthing the words soundlessly. "So innocent-looking," he added.

The suggestion in his words made my heart trip and my hands rose quicker until my open palms climbed to his abs. My looks were more than a little deceiving. I proved as much as I hooked my fingers quietly under the waistband of my stepbrother's underwear.

Parrish bared his teeth and closed his fist around strands of my hair. It didn't hurt; it was only a gesture, meant to show me where my place was.

I blinked at him pleadingly, waiting for his further command. But he merely nodded, and that was enough to make my cock pulse hard and fast.

I shivered as I inhaled, pulling his shorts and underwear down. His hair had been shaved perhaps a week ago, not even a finger's width covering the skin around the root of his cock as I revealed it, inch by sexy inch.

Parrish sucked air between his gritted teeth and tightened the grip on my hair, basically telling me to stop the teasing. He was the one only who could tease; my job was to suffer the sweet torment he cared to impose upon me.

I obeyed. Every cell in my body relaxed with satisfaction at that. It was like the entire world went back to order.

I pulled the waistband over his dick and watched it lustfully as it straightened in front of me. My heart climbed into my throat, pounding excitement into every shred of my being. Still, upright, hard as marble, he was eight or nine inches long, and slightly thicker than my toy, promising me the time of my life.

I like it rough. His words echoed in my head as I let his shorts and underwear fall down his legs and wrapped my right hand around the base of his cock.

Unable to wait, I stroked him once and leaned in with my mouth opening wide.

"Easy, boy," he rasped, tugging my head back carelessly. Fuck, he spoke to me like I was a puppy or something. And it made the hairs on my neck hackle. "Use your hand."

I stroked him, blinking my agreement, and biting my lip to prevent a pained whimper from bursting out of me. I worshiped his tattoos with my greedy eyes while my hand moved back and forth along the length of his hard cock. And each time he pulsed in my hand, I felt pride spark inside of me.

I was sure he could see it on my face, because he loosened the grip on my hair and began patting the back of my head.

And when my free hand, which I had been holding on the side of my leg, moved to my stomach to feel the tingling skin on my abs, and sliding down to where my hard cock was desperately trying to break free, Parrish clicked his tongue quickly. "Easy," he whispered. "No touching until I tell you, Levi."

My eyes went wide, but I knew my pupils dilated as the meaning of his words sank in. I licked my lips insecurely and nodded reluctantly. Or feigned reluctance, at least. The truth was far more complex. My body screamed for something more. It was desperate for every twisted indulgence I could get from him tonight. But the denial of pleasure excited me in more ways than one. It promised me something grand and unforgettable, even if it was unforgivable.

"First, I'm going to make you choke on my dick," he purred, rounding his lips and breathing through his mouth, his throat open so that air was flowing almost silently. "Then, I'm going to destroy your hole so you never forget the time you played with fire."

A moan rose to my throat, but I stopped it there. It hurt on its way down as I pushed it with all my will. My only reply was an indulgent squeeze around his cock. It visibly edged him a little closer to his release, though he didn't appreciate it nearly as much as he should have.

"Bad boy," he said as he swatted my hand away and took his cock in his own hand. The other, which had been patting me, circled around my head and he pushed his thumb inside my mouth. Like he was examining a toy, his thumb stretched my lips and moved them this way and that, until he pushed it deep inside of me, pressing my tongue down and holding my chin with the rest of his hand.

I didn't gag. I might have had a dry spell and my sex life might not have been spicy in the past, but I wasn't completely out of shape. I'd had my toy and I'd gotten my money's worth out of it. Distantly, I wondered if Parrish would be jealous if he knew about that.

I watched him stroke himself so excruciatingly slowly that my own chest was squeezing tighter. Here stood the master of bedroom tension, the overlord of teasing and denying. I hated how much I loved it.

My knees stung against the bare wooden floor. I sealed my lips around his thumb and sucked it, making one corner of Parrish's lips twist upward. He ran his other hand over his short, coarse beard and I waited patiently, imagining its burn in the most sensitive of places on my body.

When he was done thumbing the inside of my mouth, pleased with whatever conclusions it had helped him make, he nodded. "Open your mouth, Levi. Open it wide."

I did. At once, my throat constricted and airflow stopped. It was somewhere on the periphery of my consciousness that breathing was somewhat important for sustaining life, but I didn't bother with it until it grew crucial. In the meantime, I stretched my jaw as far open as I could and did my damned best to hide the shivers that ran down my arms.

Parrish held his cock again and brought the tip to my lips. He didn't insert it. Oh no. Nothing with Parrish was as simple as that. He pressed the tip right against my lower lip and dragged it left and right until my tongue reached out to meet it. The saltiness of his precum dominated my senses the moment when I became aware of it.

Fucking finally, Parrish placed his hand behind my head and did precisely what he had promised. Though he eased himself inside of my mouth gently, at first, and allowed me to savor everything from the sweet and salty taste of him to the smooth feel of his dick on top of my tongue, he soon swayed his hips closer, penetrating my throat deeper with each move.

I managed to breathe in intricate little bubbles of air while Parrish was pulling back, but I choked on him with growing frequency. He rose to his toes, tilting my head back, fucking my throat from above like he somehow knew every last idea of what rough and dirty sex meant to me.

He stared into my wide eyes. His were ablaze, burning brighter each time he shoved himself deeper and claimed more of me for himself.

A gargle broke out of me and Parrish frowned, but the grin that crossed his face for a brief moment spoke volumes. I, too, felt it. I felt the thrill of having to stay quiet. I felt the high of fright and relief when the choked sound burst out of me and over his thick cock. And I found myself, too, perking my ears for any sign we might have been overheard.

Nothing. Chatter and laughter downstairs. Snoring in the room next door.

Parrish put both of his hands around my head, pulled back, and somehow seemed larger still. He inhaled, his chest rising as he twisted his eyebrows in a mixture of pleasure and pain. Slowly, he impaled me as deep as he could, as I scrambled to open my throat for him. No air could pass in or out of my lungs and my vision blurred with tears. I craned my neck, giving him a better angle for another fraction of an inch, and felt the trickle of saliva escape from a corner of my mouth.

A noise, like a breath with just a tinge of voice, left Parrish's lips, and he relaxed. He was back on his feet fully, pulling out of me, and reaching for his cock to stroke it hard and fast, looking like he was soothing the biggest hurt you could imagine. And I breathed deeply, all the while he slowly sank onto his feet.

Once he decided I'd had enough of breathing, he leaned in and pressed his lips against mine. He kissed me deeply, rewarding what he must have seen as good behavior. And a sort of pride I hadn't known before filled me to bursting. If it were not unimaginable, I would say it was the kind of pride a younger brother felt when the older one praised him.

Was I so hungry for that? Had my life been shaped by my expectation that Parrish should notice me? Parrish, the object of all my desires? Or Parrish, the stand-in for a big brother I had never had? Or did one make the other possible?

I had no time to wonder.

Parrish pulled back from me as my brain swam in hormones and the room spun around me. My lips moved in kissing motions for a heartbeat longer after Parrish broke contact and this made him smile. "Be a good boy and get on the bed, Levi," he said. "I'm going to fuck you senseless."

I whimpered right there and then. And neither of us cared for the risk that came with making noise.

But, as soon as the little sense I'd had left returned to me, it was ready to get lost again when Parrish wrecked me. I scrambled to my feet and lay on my stomach, crossing my arms under my head and pressing my mouth and nose tightly in the fold of my arm.

Parrish followed, kneeling on the bed behind me and taking his time to watch me. He sure liked observing me from behind. And from the front, too, if today's jealous glares were any indication. I cherished his jealousy, even if I didn't want to encourage it. It made me feel conflicting, mutually exclusive things that should not exist at the same time. It made me want to bicker and sneer and tell him jealousy was a lousy trait. But it also made me feel so special and wanted and privileged that he would wish to break an innocent — if annoying — nose just to make it clear I was his.

Parrish tucked his fingers inside the waistband of my cotton shorts and briefs, just above the pronounced curve of my ass. He dragged them down slowly, revealing more of my smooth, white skin under the light of the lamps around the room. A deep set purr from his throat filled my ears and made my heart three times bigger.

He wasn't so gentle with me now. He yanked the clothes down, catching and pulling my aching, itching cock with it, until I almost yelped, catching myself a fraction before the cry burst out of me. But the next moment, unbearable warmth washed over me and I felt like everything was as perfect as it could be. Parrish was sliding my clothes down my lower legs, freeing me of their confines, and my dick was pressing hard against the soft mattress.

"That's right," Parrish said as I lifted my feet to help him finish the work. My clothes dropped near my head in a small, messy pile, and Parrish set his big hands on my hips. "What a good boy you are," he said just before he yanked me back and forced me on my knees. "You're going to like this."

It was the heat of his breath that alerted me to his proximity a moment before he buried his face between my tender cheeks. His hands moved from my hips to my ass, kneading and spreading my cheeks all the while he licked and slurped, ate and tongue-fucked my rim.

His left hand soon moved from my ass, between my legs, and to my cock. He closed it from beneath me, my balls settling on his wrist, and stroked me so desperately slow that I felt compelled to thrust my hips a time or two. All I got in return was a tighter squeeze around my cock and his nails digging into my cheek as punishment for disobedience.

He ate me ravenously and for an endlessly long while. My head was spinning with appreciation and desire. Whatever he was making me into, I was happy to transform. A good boy? *Yes, please*. A slut for his cock? *Fuck me now and never stop*. I just wanted this to last.

My arms, back, and ass prickled as shivers ran in every direction over my body. Every last part of me tingled as Parrish worked me skillfully and resolutely. And then, like the total master of my body who knew my needs before I needed them, he released my cheek and circled his index finger around my rim. Once, twice, and I cried into my folded arm with pleasure when he buried it inside of me.

"So fucking hot," he whispered against my wet skin, letting the tip of his tongue soothe my hole as he penetrated it with his finger.

He stretched me so with one, then two of his fingers, until I wanted to cry with lust and desperation for more. I wanted his cock so badly that I seriously felt like I might faint if I didn't get it soon.

"Such a tight boy," he said and I found myself stretching my arm behind my back and grabbing his wrist.

Harder, you motherfucker, I grunted internally. *Fuck me harder*.

A pleased wave of laughter rolled out of him and against my butt while I jerked his hand closer, pushing his fingers deeper into myself.

"And so eager," Parrish said, then he fucking bit the side of my hand. It wasn't hard, but it was surprising enough that I almost shouted.

And when I jerked my hand away, he pulled his fingers out, rubbing them smoothly up and down my crack, all the while teasing my cock with the slow pace of his stroking. "Turn around. I want to look you in the eyes while I fuck you." He got off the bed and reached for his duffel in the corner of the room, rummaged briefly around it, and brought back a bottle of lube.

He didn't need to command me twice. It was easily the weight of his words that tipped me over and I rolled onto my back, legs spread and dick swollen. He looked at my face, then my torso, and finally settled his gaze on my cock.

He lifted his eyebrow. "I thought you'd be smaller."

I snorted. "Are you displeased?" I asked teasingly.

He cocked a corner of his lips and hooked his hands under my legs before I knew what was up. He yanked me down the length of the bed. My head slid off the pillow and I watched the ceiling with an indestructible grin on my face.

I dropped my gaze to Parrish's dark features and all the allure of his wicked smirk as he lifted my legs. His cock settled between my cheeks and he rubbed himself against me. "I'm not at all displeased. You're far better at this than I expected."

I said nothing to that. If he imagined I'd had a lot of practice and that sparked jealousy that made him competitive, I wasn't going to complain. He was more than welcome to outperform the imaginary lovers that might have trained me so well. He didn't need to know it had mostly been me, my trusted dildo, and an abundance of late-night porn.

But as Parrish bent my legs, knees almost reaching my shoulders, and let his weight work in his favor, I felt the moans swell in me. His cock was rubbing against my hole hard, even if he was still seductively slow. And I couldn't hold it in.

The intensity of his gaze, so fully on me, was what tipped me over and I whimpered.

"Shh," he said, taking my feet in his hands and setting them onto his chest for support. We depended on one another for this to work. And I was more than willing to depend on Parrish Turner.

He reached for his cock and stroked it, then squirted a few drops of lube over his fingers and slicked himself for action. But when the tip of his cock even grazed my hole, all the silencing he'd attempted failed miserably and I moaned against my better judgment.

Parrish grunted, then reached over to where he'd left my clothes, lifted my briefs, and balled them. "I told you to be quiet," he said darkly. He pressed the ball of fabric against my lips and lifted his eyebrows as if to say: "You know what to do."

And I did. I opened my mouth wide for him to stuff it with my briefs. And good thing I did, because when he pushed his cock into me, my jaws clenched against my will.

It wasn't painful. Not after the work he'd put into preparing me. But it was overwhelming in a totally different way. My chest filled with air I inhaled through my nose and my briefs soaked up the moan that escaped from my throat.

Parrish held my hips while I pressed my feet hard against his inked and muscled chest. He yanked me down, impaling me on his length until my eyes widened and I got what I was promised. Rough fucking to leave me senseless. Never to forget the time I played with fire. But all it did was make me want to carry a lighter wherever I went.

Parrish buried his cock inside of me after a few probing swings of his hips. Every bit of me stiffened, but I worked to relax my hole and let him in. His jerky movements didn't allow him to pull his cock far. Instead, he found my special spot and used his length to rub hard against it.

Every push into me rippled through my body. My dick throbbed and my voice soaked my briefs with muffled moans and cries for more, more, more. And like he could hear me or read this off my face, he rammed me harder and faster, pulling his cock further only to reach deeper inside of me.

And every move he made, brought me closer.

Parrish could command me not to touch myself. He could tell me. He could bind my hands. And I would obey. But there was nothing in this whole wide world that could stop the overwhelming feeling when he decided I was ready and he worked my prostate until I truly was senseless.

My balls tightened and my cock pulsed. The sensations merged and flooded me. The stretching and the grinding; his proximity as we merged into one being, forbidden to exist in such a way as we did; the harmony of two souls colliding into one.

My neck craned back and a grunt choked in my throat. My head sank deep into the mattress as I arched my back what little I could. There. There. Just like that. He rubbed against it and pushed it and pressed. And, when I could no longer hold it back, I let it happen. My cock pulsed just as my hole did.

I wanted to talk dirty to him. I wanted to plead for him to fill me, now, while I was coming.

But I couldn't.

All sounds drowned in the fabric that filled my mouth.

And I let myself ride this high.

Parrish grunted softly, but his fingers dug into my hips harder as he strained to stay quiet. My cock pulsed faster, cum squirting all over my body, my hole clenching around the root of his length that filled me.

And it did it to him at last.

Parrish's cool, if a little pained, expression crumbled and fell. His cock throbbed inside of me and he filled me with his cum. Holy shit, how I had wanted him to do just that.

He yanked me down his dick once more, then paused, holding himself inside of me until his cock stopped pulsing. Then, he exhaled almost silently, but sweat covered his gorgeous face just as it covered all of me.

He breathed quickly through his mouth, while my nose worked for air loudly. It made Parrish hurry to pull the briefs out of my mouth, and he leaned and pressed his lips against mine. "You were perfect, you dirty boy," he murmured over my open mouth. "You and I are gonna have a lot of fun."

His cock slowly left me, though I wished it didn't have to. What remained was knowledge of the thing we'd done; something we could never undo.

Something I never wanted to undo.

And, for what it was worth, Parrish didn't get off the bed. He didn't put his clothes on and stroll out with a lazy smile that taught me never to trust again.

Instead, he collapsed next to me, turned me like I was his body pillow, and wrapped his right arm around me. His torso pressed against my back, sweat sealing us together, his cock softening between my cheeks.

And he held me.

"You're mine, Levi," he whispered. "Don't forget that."

Shivers ran down my arms. My toes tingled. And all I could do was breathe and close my eyes and let him claim me.

Chapter Ten
PARRISH

I muttered obscenities into the pillow. The sunlight, magnified by the window, was as intent on blinding me this morning as it had been every day so far.

I was just getting ready to wake Levi up and complain. 'Can't we ever use the goddamn blinds?' But then, my heart leaped all on its own, and every negative thought evaporated from my mind.

For one instant, it was like I liberated myself.

We had done things last night that I would remember until the day I died. But which I should also take to my grave quietly.

Oddly enough, there wasn't a single regret in my heart. Levi had been everything I had failed to imagine he could be. Attractive, yes, but also fully receptive of whatever I had asked of him. Ah, and so very talented. It was rare to run into someone as adventurous as that and rarer still to find him in my own family.

I blinked myself awake and discovered that Levi wasn't even in the bed.

We'd cuddled for a long while last night, then showered together when I'd asked him for his hand and led him into the bathroom. Afterward, I spooned him from behind, connecting our bodies wherever I could. He fit into mine like a piece of a puzzle. Where my knees bent, his legs folded; where my stomach expanded with every breath I inhaled, his lower back curved to fit in.

I had no memory of Levi getting out of the bed. I had been knocked out the entire night. Now, I got up and found a pair of boxer-briefs and everyday shorts, put them on, brushed my teeth, and made my way downstairs.

I was mostly in search of coffee, but I found something better. Most of the house was still asleep. The cool morning air wasn't yet giving way to the heat of the day. And out on the back porch, Levi sat cross-legged on the large patio sectional that was connected to the wall of the house. He was completely lost on what he was doing, which was something I had never seen him do. He had a sketchbook open in his lap and his right hand frantically worked.

The weight of our sins crashed onto my chest in that instant when Levi became aware of me standing by the door frame. He lifted his moss colored eyes to look at me, roses blooming on his cheeks. "Hey," he said, barely louder than a whisper.

I lifted my chin in return. "You sketch?"

He quickly closed the sketchbook. "Oh, no."

Though different feelings splashed within me this way and that, I couldn't help myself but grin. "Lemme see."

"No way," Levi said, setting his sketchbook on the other side of his seat so it was out of my reach. It would have been if I had any reservations about invading his personal space.

I moved like a panther, appearing right up against my stepbrother in the next beat of his heart, reaching for his sketchbook while distracting him with my proximity. My bare chest all but pressed against his face as I bent down, snatched the object of my curiosity, and skipped back.

"Don't do that," Levi whispered a little harshly. "Not out here."

"They're sleeping," I said.

He shot a look over my shoulder, in the general direction of our parents' bedroom. I got the message, but not exactly the feeling that must have been sent my way. I wasn't afraid the way he was.

Instead, I shrugged guilelessly and dropped into a chair, elbows on the armrests, thumbs feeling the quality paper of the sketchbook as I flipped from the empty pages in the back closer to the filled ones of the first half. "I had no idea."

"It's nothing," Levi said, stiff and defensive. "I couldn't sleep. I got bored."

I found his work and stopped dead in my tracks. My eyebrows twitched and I cocked my head, not entirely able to believe my eyes. "This..."

"...sucks, I know," Levi said, unfolding his legs and reaching quickly for the notebook. But I was faster in pulling it out of his reach, flipped a few more pages and bit my lip. "Give it back."

"No," I said bluntly.

"Parrish," he said with all the command he could muster. Was he forgetting that he was *mine*?

"I'm not giving it back," I said and met his gaze with a steel one of my own. He sat back, surrendering, blinking and heating up in reply to the finality in my voice. It wasn't up for debate.

Levi swallowed, lips pursing with unspoken disagreement.

"I'll give it back after you stop selling yourself short," I said after a long pause. I set the sketchbook in my lap and flipped a few more pages. Studies of hands, feet, arms, torsos, random objects. "Great shading work," I muttered more to myself than to Levi as I examined one particular sequence in which he sketched an orb nine times over, each hit by light from a different source and angle. Soft and stark, left and right. "Crosshatching could use practice," I said, flipping pages again to where he had half a portrait done in that particular style. "But this is promising. This is very promising." I looked through his lackluster attempts at animals and his passionate studies of the human figure. "There's a pattern," I mumbled. "You know your strengths. That's good." Finally, I looked up from the page to where Levi was stewing in embarrassment. "Do you have an idea of your style?"

He snorted. "You're looking at five years worth of doodling," he pointed out emphatically. "I don't know what style means at this point."

I narrowed my eyes. "That's a lie."

His thin, black eyebrows rose. "Excuse me?"

"Where's the *real* sketchbook, Levi?" I asked, a coy smile tugging on the corners of my lips.

"I don't know what you're talking about," he said breathlessly.

"Sure you do. These are all studies of this detail and that. Not one attempt at something real." I closed the sketchbook, still holding it in my hands. If I was anything, I was a man of my word, and I wouldn't return it until I heard him agree he was talented.

"I'm not ready to try something..."

I sucked my teeth to stop him right there. "There isn't a person living or dead who just blindly practiced until they were ready without ever trying to really sketch. You were practicing for something, right?"

Levi frowned at his defeat and rolled his eyes. "Fine. I have it. You can't see it."

I didn't need to. It was probably brilliant. Promising, at least, if not fully baked yet. A smile crossed my face. "Keep at it."

"What for?" he asked, suddenly somber. "It's not like I can do something with it."

I sighed. "The number of times everyone told me that while I was growing up," I mused, shaking my head. "And now, I'm going to try to open my second parlor. If the fifteen-year-old me could see it...ah, he'd die with envy," I finished and laughed.

"Yeah, but..." Levi shrugged like there was something obvious. And when I lifted my eyebrow in question, he said simply, "You're an artist."

"I became one," I corrected. "You have a gift, Levi."

He snorted.

"Even if you can't see it, it's there." My tone was dropping lower as movement somewhere inside the house ticked the back of my consciousness.

"Fine. Whatever. It's not like I'll ever use it. I pick the pencil up once in a million years and kill an hour. Don't try to convince me that it's any good," he said, a little snappy, and crossed his legs again. While he was at it, he crossed his arms, too, and looked away from me.

Annoyance flared through me. "What is it with you?"

"Nothing," he said. "I'm just not good at it."

"That's not it," I said, my guts turning to steel. "Tell me. What are you really ashamed of?" I narrowed my eyes at him.

"Shh," he snapped.

I balked and opened my mouth, then lowered my voice. "Do you regret it?"

"No," he said.

"Regret what?"

Levi turned to stone and I rolled my eyes at the sound of Harold's voice. The door of their bedroom shut and he stepped out onto the patio, then moved toward the table to pour himself a mug of coffee. "What are you on about?"

Levi's face turned red.

I assumed a deadly serious expression and looked Harry in the eyes. "Data science," I lied. "He threw away his talent for something that's only profitable."

"Nonsense," Harold said and slurped his coffee as he sat down in the same spot he'd had his morning coffee in since the day he'd married my mother. "Why should he regret a respectable diploma?"

"I don't regret anything," Levi insisted, his gaze meeting mine for the briefest of moments.

I lifted my eyebrow just enough that he would notice.

His lips tightened as if to assure me he was telling the truth. He meant it. There were no regrets about last night.

"What talent are you talking about?" Harry asked. The question was thrown at me.

I lifted the notebook without handing it over. Yeah, I'd noticed the tattoos on his studies of hands and arms. They were few, because that was how many I'd had when he had last seen me. There was no way I would let Harry see Levi's hidden interests. "Looks like Levi is a secretly gifted artist." When Harold's eyebrows quivered, I added: "You should be proud, Harry. He's enormously talented."

Harold looked between us, then stuttered. "Of course I'm proud of him. Aren't I, Levi?"

"Sure, Dad," Levi huffed, suffering between the two of us like we were literally talking about last night.

"You wouldn't think that information tech is something to regret, would you?" Harold asked, but it wasn't directed at Levi. It sounded more like he used it as an opening to a lecture. "Just because it's a highly valued skill, learning it doesn't mean you're selling out." As he spoke, I realized the lecture was intended for me to hear, not Levi. "It's all nice and good to have fantasies, but when the real world comes calling, it's those who have something to offer, a commodity to trade, that prevails."

I couldn't hold the grunt down. "Unless you're resourceful," I said. "In which case, you don't serve anyone but yourself, and you love what you do. Or, you know, you marry well."

Harry winced. He'd slowly but surely abandoned his job after marrying Margaret. It had been her idea, for the most part, for both of them to retire early, but Harold hadn't had a hard time leaving the commodity he could trade. Once they'd merged our houses and their finances, they had sped through the few years of extra work and decided they were ready to live off of their portfolio. Not that I cared which one of them had contributed more. Especially since it was the inheritance from my grandparents' that had made it possible for Marge in the first place.

But Harry still turned a few shades redder and stopped talking.

What followed was the most awkward breakfast this house had ever witnessed. Margaret prepared French toast, boiled eggs, a variety of fresh vegetables, cheeses, jams, and cold cuts, while Harold busied himself with the newspaper. Natalie appeared, only to roll her eyes and huff that Jarred was insisting she simply had to show up as soon as possible to entertain one of the aunts. And our own aunt, Lauren, appeared with a sore head and no recollection of bursting through our bedroom door the night before, belching at the sight of food and downing coffee like a camel. Nevertheless, as soon as she had appeared, Levi had gotten even quieter. As if being seen by her carried the risk of sparking a memory that had never formed in her head. Possibly a memory of our bed squeaking once the wrong way or his whimpers escaping him against all his efforts.

It was after breakfast, while Lauren sunbathed in the backyard and Margaret set out to prepare everything for lunch with Harry cleaning up, that I tapped Levi's shoulder. "Come with me," I said.

He blinked once, as if taking a moment to consider, but nodded without protest. He never asked me where we were going or what we would do there, and I didn't say. I didn't have a clear plan, but I needed to have him someplace private, someplace we could talk plainly.

He gave me enough time to put on a T-shirt and followed me wordlessly out of the house. My feelings warred in me, the goods and bads clashing and playing a desperate game of tug of war. The breakfast left me feeling spiteful, but Levi's quiet obedience gave me hope. Still, he wasn't letting himself go just like that. It was a good ten minutes after we'd left the house that he spoke. "You know, it's easier if you don't contradict everything he says."

"What?" I murmured, my mind elsewhere.

"If you don't draw too much attention to yourself," Levi explained.

"Like what you're doing?" I asked before I could stop myself. A lifetime of careless remarks made it all too easy to be brutally honest with him. And the same went in both directions. "Hoping if nobody notices you, nobody will find out about college?"

We walked shoulder to shoulder. I turned my head to face him and looked down into his eyes only to find sparks of low simmering anger there. "Like that, yeah," he said dryly.

"Sorry," I blurted. "I didn't mean it like..."

"No, it's right," he said. "I often bury my head in sand." He shrugged and looked ahead at the rows of shops on both sides of Main Street, which led to the old, neocolonial town hall. "There's too much at stake, Parrish," he said meekly.

"I thought you had no regrets," I said.

"And I don't," he snapped like he couldn't believe I needed to ask again. "But I don't want to advertise it, either. They can never find out about this. We..." That was the first time either of us had used that pronoun in such a way. We both noticed the twisting of its meaning as it happened. "We have to be careful," he finished.

"As we are," I said. "You worry too much."

"Don't lecture me," he said. "Not you."

"I'm not," I said honestly. My voice was quiet so that only he could hear me, and low in a way that would make him want to squirm and bite his lips. "While you're mine, I'm taking that worry away from you, Levi. It's mine to deal with."

He had nothing to say to that. It was better that way. If he asked me how long he would stay mine, I couldn't answer him. I wasn't going to think about it. In the real world, far detached from my imagination, we only fucked once. I needed to remind myself about that.

"I'm not saying it's not complicated," I went on, pausing at the stoplight and waiting with Levi one inch away from me.

"Then, what *are* you saying?" he asked bluntly.

The light changed and we moved forward. I inhaled sharply and spat it out without any double meanings. "I don't want it to be one and done," I said. "I want to have you again. And again. And as much as I can."

He didn't ask me for how long and I couldn't tell him. Our paths would fork at Natalie's wedding. Would we even last that long?

Levi was quiet, as if pondering, while I led the way that cut the journey shorter, through the alleys and onto the right bank of Rushing Brook. The water level was low and nobody was around, either to fish or dip themselves in the river. A few pedestrians were crossing the bridge, but they were of no concern to me. I led Levi down the stone steps to the narrow promenade near the water, then toward the bridge. It was a stone structure, old but well maintained, with three arches and enough width to shield us from sight of any prying eyes.

We stopped in the shade of the bridge and I faced Levi. "So?"

"So what?" he asked.

"What do you say to that?"

He scoff-chuckled. "Are you seriously asking me that? Obviously, Parrish. Obviously, I want more. But I..."

I didn't let him give me any buts or clauses. I pushed him with my entire body and pinned him against the cold stones of the bridge, leaning in hungrily and pressing my lips against his.

The kiss seared us both, but I didn't care. I wanted to have a taste of him so badly that I would have risked it out in the open had the bridge not been this near. I would have had my way with him on a bench in the park or behind the brewery.

I kissed him until he moaned into my mouth and I smiled against his. Then, I pulled my head back, and looked deep into his glazed, mossy eyes. "Obviously, you want more, but what?"

Levi took two breaths then smiled, letting only the hint of his dimples touch his cheeks. He lifted his hand and ran it over my beard with surprising fondness. "To be honest, I can't remember what I was going to say."

A dark grin crossed my face. "Lucky me."

Chapter Eleven

LEVI

As our first week back in River Bend came to an end, I found that everything in my life had changed. Except, nothing seemed different whatsoever. And that was precisely what painted every experience of every moment of every day.

Parrish was the spark that lit the fuse I hadn't known was in me. Ingenious ways he came up with just to draw us away from everyone never stopped amazing me; and it even more amazed me that he could kiss me with more passion than the day before, whenever he found a good spot for such a thing. As often as not, the right spot was our bedroom, which we began locking whenever we were both inside, even if nothing was taking place in there. But even so, Aunt Lauren would occasionally get it wrong and try our door instead of hers. "Is she seriously drunk again?" Parrish once whispered into my ear in between licking it.

By this time, it didn't even kill my mood or drive to remember the rest of the family was in the house. We were getting ten or twenty minutes of privacy at a time, not enough to gorge in one another's bodies as we might like, but just enough to fan the desire. "She's heartbroken," I replied, more busy with running my hand through the hair on the back of his head than thinking of Lauren's heartache. I was sitting in Parrish's lap, facing him, and grinding him until he was so hard he was close to willing to beg. And, in a sweet turn of new routines, I pulled back just then. "We should go downstairs. Dinner's almost ready."

Then, we would sit and eat together with the living reminders of what we were doing was wrong.

But as soon as I came close to surrendering to despair and fear, Parrish would turn restless and find us an excuse to march out of the house.

"See that bookstore there?" he asked me on one such excursion.

"Mrs. Crane's?" I asked.

"Yeah," he said fondly. "Around the time I was thirteen or fourteen, and you were probably still learning how to walk—" he looked and me and grinned, "—I was too young to let all hell break loose like I could later, so I went to Mrs. Crane, often pretending I needed someplace quiet to read or do my homework or whatever lie I could come up with each day. And she always took me seriously, showed me this loft above the store she imagined for readers. It was rarely used. Mostly kids like me came around and read books they couldn't persuade their parents to buy. Mrs. Crane didn't mind. That was my hiding place. I'm pretty sure she knew all along I just wanted to crawl somewhere and be alone, but she slowly got me interested in reading. A bit of this, a bit of that, until I really liked fantasy. For a short while, just before I discovered how good it felt to destroy shit and get away when you're an angry teenager, that was my whole world."

I stared at him with a mixture of profound respect for him and deep hurt for the fact that he'd felt like a stranger in his own house.

Parrish went on, talking about the books he liked, the books he hated, and the slow death of the reader inside of him over the years. "I liked raising hell a lot more," he admitted in the end. "Not that I stopped. Obviously." He looked at me like I was the hell he was raising.

And right then, I was willing to be.

But it kept shifting like the wind changing its direction. Wherever I found myself, excluding those quiet, private minutes with Parrish and Parrish alone, I was tapping my foot on the floor or my finger against my lip. I was touching my increasingly messy hair and rumpled clothes, or toying with food on my plate for the lack of appetite.

For all the passion my time with Parrish behind the locked door fed me, all the other times starved me. Every moment of pleasure came with a price I needed to pay. And I thought he could sense it. I thought he felt the same. But Parrish was fiery and stubborn; if he was bothered by the enormity of our transgressions, he wasn't going to say that aloud.

All we had done only made me want more. And it was so soon that I became addicted to Parrish. Because, once he gave me the attention I had wanted all along, I didn't dare imagine going back.

There had been nothing in my life I had ever craved quite like this.

And I wasn't going to give it up.

My resolve strengthened as we had our dinner on Saturday. Whether he knew what he was doing or not, I never asked, but Parrish forced me to make a choice for myself. Was it possible that he could see the haunted look I carried all day long? Could he see into my soul and understand me without ever uttering a word? I doubted it, to be honest, but the evidence was piling up. And so, we wined and dined and Lauren went a little further than she normally allowed herself when she was around family. Between one hiccup and another, Lauren turned to Parrish, who was on the sectional on the back porch, right across from me. "Will you come around again any time soon?" she asked.

The venom in her voice was unmistakable. For all of Margaret's attempts to conceal her own distaste of Parrish, Lauren let loose.

"Probably," Parrish said, taking me aback. I'd honestly expected him to say he wouldn't show his face in this town again, that a Bigfoot sighting was a more likely outcome.

Nervous shifting around me, mainly from Dad and Margaret, clued me in. Parrish knew people far better than I ever could. He knew his presence here bothered them more than his distance.

He glanced at me very briefly, but long enough that the spark of mischief flared in his brown eyes, reminding me of what he had been like back when I had first fallen for him. My heart throbbed sadly as I thought of all the time lost, but I didn't have enough time to dwell on it. "I've got people here," Parrish said, lazily pushing his leg under the covered table until it brushed against mine.

The thing about Parrish was that he loved comfort. He loved it so much that he had gone to senator Wilkinson's mansion in cotton shorts and rubber flip-flops. So, when around the house, he wore the bare minimum of clothes, letting me secretly drool over the tattoos on his torso, and easily sliding his foot out of the slipper to do unspeakable things with it.

"Natalie's not leaving," he said. "I'd like to see her more often."

The back of his foot hooked under my bare calf. While I wasn't nearly as free and comfortable with my body as Parrish was, I also liked my comfort around the house. I wore a sleeveless T-shirt, cotton shorts, and a pair of sneakers on short socks. This gave Parrish plenty of bare skin to feel.

Natalie smiled at Parrish from the far right side of the table.

"And you're not as bad as I remember, Levi," he said, his foot rising a little higher as he leaned back and twined his fingers behind his head. "I could see us catching up. When you're in town again."

My heart dropped, for a moment only, at the hint I might be revealed, but Parrish shot me a lopsided grin and looked around the table.

A flood of images washed over me. Stealing kisses and moments, living on borrowed time, meeting up every once in a while. Would I live my life like that for Parrish? I was too scared to answer that, because I knew I would. I would let him have me however he liked.

"It's good you boys are getting along," Margaret said. But, when I looked at her, I found her lips still and her smile icy. She tried and failed to make me believe she meant it. And all this because Parrish didn't fit into this fantasy of a perfect family she had imagined around herself. He was better off as the son who was succeeding in New York, too busy to visit. *Oh, he calls, often he calls, and sends his love. He misses the town so much. Yadda-da-doo. Blah, blah.*

As these things crossed my mind, every bit of tension left my body. I relaxed and Parrish felt it on his rising foot. His toes reached over my knee and along my inner thigh.

I wished to squirm; the urge was strong. Breathing became optional. Every bit of me tingled as Parrish pressed his foot hard against my thigh and dragged it higher, closer to where my cock was getting rapidly hard and greedy for my stepbrother's attention.

And this was what he did. He made me choose. Stay or leave. Let him or deny him. It was Parrish or the rest of them. And Parrish was looking at me in a way only I understood. Seemingly distant, like he was lost in his thoughts, he was reading every twitch of my muscles and counting every breath I drew.

Next to him, Lauren was hiccuping and Margaret was holding herself tightly so as not to appear rude. Dad's face darkened as if he could see the devious things Parrish was doing under the table. What really worried him was that Parrish was even remotely interested in seeing me again, and I wasn't loudly against the idea.

I never would be.

See me all you like, I thought, hoping Parrish could truly read my mind. *See me. Take me. Have me. I'll wait.* Shivers ran down my spine when his foot reached my crotch and Parrish sighed with satisfaction. But I relaxed. I couldn't tell you how.

My face was heating up, but not with shame. Not really. It was the thrill of being right there, under their turned-up noses. They couldn't see what was happening from the enormity of their egos.

Fuck, I thought weakly. *It's you I want.* And all the rocking emotions welled in me and threatened to pour out in his direction. I made the choice. After days of following him wherever he cared to take me, I finally knew. Not that it made any difference. But if it came down to it, I would choose him.

"I was thinking," Parrish said, his foot rising along my hard length, rubbing me softly. "I'd like to drive up to Lake Crystal tomorrow. Walk around the town, grab a bite, spend the night. Anybody want to join?"

Natalie groaned. "I doubt it. Jarred's been pestering me to help organize his bachelor party."

"Bachelor party?" Parrish frowned.

Natalie shook her head dismissively. She was tired of this bullshit, obviously, but I couldn't offer help. I was too far gone in fantasizing of Parrish as he casually stroked my hard cock under the table. I had to hold my breath, else I would moan like a whore. "It's a redo," Natalie was saying distantly. Or maybe I was the one who was distant. Completely lost. Afloat or adrift. "A rematch, he calls it. The last of his freedom." She scoffed at that with the expression of someone who was very tired.

Parrish snorted. To him, I was fine-tuned. His voice, even like that, went straight to me. "Anyone else?" he looked around the table while I watched his chest rise and fall.

"I don't think so, darling. We're far too busy," Margaret was saying.

"Busy, busy," Dad echoed.

"I'll go."

Parrish hardly looked.

For an instant, I wasn't sure if that had been me or Lauren saying that. I was outside my body. I was flying across the state to Lake Crystal and enjoying the anonymity with Parrish.

"...have to study?" Dad's voice faded in and I realized I had offered to go with Parrish. Nobody else had. It was a relief. If he'd gone with Lauren, he would have returned miserable because his plan backfired. "Levi?"

"Study what?" I asked without thinking, without breathing, and without looking away from Parrish's blazing gaze.

"For your exams," Dad insisted. "What's the matter with you, Levi?"

"Oh." Every muscle in my body was tensing as Parrish's foot increased the pressure. Fuck, I wasn't even close, but it felt so good. I would surrender to this grueling, excruciating pace for the entire night until he got me where I wanted to go. But I had to ignore it, for a moment at least. "I'll handle it. It's just a day or two, right?"

Parrish nodded, completely casual, like he wasn't sinning enough under the table to turn the devil away in embarrassment. "We'll make it a boys' night out."

Dad grumbled something, then inhaled sharply. "Very well. I don't want you boys doing anything funny."

Laughter nearly raptured me, but I swallowed it down. "I never do anything funny," I said, forcing my most expressionless face on full display.

Parrish began to move his foot back and my legs closed around it before he was free. He grinned, seemingly at nothing, without acknowledging me, and left his foot limp where it was. To that, I rubbed my thighs together and around him, shifting in my chair, until his gaze turned so amused that anyone could see something was up.

I released him.

"Right," Dad muttered. Whatever was going on in their heads, I didn't care. Just this once, I would do what I wanted. I wouldn't be burdened by the fantasy I was made to play along with or by someone else's expectations.

And, one day soon, when this all came to an end, I would have that lesson with me. I would have this little defiance.

It was the next morning, after Parrish had repeatedly refused to finish what he'd started under the table, and made me promise I wouldn't touch myself, that we packed after breakfast and got into the car.

The drive wasn't terribly long, but Parrish wasn't hurrying one bit. He drove slowly, talking about sketching of all things, and giving me ideas on how to practice crosshatching for better results.

The rolling, windswept hills around us grew steeper as he drove and spoke. We were well away from River Bend and the invisible cages that kept me trapped.

"You're smiling," he said abruptly. "What's funny?" There was expectant humor in his voice that only made me grin wider.

"Was I?" I asked, honestly in need of an answer.

His lips stretched into a smile. "You were. Ten minutes or longer. I figured it had to be a really good joke."

I shook my head. "I didn't realize."

And, as I tried to flatten my lips, my entire expression, Parrish clicked his tongue quickly. "Don't stop. It's nice to see you smile."

Even if I wanted to stop now, I couldn't. It was stronger than me. It pulled at the corners of my lips and revealed my teeth to him in a disarming and surrendering way. Gone was the animosity of our lifetimes. In its place, I found something far warmer. Something I dreaded to name because I wasn't yet ready to accept it.

And though my smile stayed, creeping doubts made themselves ever so slightly known in the far reaches of my mind. This, like everything, had an end. And it was in sight more likely than not.

What happens to us when Natalie gets married? I wanted to ask. *Will you really come around once in a while just to make me feel this way? Will you remember how you made me fly?*

And for all the choosing and deciding I had done last night, I wasn't ready for his answer.

Chapter Twelve

PARRISH

The drive to Lake Crystal was interesting. Levi kept smiling to himself and looking out the window to conceal the goofy grins. They were interrupted only by my hand occasionally on his thigh and his strangled whimpers, followed by curses at the cruelty of last night. I had kept him on the very edge, balancing him, teasing him, getting him so hard that he whimpered in pain, then pulling away from him. I had nibbled on his ear and pinched his small, brown nipples, and feathered my fingertips along his bare thighs all night long until he clutched the linens and whispered he would cry out loud if I didn't either stop or get him off.

"Try me," I'd told him. "Cry and see."

He'd pouted and endured my savage torture. Last night as much as now, in the car.

By the time we arrived in Willow Bay, after some two or so hours of driving, Levi was crossing his arms at his chest, cheeks rosy and his frown set. "You're the worst," he told me.

"You'll thank me later," I said confidently.

It softened him right away. He cracked that boyish smile and rolled his eyes at me. "You better deliver."

"You know I will, baby boy," I said, my darkest, sexiest voice rumbling from my throat.

It took a moment before he remembered to breathe.

I left the car in the reserved parking spot in front of a quaint bed and breakfast. The wood cladding on the exterior of the house was light green, with white balustrade around the porch, and a tall, pristine red roof.

Inside, we were greeted by the owner, who had three such houses in her care. She showed us the living area downstairs and the spacious bedroom with a large, modern bathroom connected to it, upstairs. There were roses on the bed and chocolate on the pillows. "I'm sure we won't forget this romantic getaway any time soon."

Levi tensed next to me, so I threw my arm over his shoulders and pulled him closer. *It's okay*, I messaged him silently. *Nobody knows we're stepbrothers. We're just another couple*. A couple...God, that word made me feel too many things at once. It injected fizz into my veins just as much as it made me frightened of something intangible and foreign. But it gave me this stupid sort of hope that made my heart throb too. Whether he heard my thoughts or not, Levi relaxed under my arm, our inner sides pressed together. He even wrapped his arm around my waist.

The landlady left the house and I shut the door behind her, only to turn around and see Levi leaning back against the wall, thighs pressed tightly together, and hands holding one another behind his back. He had that glassy look in his eyes that said he was willing to be handled.

I purred a chuckle.

"What? It's why we're here," Levi said defiantly, as if offended I would even find it amusing how eager he was.

"Sort of," I said.

"What do you mean?" he asked.

I gave him my most intense gaze. It seemed to make him lose his balance. Literally. He swayed a bit and steadied himself. "We're here because I know you can be quiet. And now, I want to hear you scream."

This tipped him again and he had to shift his feet to stay up. "What are you waiting for?" he whispered.

I stepped toward him and took his hips in my hands. When I pulled him closer, I felt how hard he was. Not gonna lie, I was getting hard too, but Levi was beyond lost. "If you wait until tonight..."

He let out a strangled whimper.

"I'll make it so worth your trouble," I whispered and bit his ear, then kissed the length of his neck.

"You're going to kill me, Parrish," he said. "I swear, you'll be the death of me."

I stepped back, resisting the urge to tear his clothes off his body and have him right there on the stairs. He was too damn attractive and my will was caving in. "Come," I said, voice rough from the physical strain it took to pull back from Levi. "We'll walk around first and have a nice dinner." And so we did.

Willow Bay was a small, tourist-oriented town. Every house was like ours, decorated with blooming red, yellow, orange, white, and violet flowers that took up every inch of spare space that could be found. Even the grass was different in this place; it seemed softer. So soft you felt like rolling in it for no clear reason at all. The town itself had a couple of grocery stores, artisan shops that made all the streets smell like their handmade lavender soaps and candles, and so many restaurants and coffee places that it rivaled a wet-dream version of Paris.

The stone paved street was lit by old-fashioned street lamps when Levi and I walked out into the early evening. We turned left and headed down the street at a lazy pace that let us absorb the sights, sounds, and scents of the town. To our right, houses and shops lined the street; to our left, extended terraces looking out at the beaches and the lake that was the lifeblood of this town. Live music before an Italian restaurant pulled me in and I silently consulted with Levi, using little more than our eyebrows and smiles, to confirm we wanted to sit there. And we were in luck, as it was Sunday and not so crowded that we needed a reservation. With a few polite smiles, we were seated on the right side of the street, on the terrace that was bordered by wooden balustrades, covered with vines and nearly tipping over under the weight of potted plants in full bloom.

We toasted with red wine as a sad, Sicilian song set the mood that made my heart mellow. My guard crumbled for a brief instant as I leaned in and looked into his eyes. It took conscious effort to rebuild the walls around myself.

He is your toy, I reminded myself.
He is here for your pleasure and his own.
Give him hell. He'll like it. And so will you.
Haven't you learned a thing in a lifetime of rejection? Do what you're good at. Pleasure both of you and move along without getting any ideas.

I listened to myself and obeyed. The thing about me was that I was never wrong. Heeding my own advice was the safest way to get through this unscathed. Dad had left, Margaret had turned away, Harry had never truly tried beyond the little fathering he'd imagined was required. And every guy I'd ever taken to bed had praised my skill and promised to call later. Sometimes, they called, but I didn't answer. Other times, they just moved on, as did I.

There wasn't a shred of evidence to suggest this would be any different in the long run. I wasn't fooling myself with the idea that we could have a future beyond this little fling. But what it definitely could be, was fun. Because Levi was fun. Whether he planned them or fate gave them to us, our days had been filled with moments of privacy, in which, when we weren't too busy making out, we talked endlessly. Glimmers of his bubbly personality as I had known it a long time ago began emerging once again. It seemed like he would forget about his troubles when he was with me, and he would dive into these passionate talks of art and crafts and a utopian society in which people did what made them happy.

"Nobody knows us," Levi said, enjoying his *pollo alla diavola* just like I'd promised he would. "It feels weird." His frown was adorable. "Like, until a few hours ago, you couldn't even look at me without my pulse spiking."

I chuckled softly. "I can still make your pulse spike just by looking at you."

His eyes went just a little wide and he calmed his facial muscles down before he grinned. "Not what I meant," he said, lifting his gaze off the herb and chili pepper marinated chicken to meet mine. What was left unsaid was: "Please do."

After we ate and had another round of wine and just a tad too much serenading on the terrace, I paid the bill and gave Levi my hand to hold. He did it without thinking too much about it. His smile was unstoppable as he squeezed his hand around mine and we walked around the lake.

I wouldn't let us tire too much though. On our way back, I stopped a bike rickshaw and settled in the back comfortably with Levi at my side. The young man riding the bicycle paced us nicely, giving us plenty of time to enjoy the view of the lake.

I didn't do that. Instead, I threw my left arm around Levi's shoulders and took his chin in my right hand. Slowly, I turned his head until he was facing me and I examined his clear, smooth face. "You have become very pretty since the last time I saw you."

"I was always pretty," he said, though there was more humor in his voice than not. He didn't believe his words. "You just weren't looking."

"True. I wasn't. And you were," I said emphatically enough that he needed a moment to gather himself. He bit his lip for a moment, but released it when I leaned in.

There was no fear in him. None at all. We were far enough from the people who never needed to know about our escapades that Levi surrendered himself fully to me. I loved it; loved holding him like this, keeping him all for myself, greedily but also gently. He was a delicate one. For all his ability to keep a fight with me going, he was a tired soul, older than his years. The hissing, bickering boy was a defensive front because the real Levi was scared and wearied by the expectations put on him.

I was the man to take them all away for a few days and nights. For a few moments when, he could simply give in.

And then, I leaned deeper in and pressed my lips to his, kissing him without a single worry that what we were doing was wrong. It couldn't be. It was too good to be wrong.

When I went to pull my head back, Levi followed, not letting us part. He kissed me back, with insatiable hunger and moaned in protest when I smirked and pushed him away. "Easy, boy," I said.

It always made him blush. He was so easy to turn pink. And, whenever I succeeded, the enormity of my pride was freaking me out. Was there anything I enjoyed as much as that? Would I find it after we were on our separate ways?

I gently nudged those thoughts aside when we reached the house. I helped Levi out of the rickshaw and bent my arm for him to hold as we crossed the short distance to our door. As I unlocked it, too many images and feelings flooded me at once. Us. Future. House. Sweet and terrible expectations. His proximity. His promises. His vows.

I steadied myself and led us inside, locking the door after Levi entered the house. The lights were subdued, glowing with dark yellow warmth in all the corners of every room.

Levi asked if I would get us another round of wine ready while he showered.

I poured wine into a decanter then explored the house, its backyard, and the view from the balcony upstairs. I could see the pleasure barges out on the lake, glowing orange, with faint music traveling over the surface of the water.

His footsteps were light behind me as he crossed the bedroom floor and startled me with his speed. His arms wrapped around me from behind and I let out a panicked wave of laughter. "Stealthy."

"Mm," was all he said.

As I placed my hands on his arms, while they still held me tightly, and dragged them around, I discovered he was shirtless. My right hand fell to his leg, and to my delight, I discovered he wasn't wearing pants, either. He did wear a pair of briefs, but that mistake was easy to correct.

I strengthened my grip on his wrist, broke free of his embrace, and spun around. In an instant, he was in my arms and mine to do whatever I wanted.

I pulled the curtain over the open balcony door as I led us inside, then placed my hands on Levi's face and looked into his eyes. "You're so horny," I told him, but without mocking. Hell, I was horny for him just as much. It was pulling me apart.

Levi shrugged, pulling on a somber face. "We don't have long. We better use the time while we can."

I couldn't agree more, though the reminder that we were running out of time made something knot in my stomach. It was a quiet agreement that we both knew where this would lead. We'd known, even if we hadn't said it, that there was no happy ending for two stepbrothers who wrecked everything in their path.

And, as these thoughts filled me with simmering anger, I closed my hand around Levi's pretty mouth and looked into his eyes with destructive intensity. He nearly pulled back, but not quite.

With Levi, it was like engine combustions. We could take our fury and frustration, channel it, and burn it into the kind of energy that made God look away in despair. Levi's eyes caught the light of the lamp and he stared at me defiantly.

"Have you ever been tied up?" I asked him slowly. Turning his head left and right, examining just how sharp his cheekbones were. His chest rose as he filled his lungs with air and blinked up at me.

He shook his head the little he could in my hold.

"Would you like to?" I asked, a ghost of a smile crossing my face.

The way his nostrils flared and his pupils dilated told me what he couldn't. He nodded, like he couldn't get the words out through his throat from the sheer intensity of how badly he wanted it.

I didn't like formal clothes on me, but I could always find some use for a good tie. And right now, courtesy of an upcoming wedding, I had a very good navy blue tie in my half-empty travel bag, which I'd conveniently left on the armchair two paces away from us.

I let go of Levi, who stood still like he was carved out of stone. I slid my hand into the bag and found all of the things I needed. I tossed the lube over to the bed, then took the tie and ran it through my fingers, folding it and wrapping it around my hand.

Levi watched me, breaths quiet and shallow, eyes pooling with ground-shattering desire. But he was patient. By now, he knew that rushing it only meant he'd be edged for longer and no amount of whispered pleas would help him get there any sooner.

"Cross your wrists," I said. My voice carried the weight of command and dominance with no need for raising. I spoke clearly, in a fairly flat tone that left no room for debate. "Behind your back," I said, seeing Levi fumble with his closed fists in front of him.

His cheeks warmed with color. "Oh." And he scrambled to cross his wrists behind his back.

I watched his slender figure and the definition of his muscles. He was so alluringly trimmed, skin much paler than mine, and still untouched by needles. I'd seen his curiosity sparked so many times whenever he had a quiet moment to examine my tattoos. I'd seen the desire. *I'll show you*, I wanted to tell him every time. *When you're in New York, I'll take you to my parlor. I'll ink you myself.* But I was fooling myself if I believed we would be seeing a lot of one another after the wedding.

Gently, I pushed these thoughts away again, and stepped up to my little stepbrother. He inhaled sharply as soon as my fingers touched his wrists, but steadied himself immediately. I wrapped the silky tie around one wrist, then the other, and then both together, until there was no way he could free his hands without my help.

I stood behind him, pressing my body against his. Levi opened his bound hands and pressed them against my crotch, feeling just how hard I was. It must have pleased him, because his ears perked up.

"Does it hurt?" I asked, putting one finger around the tie and tugging on it gently.

"No." He rubbed his hands along my hard length.

"If you feel your fingers going numb…"

"…I'll tell you," he assured me, his voice airy.

I placed one hand above his left hip and the fingertips of my other hand ran down the side of his torso. He tensed as my gentle feathering tickled him.

I leaned in and pressed my searing lips on his neck, kissing him until he wiggled. Swiftly, I wrapped my arms around him, pressing one hand against his chest and the other on his tense abs, holding him tightly against myself. He was so close to naked, while I was fully dressed, and the way the tables had turned made the corners of my lips stretch into a smile. I felt every bit of his torso, slowly sliding my hands around, kissing his neck, and breathing over his prickling skin.

When my left hand reached his crotch, I discovered that he was hard enough to stretch the briefs and push one edge off the smooth and tender skin of his groin. My fingers ran over his bared tendon, wrist catching the tip of his cock. He pulsed and let out a soft, "Ah," which hitched in his throat.

I pulled back, my feet carrying me quickly along the bed to where the many pillows formed a pile. I snatched one, wide and thick, and tossed it on the floor not far from Levi.

He spun his head to me, asking me silently, waiting.

I couldn't resist the half-smile that lifted one side of my lips. "Kneel, Levi," I purred. He adored it when I said those words.

Like someone who'd been waiting a lifetime to hear this command, he descended to his knees with smooth flow. He sank into the pillow, tightening his fists like that would give him more balance. Looking at me for approval and praise, he licked his lips. He observed as I threw my T-shirt over my head and dropped it on the floor, then my knee-length shorts.

Biting the inside of my lower lip, thinking whether or not, I lifted the sleeping mask off the nightstand, provided by our gracious hostess for another reason, I was guessing. "Have you ever been blindfolded?" I asked.

"No," he said, voice thin with suppressed excitement.

I walked over to stand in front of him. His pretty head was at the level of my crotch and he couldn't resist looking down to where my cock pitched an imposing tent in my black underwear. He licked his lips hastily, like he was going to drool.

But I was the same. My gaze was sliding along his upright torso. He knelt like a ranger. Or like he was praying. He maintained what little stance he could, with his arms useless and him on his knees.

He nodded at me, saving us the time. *Don't ask me. Just do it*, his nod said.

I stretched the elastic band of the black sleeping mask, pulling it over the back of his head, then adjusted it to sit on the bridge of his nose. When I released it, he was still. I could tell how his body began adapting. When you took away one sense, all the others worked twice as hard. And that was the idea. He was going to listen and taste and smell; he was going to feel me without a need to look.

He shivered when the back of my curved index finger ran down the side of his face. And he followed my lead when I lifted his chin and leaned down to kiss him deeply. I enjoyed him when he was fiery and rash and stubborn, but I adored him when he was obedient and completely mine.

I kissed him greedily, exploring his mouth with my tongue, and taking a military style kneel on one knee to level myself with him. My hands worked him; one caressed the back of his head, the other teased his ribs, stomach, arms, and thighs, wherever it went. I kissed him until he swayed with lust and whimpered into my mouth. Then, I knew he was ready. And though I didn't need to, I still made sure he was rock hard by brushing my open palm over his cock. The area where his briefs were stretching the most had a small wet spot that made me drool.

I wrapped my arms around him, hands meeting on his left hip, and took the side of his briefs, then tore them with all my strength. The fabric ripped quickly, requiring only one more tug to tear the last bit of the seam, freeing Levi's left leg completely and making him inhale sharply in surprise. "Fuck," he murmured with pure admiration as his chest shuddered.

The other side of his underwear didn't bother me. His briefs slid down his right leg to his knee and onto the pillow, his cock pulsing and stiffening, upright and swollen like I'd never seen it. The tip glistened with precum.

Levi shivered and tensed when I ran my thumb unexpectedly over the slit from which his precum trickled. "I want you to taste yourself," I whispered.

"Uh-huh," he managed.

"Open your mouth," I said, still making him shiver as I gently rubbed my thumb in the mess I already got him to make. He obeyed, opening his mouth wide and extending the tip of his tongue out.

I brought my slick thumb to his lips and held his chin with the rest of my hand, dragging out every sensual moment of this game we played. I took him in my hand, feeling him throb with every contact between his tongue and my thumb. And when I pushed my whole thumb into his mouth, he sucked on it hard. His cock was so deliciously stiff that I feared giving him two firm tugs would get him to spray the walls.

"Jesus, you're hard as fuck," I told him.

"Mm-hm," he managed, sucking on my thumb evenly.

"You love this, don't you?" I husked.

"Mm-hm." He opened his mouth and spoke clumsily over my thumb. "I love it."

I let go of his cock and lifted myself to my feet, then pulled my thumb away. "I have better uses for your greedy mouth, little bro," I said.

Air hitched in his throat and pinkness blossomed in his cheeks. He moaned faintly and I let out a sinister laugh.

"You love that, too, huh?" I asked. It had been a throwaway comment. Something that I'd just said, among a sea of filthy things I was saying to him all the time. But it made all of him twice as alert.

"I do," he whispered, like he was admitting to something very embarrassing.

"Don't be embarrassed," I said. "It's just a kink."

He bit his lip hard.

I dropped my underwear, stepped out of them, and held the back of his head. He opened his mouth for me with no need to be told. "Slowly," I told him, holding my cock with my other hand and rubbing the tip against his lower lip.

He inhaled through his nose, lips stretching into a silly grin, and extended his tongue to welcome me.

I pulled back.

"Stop teasing me, Parrish," he protested painfully. "Fuck my throat already or I'll die."

A deep rumble of laughter left my throat. This was why I'd brought him somewhere nobody would hear us. "Ask me again, little brother. And nicely."

He inhaled a shallow breath of air and licked his lips. "Please, Parrish," he said. "Fuck my throat."

He left his mouth wide open as soon as the last sound rolled over his teeth and I took the hint. My cock slid into his mouth, feeling his lips seal around it, and savoring the warm wetness of his tongue. It took four or five gentler sways of my hips before Levi relaxed his throat and accepted my length, and far more of it than the first night when he'd already impressed me.

Whoever trained you did a great job, I wanted to say, but the possessiveness in me wouldn't let me say those words.

I closed my fist around his blond hair and held his head in place, fucking it like a rubber toy, but one that made the sexiest choking noises and sniffed whenever it had a moment to breathe. In a matter of a few minutes, Levi was hyperventilating as soon as I gave him a chance, and his saliva had made his chin shiny under the faded orange glow of lamplights.

"Fuck, you're so big," he blurted. He licked his lips in a futile effort to clean himself up, now that he couldn't wipe his chin with the back of his hand. His shoulders pulled back when he realized it wasn't going to happen. "I'm so wet," he said, half amazed at the state he was in.

"I like you messy," I said, bringing my cock back to his mouth, smearing the wetness around, and making him swallow me until his throat constricted around me and forced me out. "Stay like that," I commanded, then walked around him to the bed and grabbed the lube.

I held it in one hand, while resting the other on the back of his neck. He knelt still, his back turned to me, and waited in silence. I lowered myself down on my knees, dropping the lube by his side, and dragging the back of my fingers down his spine. His creamy skin prickled.

I cupped his ass in my big hands, massaging the cheeks until he moaned with pleasure. My right hand slid under him, feeling his hardened taint, his smooth, tight balls, and his swollen dick. Precum trickled down his length, leaving his roots and balls all slick.

It wasn't easy for me, either. I craved his body and his cries of joy; I was hungry for pleasure I had never felt before Levi; I was dying for the release almost as much as he was. But I was in control of my feelings. And watching Levi fall apart was just so much more fun that way.

He couldn't stop himself from trembling with this shattering need to come. But, later, when I would tell him how well he had done and how strong he had been, he would have the brightest smile, and it would make all this torment worth it.

"Are you ready, bro?" I asked, whispering the last word so that his shoulders stiffened and his cock pulsed.

"Fuck yeah," he gasped.

I poured lube over my index and middle fingers, crawled closer to him, and wrapped my left arm around his chest and shoulders, while sliding my right hand between his cheeks. His tight hole pulsed when my fingers brushed over it. I circled it skillfully, exploring, waiting for him to relax. I rubbed it until he opened to me, muscles loose and waiting. And I pierced into him with one finger, immersing myself into the heat of his body as he embraced me.

A moan dragged slowly over his lips as his hole tightened around my knuckle.

"Relax, sweet baby boy," I whispered into his ear.

And he did, embracing my middle finger in two throbbing heartbeats. Slowly, I pulled my hand down, then back up, fingering him from below, and squeezing whimpers out of him.

Levi panted once I quickened my pace. My hand worked him from underneath, impaling him swiftly and ruthlessly, probing and stretching. Every once in a while, his focus would drift, and he clenched, making himself cry out, mostly because it made his cock pulse and, right now, he was so hard that even the slightest twitch ached.

My cock was pressing just above his ass, skin on skin and pulsing, spitting precum nearly as much as Levi was. I fingered my stepbro hard and fast and for a long time until he began hyperventilating and the burning sensation climbed up my arm. Even then, I persisted, and added another finger, readying him for my cock.

"Fuck me, Parrish," he panted. "Please. Please."

I tightened my left arm around him, feeling the tension in his defined pecs, and feeling the pounding of his heart. He was all slick with sweet sweat, hair tousled. His bound hands jerked and he took my cock, stroking it with revenge. His grip was tight, as ruthless as my hand that worked him, and filled with purpose.

I bit his ear hard and growled, then pulled my fingers out. "You won't last a minute," I grunted, slapping his hands off my cock, taking it myself, and stroking it twice with my slick hand, then ramming it into Levi.

He yelped once, then moaned so loudly that it made the entire trip worth it in an instant. This was exactly what I wanted to hear.

"Fuck. Yes!" he cried out. "Harder, please. Just...fuck me harder, Parrish."

I grabbed his hips, his torso leaning forward. My right hand quickly clasped his shoulder to give him balance and keep him from falling over. It was sort of like a sexy trust fall, and it was the first time I had a blinding realization that Levi trusted me. He trusted that I would catch his shoulders if he fell forward, helpless without his arms.

I kept my left hand on his hip, tugging him back onto myself, and burying my cock balls-deep into him.

Levi spilled a litany of profanities, begging to be ruined, savaged, and destroyed. And the tables turned suddenly, with Levi spilling out the commands, and me more than happy to obey. The fine order of things and the balance of power had gone out the window, and we existed in a mess of pleasure where each dominated the other for one exact goal.

And Levi tensed all over. Every fiber of his being was alight, glowing, pulsing, trembling. His entire body was flickering as he held his breath, then let all that air out in a long-drawn moan that made me want to steal him away and keep him for myself in some remote, mountain cabin, where he could moan all day long and never worry he'd be overheard.

The rapid tightening of his hole around my dick made a million different sensations explode all over my chest, and I gave in to it. I surrendered to it. I filled Levi with my hot cum just as he sprayed the floor and let his voice go on and on, fluctuating and jumping with each thrust of my hips. And even when I was empty, when the last drop of me was his, I rammed him still. The smashing, slapping sounds had the wet quality now, and Levi let his body relax and endure, but his fists were clenched hard. "Yes! Ah! Yes!" he repeated on and on and on until I felt like the last drop of energy my body had was burned.

I pushed myself in and made myself comfortable. I wrapped both my arms around his chest and held him hard as we caught our breaths. Hearts pounding, sweat dripping, and cocks turning flaccid at last. I pulled out of him some time later, soft and exhausted, then tugged on my tie and released him.

I was careful around him, supporting him with one hand while taking the blindfold off with the other. He squinted and blinked, but wore a deadly handsome smile and a glaze over his eyes that told me he was well and truly pleased.

He rubbed his wrists gently and uttered another, "Fuck." Then, with his hands in mine, he got up, and followed me into the bathroom. The spacious shower steamed the entire bathroom within moments, and I soaped us both up, kissing him more often than not. I washed him from head to toe, slowly, thoroughly, massaging the tension out of his shoulders and whispering sweet and filthy things into his ear.

And, when the soap was long gone down the drain, and we stood under the pouring water from the big shower-head mounted to the ceiling, Levi nestled in my arms. He pressed his face against my chest and I hugged him. We stood in silence, only the splashing of water around us, and savored the moment.

"Can we just...stay here? Forever?" he asked, though there was a smile in his voice, and that wasn't really a question. He was smiling at the impossible idea.

My heart tripped, then inflated, and I held him tighter.

If only we could.

Chapter Thirteen

PARRISH

Levi slept.

It was a rarity, but not impossible, that I woke up and discovered that he was deep asleep. Even the dark circles around his eyes were paler than they had been seven or eight days ago.

And, while he slept, I prepared a batch of French-pressed coffee and hopped down the street to a bakery to get us breakfast. Unsure of what to choose among the hot, fresh products, I asked for some of pretty much everything. Sweet and salty and savory, plain and filled. Puff dough bundles stuffed with Brie and prosciutto together with Napoleon cakes. And I hauled it all back to the house like I was making Levi's wish to stay here forever come true.

When I returned, Levi was already on the balcony, wearing a pair of tight shorts that emphasized the curve of his butt. He sat cross-legged on one chair, sketching again.

I couldn't help but chuckle. "I'm seeing a pattern," I said.

He lifted his curious gaze at me and blinked.

"You're inspired after every good dicking," I said.

His eyes sparked, but he suppressed his smile and replied knowingly. "You're wrong."

"How so?" I asked, raising an eyebrow in challenge.

The smirk beat him and shone through. "It's only after the best dicking."

I laughed out loud. "I see you sniffed out the coffee."

"And had too much of it already," Levi said, lifting a hand to show that it was shaking. It wasn't. He pouted and shrugged and picked up his pencil again. "If I didn't know how much you'd gloat, I'd tell you that your crosshatching advice was spot-on," he said, busy crosshatching the way I would. Then, he lifted his deadpan face to me. "But I know better, so I'm not saying it."

Even though there was only a ghost of a smile on his lips, his dimples came to life.

I felt air slowly drain out of me.

Hollowness replaced my stomach.

Levi was none the wiser, returning to the sketchbook, as I stood there, gazing at him with stinging eyes and a welling sense that something was terribly wrong. Not wrong. It didn't exactly feel wrong. But I was starting to be afraid.

It was hard to make sense of it. When pushed, I couldn't find a single thing wrong. I refused to believe that being attracted to Levi was wrong just because his father married my mother. No one had ever asked us how we felt about that. Why should we pay for it?

And yet, I felt like there was an oncoming storm. Like there were guns and knives lurking just outside of my field of vision. Like there were dangers so immediate that I needed to throw myself in front of him and take the bullets, and take the stabs, and take the punches to my gut, right now, if I wanted to save him.

That was what felt wrong.

It was a pleasant, warm morning. There were hardly any sounds anywhere. The lake water was splashing on the shore. Birds were chirping. There was nobody out there, waiting to attack.

But, in that one dimpled smile, Levi had me falling to my knees. He had me silently vowing to stand in front of him and face any danger with my head held high.

"Are we eating or will you just hold it like the tease you are?" Levi asked, smirking at me and pointing at the bag with the back of the pencil.

It was like someone had plucked me from a cloud and dropped me onto the balcony. "Yeah," I said, trying to get myself familiar with the place I was in. I bumped into the chair, then into the table, too, until I finally decided it would be smart to just sit the fuck down and shut the hell up. At least until I understood what had just happened in the depths of my soul.

I didn't have much time to figure it out. The cream from the Napoleon cake left smudges around Levi's lips and he kept shooting embarrassed glances my way as I stared in awe. *How the fuck are you so adorable?* I wanted to ask. Nay! I wanted to shout and threaten and get a clean answer from him. *How did you bewitch me?*

Levi ogled me one more time after wiping his lips. "Is there more?" he asked, licking the corners of and then smacking his lips. "I think that's all. Right?" he lifted his hand to wipe his mouth just in case, but I leaped forward before he could.

My lips pressed hard against his. The sensations mixed, mingled, and exploded like a million firecrackers in my chest. The sweet cream taste of the cake and the subtle note of coffee, mingling with the freshness of his body wash and cologne, mixed together with the sudden realization that I was ready to die for him, made my eyes wet and made me want to suck the soul out of him with this kiss.

Once I pulled back, Levi licked his lips. "That was...wow." Wide-eyed, he gazed at me, then grinned. "You can do *that* again."

I nodded and tried to put a smile on my face.

It took me a while longer to recover from the disruption that such strong emotions, none of which I could fully recognize or understand, caused.

Gradually, I eased myself into the leisure and luxury we carved out for ourselves for this one day. Until tonight, I was determined to treat him like royalty. I knew he could serve for pleasure, but I wanted him to get the pampering he deserved.

The entire day, walking, talking, swimming in the lake, feeding him strawberries on the beach while baking in the sun. I could give him both heaven and hell. I could make him kneel, but I could also make him fly.

We lay on our towels, eyes closed, skin tight from all the sunshine, breaths lazily shallow as we enjoyed the moment. "Has anyone ever told you how good you are?"

"What do you mean?" Levi asked. "Margaret won't stop telling me."

I chortled. "Christ, no. I meant in bed, Levi."

"Oh," he said, then laughed out loud. "Let's never mention this again."

"Agreed," I said. "But has anyone ever told you that?"

"*Not* Margaret," Levi insisted, riding another wave of laughter. "Actually, no. I mean, yeah, but I'm not sure I believe him."

The muscles in my neck tensed when I fell into my own accidental trap. There had been someone else who'd had him. Not that I cared that Levi had had sex. It wasn't like that at all. I just didn't trust this faceless, nameless man who'd been with Levi. I didn't trust he had understood Levi's true needs. "How did you get this good?" I asked. "You don't have to answer," I added quickly, realizing how bad that had sounded.

"No, no," Levi said. "I don't mind telling you. I just figured...you get jealous, you know that?"

I smirked. "That's true. But I won't." Still, my guts twisted at the thought of someone failing to give Levi the high I could, but trying anyway. Even more so, I detested the idea of someone else doing it in the future, when I was no longer around. It had to happen, eventually. It wasn't like I really could run away somewhere remote with him.

Levi let out a satisfied sound, like he was musing about something so pleasant that he couldn't hold it in. "Darren," he said.

"Uh-huh," I said, hackles raising. This was a terrible idea. I didn't want to know his name. I wanted to stand in front of Levi and push Darren away, bark at him until he gave up. "Must've been pretty good," I muttered.

"Oh yeah," Levi said with unfiltered joy. "I wouldn't say the best, but a close second, for sure." And even though I knew he meant me as the best, I was deaf to it, focusing on the fact that there even was a second, let alone a close one. "The things we did. And a lot of it. Like, sometimes twice in a row. You know? Like us when everyone's asleep in the house."

I sat up, my stomach turning upside down. "I'm sorry. I can't. Nope, nope, nope. I don't want to know."

Levi blinked innocently at me, like it was a surprise.

I took a calming breath of air while he sat up to level with me. I looked into his eyes and instinctively covered his hand with mine on the ground between us. "I'm sorry I asked. And I'm sorry I'm like this. We're both young guys. I'm glad you had good times in the past. I did, too. But I just don't want to hear about it."

"Oh. Okay," he said.

It wasn't enough. I wasn't explaining myself correctly. "Look, it's just that I get very possessive when I..." *When I what? Care?* That would only get more confusing. "Ah, can we just leave it?"

Levi nodded, still so innocent that it was starting to get fishy. And when a spark of naughtiness flared in his eyes, I frowned. The smile — not even a full, proper smile, but a tiny flicker of his facial muscles — tipped me over. "What?" I asked.

"Nothing," he said, shaking his head determinedly. Then, "It's just that you're funny. You're so competitive." He chuckled. "If you knew Darren, you'd probably changed your mind."

I waved my hands and shook my head, panic spiking in my chest. "No, no. Thank you. I'd rather not. I'm sure he's a great guy."

Levi snorted.

"Okay, yeah, I hate him, but not because it's him. It's because I'm fucked up like that and I kinda want to kick him in the balls if you so much as say he gave you a mean look once," I said.

Levi started laughing. Quietly, first, then louder. "Poor Darren," he moaned between the laughs.

I stared at him, finding nothing funny about this. Was he telling me that Darren had, in fact, given him a mean look? Was Darren poor because he was going to get punched in the nuts? "What's funny?" I asked, my face contorting in mild annoyance that poured to this shapeless, faceless idea of Darren.

"It's just..." He tried saying, laughing harder. "Oh my god."

"Levi?" I growled.

Finally, after another two fits of giggles, Levi wiped the tears of laughter from his eyes, which now shimmered with the greenest green I'd ever looked at, and shook his head pitifully at me. "Darren's my dildo."

I opened my mouth to say something, but choked on the first syllable.

"Darren the Dildo," Levi said. "And he never, ever laid a finger on me, Parrish." He said this with such a serious face that I had to commend his acting skill. If I could commend anything. Or think. Or blink. "As for being mean...well, I sometimes imagined him telling me I moan like a slut." He shrugged, then lay back and wrapped his hands under his head. He chuckled once again, but it didn't last long.

"You asshole," I grunted, jumping off my towel and onto his, sitting down on his crotch with all my weight, and digging my fingers into his ribcage. "I was already on my way to find the guy!"

Levi squealed and cried and protested, but I overpowered him, tickling him senseless. I grabbed his wrists and lifted his arms above his head, pinning them against the ground, and staring into his eyes.

His laughter subsided and he gave me that glassy look of desire, and breathed through his parted lips. "You'll find him in the drawer under all my underwear back home," he said.

I leaned in and kissed him, silencing whatever teasing I saw rising to the surface. I kissed him hard and fast, then climbed off him before someone's sheepish Aunt Mable clutched her pearls and fell over. I lay on my side, watching him, as he took a deep breath of air and let out a satisfied little moan. "And, as for guys, there's no one to be jealous of," he said, turning a serious look to me.

"I hooked up with college bros now and then and I can't tell them apart when I think about them. Not that I sit idly and daydream about any of them. They were just distractions from how crappy everything else was."

"College, you mean," I said softly.

He snorted. "I fucking hated it. Around my second semester, I realized I wasn't meant for that. Sure, I could learn the shit, and recite the knowledge for oral exams, and get high grades most of the time. But I hated every moment. But just when I realized I couldn't go on, Dad and Margaret started flaunting me around. Soon everyone thought I was a prodigy of a thing they barely understood. And..." He shrugged. "It sucked." He finished.

"They do that a lot," I said. "And I'll cut my dick off if that's not half the reason Natalie's marrying that asshole, Jarred," I muttered grimly. "They push and push and push until they have their way or break you in the process." The same protectiveness I'd felt this morning filled me to bursting now. "Be careful with them," I said. "I mean it. They'll start pulling strings and calling favors from people they consider influential. If you let your guard down, you'll wake up one day, working as a clerk in the town hall, thinking about where the fuck your life had gone. And they'll stand there, boasting how you're thick as thieves with the mayor."

Levi snorted. "Christ, that sounds accurate."

"I'm telling you," I insisted, a rising tide of panic sweeping me off shore. "You can't let them control you. Promise me."

Levi blinked, finally sensing how deadly serious I was. "I promise."

"Good. They're selfish people, Levi. That's not easy to see in parents. But the sooner you accept that, the sooner you can live your life the way you want to."

"Like you," he concluded.

"Nothing wrong with me," I said defensively.

"I didn't mean to say...of course not." He fell silent.

I shook my head. "I'm sorry. Of course you didn't mean that. Frankly, I'm used to being an all-purpose bad example around there. They can't wrap their heads around the fact that I wake up happy. And even happier for not having them guide me by the hand."

"Are you happy?" Levi asked.

A smile spread across my face. "Yeah," I said. And I was. In general, but also in this very moment. "I love what I do. I'm good at it. What more can I ask for?"

Levi shrugged. "Dunno. I was good at analyzing data, but I was lonely."

The thought made my throat constrict.

"But nobody ever got me interested in dating. Or even being a really good friend, if I'm honest," he said.

I had good friends. I had close friends and distant ones I still liked very much. I had clients who'd become my friends over time, and from every area of life. A tech startup entrepreneur and a rent boy that worked on my block; an elderly BBQ joint owner and chef, as well as a young stripper. But I had no one special. Ever. And I told him so.

Instinctively, my hand went to his, and I held it.

For a long while, we lay there in silence, holding hands, until Levi finally whispered. "Maybe this is why."

DESTRUCTIVE RELATIONS

I swallowed. "What do you mean?" I asked, though I knew.

"We're fuck ups," he said, laughing dryly. "Just look at us. We're one step detached from incest and I don't fucking care. I'm loving every moment of this. I feel more alive than ever when you tell me you're going to choke me with your dick or command me to kneel. Christ, Parrish. This is why we can't have relationships."

"Can't do anything about that," I said, holding his hand evenly. I didn't care that he was my stepbrother. If anything, that was what made him so much more irresistible those first few days. Then I got to know the hidden side of him and I enjoyed him so much fucking more. I enjoyed being silent with him and watching him as he sketched. I enjoyed every thrust of my hips and every whimper off his lips. I enjoyed the way he snored like a puppy, once or twice, for no longer than a couple of seconds at a time, when he finally slept. And most of all, I enjoyed the change in his glow; his skin was smoother and his eyes brighter, every day a little more.

As the sun dipped under the horizon, and I took Levi's hand and walked the streets of Willow Bay, kissing him by every lamppost I could, we knew our time in heaven was ending. In this slice of private heaven, at least.

I'd only just kissed him deeply and directed him to walk with me to the house to get the car, when I spotted them. Levi saw them, too, as plainly as I. He froze, eyes widening in fear, as two familiar faces turned the other way in haste.

"They saw us," he swiftly whispered.

Senator and Mrs. Wilkinson crossed the street some ways ahead of us, not looking back. They were talking to one another, but a rising sense of dread filled me fast. "They didn't," I growled, like it would be true if I insisted hard enough.

"They saw us. I'm sure they saw us," Levi hissed with panic.

"Calm down," I said. "They didn't even stop. They saw nothing."

Levi turned his frightened gaze at me. He looked so helpless that I wanted to run and trample the Wilkinsons for daring to scare him like this. I wanted to wrap my arms around him, but couldn't risk it in case they returned and actually saw us. "I promise," I said. "If they'd seen us, they would have at least said hello. He's sleazy. He would have hinted he saw something, I'm absolutely sure of that."

"Are you?" he asked.

"I am," I said firmly. "Don't be afraid."

He nodded hard. The frightened expression melted away as I felt the storm calm down inside of me. No way they'd seen anything. But by the time they'd come up from around the corner and checked the traffic, we were already well apart. And they hadn't even paused. They had been looking for cars that could run over them.

I nudged Levi to walk to the house and the car.

We didn't talk of it anymore.

We didn't talk about anything as I drove slower than ever, dragging out these few miles of aloneness as much as I could.

I detested the thought of going back into that house, sneaking around with him, pretending I wasn't bothered by all the snide comments and whispers behind my back.

But that was what I did. And I did it with a happy smile on my face. I endured the goodnight chats once we returned to total peace and stillness at the back porch. Nobody had called Marge or Harry to tell them they'd spotted us. Lauren was drinking away in one corner, scrolling on her phone, near tears most of the time. And I endured the fact we needed to lock the door. And I endured it when I had to bite my lip that night as I buried my cock inside Levi, my hand covering his mouth, as we struggled to keep the stillness going.

We moaned silently, letting our eyes express the depth and intensity of our passion.

That night, and again the next day. Our time together was running out no matter if we had been spotted or not. I would rather it all stayed secret for Levi's sake, but we were going to part ways soon no matter what.

And I made it my mission to take every spare moment and make it into something dangerous and magical.

Chapter Fourteen

LEVI

His hand clasped my face as my bare chest bumped against the door of our room. He gripped my hip with his other hand, sliding into me with brutal intensity and merciless purpose. Be it the fright that we were nearly caught together or the sheer desire for Parrish that welled in me, I embraced him, moaning silently into the seal that his hand made over my mouth.

Parrish jerked his hips forward, impaling me hard with his length. As we stood, my back turned to him and curved a little, the angle made it so fucking easy for his cock to rub against my prostate and make me want to cry out with pleasure.

He wasn't letting that happen.

The house was full of people.

Oblivious people.

A moan escaped through my nose and Parrish buried his face in my neck, shushing me and opening his mouth to breathe quietly. The heat of his breath washed over my bare skin as he pounded me against the door. I clawed at it, distracting myself from the desperate need to tell him, as loudly as I could, to fuck me harder. My hips, thrust back at him, would have to do the talking for me.

Parrish could hold me from my climax for ages. He could stretch me so thin I was transparent and tearing apart. He could drag it out so long that I was willing to cry and beg for the sweet release.

But he could also grip me tightly and ram into me with purpose. He could set his mind to it and fuck me until I sprayed the door and the floor with my hot wetness and collapsed to my knees once he filled me full of his. And that was what he chose now. Fucking me harder and faster until my cock throbbed and twitched with every move of Parrish's body. He held his hand on my mouth so strong that it pushed in between my teeth. And I bit him. Not to make him feel pain from my teeth. Far from it. I bit him to keep myself quiet. And it made him grunt and growl and fill me with his cum right when he pushed me over the edge and allowed me the pleasure of my orgasm.

But the joy of savoring it for another few minutes quickly turned to ash in my mouth. "Where are they?" a voice boomed. "I won't hear it. I won't. Bring them here.

Bring them both. You're mistaken. They'll tell you that you're mistaken."

Hurried footsteps rose along the stairs and neared my room. The knock on the door kicked air out of my lungs.

I either pushed Parrish away or he stepped back on his own. I didn't know in the mess that was happening in my head. I was still short of breath from the best orgasm I'd had all week. I bent down and yanked my underwear and shorts up from around my ankles where Parrish had left them.

He wasn't rushing with his clothes, though he was putting them on. Lazily, he turned his T-shirt the proper way after he'd pulled it inside out earlier in haste, and looked at me while Margaret knocked on the doors. "Levi?" she called.

"Coming," I said, panic dripping from my voice.

"Hurry, darling, the senator is here," she said, worry palpable in hers.

"He's coming," Parrish snapped. "We both are."

That made Margaret fall silent and leave.

I directed my frightened gaze at Parrish, muffled voices from downstairs having no clue at all. "What do we do?" I whispered. "They saw us. I knew they did."

"You don't know that," Parrish said, surprisingly calm.

"I fucking know," I hissed. "Don't be stupid. What else could this be about?"

Parrish made two quick steps toward me. All the allure of him was still intact when he towered over me, even if he was doing it threateningly and in anger. "You keep your mouth shut. You keep it shut with whatever they say. Deny it. Deny it with everything you've got. Tell him he must have forgotten to take his pills. Tell him he's crazy if you must talk. But try not to." His voice was so commanding that I could only nod. But he must have seen the fear in my eyes; the debilitating terror that made it impossible for me to move my feet. He took my shoulders in his hands. I half thought he was about to kiss me, but Parrish literally shook me. "You're fine," he insisted. "You're going to straighten your back, march down there with your head high, and give them the taste of their own medicine. Act like them calling you downstairs is the greatest insult ever. And if they even utter an accusation...well, let me handle that."

And fuck if that wasn't more reassuring than a kiss.

I did precisely what Parrish told me. He walked a step behind me as we climbed down the stairs. My breaths were shaky and my heart was pounding so loudly I was certain everyone could hear it when I stepped into the living room.

"What is it?" Parrish growled. He was so much better at this. He truly did act like them intruding on his peace was a cardinal sin.

Dad's face was purple and Margaret seemed near tears. The Senator stuttered and Mrs. Wilkinson was rubbing her hands raw by dry-washing them in a corner. Jarred stared out the window, a smug grin on his face, while Natalie rolled her eyes. She caught my attention the most, because she looked like she couldn't believe there was drama. We only lacked Lauren, who was, judging by the dusk glow outside, probably clinging to some table and crying over another heartbreak. Any day now, a man would sweep her off her feet and she would swear he was the one. The cycle never ended.

"Huh?" Parrish repeated, challenging the first one to speak. "I was showing Levi how to crosshatch shade his works and you just had to call us now."

Jesus, I thought. It was impossible to replace the thing we'd been doing with the thing he insisted. I wasn't sure if anyone in the room believed it.

"Apparently," said Jarred with a dead smile on his face. "You two are fuh..."

"Jarred," snapped Mr. Wilkinson.

Jarred's mouth stayed open as his eyes darted to his father. He cleared his throat. "When was I supposed to find out about this?" he asked, wagging his finger between the two of us.

"Find out about what?" Parrish asked, ready to bark and bite. Whichever was necessary.

"The two of you, er, mingling," Jarred said, glancing at his father. At once, it gave him pleasure to torment Parrish and took the pleasure away that he couldn't be more graphic.

"You better mind your tongue," Parrish said, crossing his arms at his chest. "If you don't, you might lose it."

"Parrish," Margaret said harshly.

He directed his eyes to her. "Yes, Margaret?"

"Don't be so rude," she scolded with bitterness in her voice. "Is it true?"

"Is what true?" Parrish asked. "Can someone tell me exactly what I did this time?"

"You were seen," Dad said in his high-pitched, raspy voice. "Senator and Mrs. Wilkinson, here, saw you in

Willow Bay. They saw you with your arm around my son. They saw you lean in and- and- and..."

Parrish laughed bitterly. "And what?"

"Kiss him," Senator Wilkinson snapped.

"What?" Parrish asked, incredulous, but also entertained. "Did you forget your glasses?"

"Parrish," Margaret hissed. It was all she knew how to say.

Senator Wilkinson's lips quivered with anger. It was Mrs. Wilkinson, with an oddly kind smile, who stepped in. "You see, such an arrangement might...complicate things," she said. "If we are to join our families, it could reflect poorly on my husband and it could be used against him in his political life."

Parrish chuckled so darkly that even I felt the chills. "It's cute that anyone here thinks I give a rat's ass about his political life." He turned to Mr. Wilkinson. "You're mistaken, sir."

"Weren't you in Willow Bay until late last night?" Dad asked.

"Sure we were," Parrish said. "And ten thousand other people were, too. He confused us with someone else."

"Don't lie to us, boy," Dad all but shouted at Parrish.

The more you cornered my stepbrother, the more dangerous he became. He was like an explosive device. Once he was on the course to set off, you better run. And these people were doing their best to set him off.

I wondered what it was I truly felt in this moment. Where had the fear gone? The moment he had stepped up and pushed his shoulder a little in front of me, like he wanted to hide me discreetly from them all, my fears had melted away.

But there was something more. A need. An urge. As well as a sense of hopelessness. I had hoped we might have a few days more left to us.

"Don't throw ridiculous accusations at us," Parrish replied, using my father's exact tone and color of voice.

Natalie, who sat in the armchair next to Jarred, snorted and shook her head. I couldn't read her mind. I couldn't even read her face. It was her I wanted to understand the most. Everyone else was plain as day, but Natalie kept her cards close to her chest.

Was she disappointed in us? Just a heartbeat ago, we had been sitting on the beach by the lake, taking in the sun, talking with our hearts almost open. And here I was, stabbing her in the back.

"You, boy," Senator snapped, gesturing to me.

"Levi," Margaret supplied meekly.

"Levi. Right. Come 'ere." He spoke to me like he would to a puppy. Maybe that was all I was. A frightened puppy. But they were dragging me away from my human master and I wanted to tear them apart.

But I also wanted to hide and cry. I wanted to come clean and run away. What use was there in lying? They knew. They fucking knew everything.

"Levi," Parrish whispered as I stepped forward.

Senator looked me in the eyes and let it linger for a while longer. "Son, I know what I saw. And I'm not one to pass judgment. I am shocked, you see. I'm shocked, that is all. This isn't a, uh, a usual way of how things are, and it can be a powerful weapon in my opponents' arsenals. We need to know."

I winced.

"Your opponents can dig up plenty of dirt already," Parrish said. "Or is someone's winning streak in day-trading simply the product of his genius?" He pointed his sharp gaze at Jarred, vaguely accusing him of insider trading and dangling a whisper of a threat in the back. "Because it would surprise me that you're a genius on Wall Street when you can barely tie your shoelace."

"Stop that," Natalie said dryly.

Senator was deaf to it all, staring at me. I knew I was red. I knew it was from the things we'd done not ten minutes ago and the knowledge that I was still wet with his cum inside of me; I was red with the weight of our sins, too, and the fact that so many people were hurt just because we couldn't keep our hands off one another.

Were we worth more than all of them together? Jarred was an asshole, but Natalie meant to marry him. Were we more important than them? Than our parents? Than the Wilkinsons?

I looked at Parrish.

He was so beautiful.

He was the most beautiful man I had ever seen, let alone been this close to. Nobody could argue with that. And I cared for what we'd created for those few glimmering moments. I truly did. Never again would I get the pleasure and joy and thrill of chase such as that.

And even if I would give my life for him, I couldn't put our lives above everyone else's. I simply couldn't.

"It's true," I said.

"Levi, shut up," Parrish snapped.

Margaret cried out like someone had stabbed her with a pitchfork.

Dad made a step forward like he was ready to tackle Parrish.

Natalie's face was unchanged.

"I knew it," Jarred said, though nobody asked.

It was the Wilkinsons who seemed to relax a little. He gave a grave nod and Mrs. Wilkinson tightened her lips with disappointment.

"Dammit, Levi, I told you to..." Parrish started.

"But it's true," I said, staring at Parrish and watching something die in his eyes. It hurt the most to know it was the little affection he might have had for me; and just as much, it hurt to know I was the one wielding the knife that killed it. "And they already know it." I shrugged with defeat.

Parrish let out a long sigh, still watching me. If he was trying to communicate something, it didn't translate. The bond was gone. It had snapped in half and I didn't believe it was possible to repair it.

Parrish bared his teeth at me as he gave the tiniest of nods of understanding. Understanding what? I had no idea. But before I could think about it, he inhaled. "I knew you'd turn on me, you little shit. I'm glad I faked everything for a nice, juicy squeeze."

A murmur of shock and disapproval passed through the room, but I was too stunned to speak.

Parrish laughed bitterly. "What? You thought that was real? Jesus, Levi, you're dumber than I thought. And easier to fool. You must have been so pathetic if it was this easy to get you to trust me." That deadly laugh, again. He shook his head at me as my eyes stung and widened. "Yeah, I see you believed me. Didn't they warn you against that?" He turned to Dad. "Harry, didn't you warn him I couldn't be trusted? Just last week, I could have sworn you told him."

Dad's lips quivered with hatred and rage. "Is this all just to get back at me?" he asked. "Is it, Parrish? Because, remember this, I would throw you out of this house all over again."

"To get back at you?" Parrish asked. "Christ, you're all so thick. I was *bored*. I was *bored out of my mind*. You're all so fucking quiet and boring and just saying 'senator this' and 'senator that.' I needed to pass the time." He made a step forward, patting Dad's shoulder. "Nothing personal, buddy. You do my mom, I do your son."

Dad grabbed Parrish's T-shirt and shoved him back as Margaret leaped to stop this from getting physical.

What the fuck was he doing? He couldn't be serious. Could he?

No.

But...doubt filled me to the brim.

"And you," Parrish said to Margaret, dusting himself off and stepping away from everyone, not even glancing in my direction. "You were always on their side. Now you know what it feels like to be betrayed." He scoffed in his throat and looked at the Wilkinsons. "Your political career is already in the gutter, old man. You never left the state."

Senator Wilkinson's eyes flared with pure hatred. Only truth could spark that. "Careful, boy," he snapped. "We have connections."

Parrish snorted at those connections. "Well, I had my fair share of fun," Parrish said, like he was announcing he was ready to leave, and crossed his arms at his chest. I wanted to beg him to forgive me, though I didn't know what I'd done wrong. I didn't know what I'd done to earn all this.

At the same time, I wanted to scratch him to pieces for leading me on. If that was what he'd been doing. It was so hard to parse truth from lies. My big stepbrother was so good at lying, after all.

"Is it just him, or do you treat all your family like that?" Jarred asked, thinking he was funny or something. "Because I'd rather pass." He only managed to glance at Natalie, insinuating that she'd been Parrish's prey, too, before I got a look at Parrish tightening his fist.

But I didn't see him leap at the fucker and hand out the punches. The slap drew my attention, first. And it was Natalie, furious, who'd slapped her fiance. "Shut your filthy mouth," she whispered with anger she could barely restrain. She, too, had heard the suggestion in his words.

Jarred held a hand to his face as redness spilled around. "You've no idea what you just did," he stammered, almost ready to cry. "This is bullshit." And he stormed the fuck out of the house. On his way, he bumped into Parrish, who quickly lifted his arms in surrender, as if to show everyone he didn't start that brawl.

Natalie ran after Jarred, though. She disappeared from the house, calling for him, and I still didn't have the slightest idea about what she thought or felt about Parrish and I.

Parrish gave everyone but me a satisfied grin. And to cease existing in the line of his vision was the most painful experience I'd ever encountered. To be yelled at or slapped or belittled was nothing compared to becoming the ghost I'd been to him all these years ago. I was nothing. "If that's everything, I think I'll be on my way."

He turned on his heels while Margaret ran to me and hugged me. "Shh, darling. You'll be fine. You'll be alright. I don't know what I did wrong to make him so cruel. I don't know. You'll be fine, baby," she whispered and whispered.

Dad, for what it was worth, tried to calm down the Wilkinsons, who stared after Jarred and Natalie in shock. "Kids. Always so passionate," he said, deaf to the irony. "They'll work it out, I'm sure."

Whether I stood there for a full hour or I returned to the approximate spot, I had no clue. I was only aware that Parrish stormed out of the house and slammed the front door on his way out. His car's engine roared to life a few moments later and the tires screeched.

Where was everyone? Was I alone?

I found myself in my room, by the window, looking at the pool. He wasn't there. He was gone. He'd been gone close to an hour.

I blinked and I was in bed, staring at the ceiling.

And again, I blinked, and it was night outside.

And again, I blinked, and everyone in the house was asleep.

I didn't know where Natalie was. I didn't know if Lauren had returned and what to do with the information if I had it. Least of all I knew what was in my heart. Where was my heart, even? It was hardly beating.

His venomous words rang in my ears and I tried and failed to accept that the outcome was no worse than what I had coming to me. You play with fire, you burn the entire house down. Only a fool would be surprised.

Chapter Fifteen

PARRISH

When Margaret began seeing this man that made her smile more often than Natalie and I had been managing, I had two things to do to keep myself occupied. The thing was, I hadn't been able to understand why she would ever need someone else. She'd had us for well over a decade to keep her company. We'd been a happy family, if only fractured. We hadn't needed a man in the house to boss us around or intrude.

But when it had looked more and more likely to happen, I normally gathered a gang of boys and did something I wasn't supposed to do. We'd break into an abandoned house in search of ghosts only to step on rusty nails or pull pranks on the hardworking — and, let's face it, innocent — people of River Bend until our mothers were pale and fathers, of those who had fathers, were having fits.

Other times, though infinitely less often, I cowered in Mrs. Crane's bookshop. I hadn't been an avid reader, but I had known about the joy of losing yourself in a different world.

Today, the scent of her second hand books knocked me back into my childhood and teen years in an instant. Mrs. Crane, for what it was worth, was still diligently stacking her shelves with all the old favorites that every kid in this town had owned a copy of. *Narnia* had been on full display for a quarter of the century, as far as I could tell, as was Robert Jordan's life's work.

"Little Parrish?" Mrs. Crane said when the bell above the door announced my entrance.

"Mrs. Crane," I said, taken aback that she remembered me at all, let alone recognized me. I didn't exactly look like that teenager who'd been hiding in here. "How are you, ma'am?"

"All the better for seeing you, my dear," Mrs. Crane said, pulling her reading glasses lower down her nose. "How have you been, my boy? I haven't seen you in ages."

I'd stopped coming here even before I'd moved away. Mischief had had a bigger allure than reading, and occasionally, helping Mrs. Crane stack the higher shelves. *Great. More guilt*, I thought. But the woman didn't seem to grudge me. What a goddamn rarity in this town. "Oh, I've moved to New York. Don't get much time for family visits," I said.

"My, my," Mrs. Crane said, squinting at my arms. "Is that a snake eating its tail?"

I glanced at one of my tattoos absentmindedly. "Oh. Yeah."

She extended her arms as if to take mine and examine it, so I stepped up and let her. "I wonder what Robert Jordan would make of it."

I couldn't help but snort. "A devout Christian such as him? I doubt he'd approve."

Mrs. Crane gave me a surprisingly mischievous smile. "You've always had a wire for irony, my dear."

I laughed, but it didn't last too long. Sadness that I had managed to bury for a moment or two roared back to life and devoured everything that was beautiful in this world. Every nice thought in my head burned away and left room for the despair that filled me instead.

"You're not here to rekindle a lost passion for books, my boy," Mrs. Crane said. It didn't carry even the slightest note of question. "Come. There's no one up there."

My heart tripped as her hands slid down my bare arm to my hand. She held it in both of hers and tugged me to pass around the counter. There was a loft above the back of the shop where Mrs. Crane had some old, worn out furniture for sitting, enjoying tea, and reading. There had been a brief period in my life when that was my second home. I would help her stack those shelves and carry boxes here and there in return for her cookies and privacy. She'd hide me up there when I had been at my most vulnerable and when facing the world had been the biggest threat a boy could imagine.

My eyes stung but I resisted the urge to fall over her and cry. I hadn't cried since I was a little boy. And I wasn't going to change that now.

I hadn't gotten a chance to bring him here, I thought as I got up to my hideout.

And when Mrs. Crane left me alone up in the loft, while promising a hot cup of tea and this morning's batch of cookies, I collapsed into a worn-out armchair and bit the back of my index finger, closed my fist tight and swallowed the screech of pain that ripped through me and begged to be sounded.

My hostess was true to her word. By the time she returned with tea and biscuits and an old copy of Robin Hobb's *Assassin's Apprentice* to keep me busy, I had managed to blink away the tears that I wouldn't let spill.

I couldn't tell how much time passed. I was holding the book she'd left me and looking at the cover, but not really seeing it. The battle was happening in my head. I'd burned the bridges just a little while ago. I'd broken his heart, hoping that earned him a roof over his head, but I had no idea what to do next.

To leave River Bend, now, in the middle of this, was somehow blasphemous. The irony wasn't lost on me that I, the guy who'd seduced his stepbrother, worried about blasphemy, but that was what it felt like. To leave him all alone was a thought that broke my heart and filled me with rage. But I was no good to him otherwise. I could only make matters worse if I went near the house.

Then, there was the only other person that mattered.

And when the bell above Mrs. Crane's door rang, I felt the familiarity swell in me. The connection between us had never wavered, despite the years, and I knew it was her.

"...upstairs," Mrs. Crane was whispering.

And, a few terrified heartbeats later, I was aware of Natalie's soft footsteps as she entered my hideout. "Parrish," she said almost like it was pure air with no voice at all.

I didn't look at her. Shame welled in me before I could bury it. *What have we done?* I wondered. The gamble had seemed worth it so long as I didn't imagine its end and so long as I didn't fret at anyone finding out. But not even I could suppress reality forever.

Natalie moved softly until she reached a couch that was as worn as my armchair. She sat on the very edge of it, lurking in the periphery of my vision, and reached over with her hand like one would to a wounded animal. Careful, eager to help but afraid of getting torn to shreds.

"Don't," I graveled. "You should leave me." A bottomless pit of despair opened inside of me. "Just go."

Natalie was quiet for a little while. I almost thought she would listen. I almost felt her decide to get up and march out of here. And out of her twisted, terrible brother's life, too. "Don't be a child."

I laughed abruptly and darkly. I'd used those exact words on Levi several times.

"I'm sorry you're hurting, Parrish," she said.

The shimmer that blurred my vision alerted me it was time to blink the tears away again. I did, inhaling shakily and lifting my gaze to my sister's dark brown eyes, same as mine. "What?"

Her lips stretched into a sad, upside down frown. "You didn't deserve it."

I narrowed my eyes. "I seduced our stepbrother," I hissed just loudly enough so Natalie would hear me. I couldn't stand the thought of Mrs. Crane overhearing that part. She was my last refuge until I mustered the strength to run back to New York.

"So?" Natalie shrugged.

I shook my head in disbelief. "How are you okay with that?"

"Jesus, Parrish, you are thick sometimes. It's really very annoying. I don't care that we're all one big, dysfunctional family Mom and Harry Frankensteined into existing, sweetie. I only care that you broke his heart when you stormed out without him."

My face hardened. That was the furthest thing from what I expected to hear. "I didn't break his heart," I whispered.

"Don't pretend to be stupid," Natalie ordered.

"But I didn't," I insisted. In order to break his heart, I needed him to feel more than attraction.

Natalie gave me a long, confused look that slowly shifted into sadness. Was she pitying me? I was too far gone in feeling sorry for myself to protest.

"He's in love with you, baby," she said, a hair louder than a whisper.

I frowned. "He...can't be," I murmured.

"Oh Parrish," she whispered, lifting her hand and running her fingers through my hair. "I knew about his feelings for you since he was sixteen. My eighteenth birthday party, remember? You had some guy from out of town to keep you company while you babysat us all. You didn't give a fuck about the party or what we were all up to. Christ, we had so much hidden booze. Never mind. You flirted with that guy all day and all day he was following you, looking at the guy like he wanted to murder him. He was so fucking in love with you, sweetie."

My vision blurred and the bitter taste of tears coated my throat and mouth. I sniffed and looked away. "You never said," I growled in a low voice, trying to make it accusatory just to deflect this whole goddamn conversation from the shimmer in my eyes.

"Don't get me wrong," Natalie said. "I love you. I think you're the best big brother a girl could have."

"But?" *Cut to the chase.*

"I didn't trust you'd be good for him," she said flatly. "Not when he got older and his crush stayed the same. Not when you left. And not when you returned for this charade of a wedding."

I chewed on my lower lip for a long while. Poor Levi. His whole life, he'd struggled between loyalty to his parents and his true feelings. My sweet, poor Levi. "You were right," I said. I'd ruined it all for him. He would have been a million times better off if he'd never remembered that I existed. "I shouldn't have come."

"No, sweetie," Natalie said. "You're wrong. And so was I." The pace at which she was patting my head increased with urgency. "Look what you're doing for him."

"I'm not doing anything," I said. "I'm running the fuck away."

Natalie smacked my head gently but warningly. "Don't be stupid. You know how this will play out. They already forgave him the moment you took the fall, even if they're awkward around him. And don't you dare hold that against him. It's not his fault things are this way. And don't even try telling me you didn't take the blame. I know you, Parrish. I know what you're like. You may not love often, but when you do, you love hard. You always have."

I wouldn't blame Levi. Not anymore. The conversation he had had with Harold that one morning, when he stood up for me, changed things. Nobody had ever done that for me. Except for Natalie.

My throat constricted. Was this love? Was that this swelling bubble of anxiety, wrapped in the warmth of knowledge that I would die for him if ever there was any need, love? God, I was a fuck up, incapable of naming the thing I felt the strongest.

"And you're loyal to a fault," she said, urgency coloring her voice. "So be loyal, Parrish."

I took her hands in mine and looked her in the eyes, killing every expression that might have gotten an idea to dance over my face. I wasn't going to let her finish what she meant to say. I wasn't going to consider returning to the house and stirring the pot. "If he really feels the way you say, he'll get over it." *There's nothing to love here. Hell, there's nothing to like about me, either.* "And he'll be better off. Harry and Marge are going to take care of him just fine." I nearly shuddered at the thought. "And he'll have you nearby if they spoil him too much.

I never should have gotten his hopes up, if that's what I did." I said the last words with as little emotion as I could.

He would be fine in River Bend.

He would leave someday and carve out a life he wanted to have.

And he would have their financial support, unlike what I'd had when I left. He had a promising future so long as I stayed the fuck away. I'd done enough damage already.

Natalie got up to leave. "You're making a mistake," she said dryly.

I jumped up after her. "Speaking of mistakes," I said, louder, and it was enough to stop her in her tracks. She knew what was coming. "Are you seriously going to marry that baboon?"

"No," Natalie said hoarsely. "I was a fool to ever think it could work."

My eyebrows quivered between frowning and rising in shock. *What did you ever see in him?* I wanted to ask, but couldn't. I was the last person on the planet who had any right to question someone's choices. I knew how fickle love and lust could be.

It took her a moment to soften, then she spoke again. "He was gorgeous and caring when I met him," she said. "It's hard to believe it, I know, but he really was. He made me feel special." She shrugged. "It's embarrassing that I fell for the act. He wanted a pretty wife to show off. And when he thought I'd swallowed the hook, the act started falling apart."

Anger flared in me. "Did he do something to you?"

"What? No," he said, frowning. She looked down to where my fists were clenching. "No, he just didn't care anymore."

"You should have let me punch him," I said venomously.

Natalie laughed mirthlessly. "He was mine to slap, Parrish. And he's mine to break things off with. Jarred and the entire family. I, uh...I don't know what to do."

I narrowed my eyes. "You could come to New York. Be with me."

She gave a soft chuckle. "It's not that easy. Mom and Harry put a fortune into the wedding."

"Let them bill me," I said firmly.

"You're doing well, but you're not that rich," Natalie said.

"I don't care. Do you hear me? I don't care about money. I'll pay in installments. I'll pay with interest. You're not going to stay here and throw your life away to please them." An image of Levi flashed in front of my eyes and my heart gave a sad throb, letting me know it still wasn't done dying. *Just die already*, I whispered to the shards of it that were scattered all over my chest.

"Maybe," Natalie said. We both knew that Harry and Marge were loaded enough to take a hit. But if they even threatened to be a problem, I wouldn't let them.

"No. You tell me now that you'll come with me," I demanded. If I could save one person from this whole mess, I might earn some redeeming points in my life. Not nearly enough, but I wasn't picky. "Natalie, please."

"Fine," she said. "But I need time. I need to do this my way, Parrish. I need to break it off, officially, before I can come. You should go back home and I'll meet you there."

"I'll go if you promise you'll follow," I said, taking her hands in mine.

She nodded and sniffed. "I promise."

I watched my little sister leave the loft where I hid and wondered at all the things I'd managed to ruin in less than two weeks of being home. This cursed town and the family that wanted to suffocate me and the boy who hurt and the girl who couldn't break free. If I could carry their burdens, I would. But I couldn't. So I did the next best thing. I did what I could to make Levi look a little better and I tried to get Natalie out of the mess I'd made.

And I could only hope she would listen.

Mrs. Crane didn't come around. The old ways never changed. Like an angry teenager, I hid up here for another hour, with her promise of total privacy. And, when I showed my face downstairs, I noticed the boxes of books in the back of her shop.

"Mrs. Crane?" I called.

She came from the back with that gentle smile I had always gotten from her, but rarely from my own mother. "Are you all better, my dear?" she asked.

I nodded, though it was a lie. He wasn't leaving my thoughts and inexplicable guilt was filling me to the brim. But I'd made all the choices already. It was too late to meddle with them now. And it wasn't like I could just pluck him from that house and make everything alright. I was the reason his world fell apart. "Do you need help with those?" I asked, pointing at the crates.

"Oh, no, no, no," Mrs. Crane said, waving her hands, then holding them together shyly. "Unless...you really mean that."

For the first time in what felt like ages, I smiled. She didn't need me to say anything, because she knew what the smile meant. For old times' sake, Mrs. Crane and I stacked the higher shelves together. She handed me the books, three or four at a time, while I stood halfway up the ladder. I dusted the shelves and sorted the books exactly as Mrs. Crane instructed, and lost myself in our work for one blissful hour.

And when we were done, we quietly knew it was time for me to go. "Oh, and Parrish," she called as I retreated. "When you're in town, do come and see this old lady once or twice."

"I will," I said. "I promise.

And, feeling an odd warmth splash through me, I found that I was having a hard time inhaling steadily. My breaths were shaky like my tired knees and my muscles were sore. But more than that, painful throbs filled my chest, and a strange idea wormed in the back of my mind. This old lady felt something for me. Something motherly and kind. Something not too unlike love.

And, if she was capable of it, maybe others could be, too.

Maybe.

Maybe...

But I didn't let these ideas take hold of me. Instead, I walked out into the night, found my car, and left this godforsaken town behind.

Chapter Sixteen

Levi

The knock on my door came just before midnight.

For a moment, I was gripped by fear. The only person I wanted to see now had left. He was gone. He had abandoned me. And I would be wise to get used to this feeling sooner rather than later.

How it crashed and burned. How it tasted like nothing more than ash. How he had walked out and left me with ringing ears and echoing words. If a tenth of it had come from his heart, it made me into the biggest loser ever.

Yet, I couldn't wrap my mind around it. I couldn't let it be true. Just hours earlier, he'd been holding me against the door on which someone was gently tapping their knuckles now. He'd been giving me the time of my life.

Outside of the bedroom more than in it. Somewhere along the way, my dreams had gotten bigger than simply having him; my dreams became grand and ambitious and filled with glimpses of a future we could never have.

I had known it wouldn't last. But that never meant I didn't want it to.

And, true, I should have been ready for it. I'd known the day was coming. And it hurt that it was over. But what truly hurt was how it had gone down. How he'd spat those horrible things into my face and walked out.

I wasn't sure if this was even pain that I felt. It was more akin to a science fiction blaster burning a gigantic hole in my chest. All was gone. My heart, my lungs. No more breathing, no more pulse. It was almost like I'd been shot by it half a second ago, and still stood, aware, ears ringing, lips parting in shock that you could play with such a dangerous thing and get hurt. I was about to fall over. Except, I didn't. I kept feeling it. I kept teetering on the edge so much that I began wishing I would just collapse and fade away.

And however many times I told myself that I was stupid to feel sorry for myself — hell, I was even stupider for being surprised by the outcome — I firmly decided to do just that. I was going to feel sorry for my ass. I was going to cry once I found the source of my tears. I was going to be grumpy to everyone and destroy what little I had left because I couldn't have it my way.

I'll be a fucking brat if I feel like it, I growled internally. *It's my heart that's shredded. I get to act like it.*

"Levi?" her voice came softly through the door after I hadn't spoken. She tapped her knuckles one more time against the wood. "I'm coming in."

She gave me a moment to cry out against it if I needed to.

I half sat on the bed, my pillow supporting my upper back and head. Parrish's pillow in my arms. Had I been hugging it? Damn. I hadn't realized. But the bergamot scent that came off the pillow once I released it made my vision blur.

Natalie entered the room as I dropped the pillow and gave me a sad, pitying look.

I didn't have it in me to ask her not to. Speaking was too much effort when I'd rather just give up and die. Or, a fate I deserved even more, I would give up and live the rest of my life in this house, like our parents' spineless puppet, numb for good, paying for the sins of these last couple weeks.

I had wanted him too hard. I'd gone too far. He should have stayed my secret fantasy even if it meant I spent my whole life wanting no one else.

Natalie shut the door behind her and walked to the edge of the bed, where she sat down and placed a hand on my ankle. "How are you?" she asked.

"Great," I squeezed through my gritted teeth. "Dad looks at my chin when he speaks to me and Margaret's bursts of sobs are down to thirty minutes apart."

Natalie pinched the bare skin above my ankle. "That's not what I asked."

I squealed. And fuck if it didn't make me just a little less miserable to feel something at all. "Ah," I breathed, pulling my legs up and rubbing the spot she'd pinched. "I'm fine, alright?" Then, I realized Dad wasn't the only one avoiding eye contact. While Natalie sat there, looking straight at me, I was looking at her knees and my feet and everything in between, just not her eyes. I scoffed in defeat. "I feel like shit. Like I should. I..." The words choked me. Here was the person who felt the true consequences of what Parrish and I had done, and she was looking me in the eyes without a trace of judgment.

My lips quivered and curved and a sob welled in me. Now, I could only whisper, and quickly before I broke. "I'm so sorry, Natalie."

Her lips parted and eyes widened. She pulled back a little as I buried my face in my hands, not to hide the tears — there were none — but to hide myself in shame. We'd cost her a future she had been making for herself. I wasn't blind; I'd seen the way the Wilkinsons stormed out like they would never look at any of us again. I'd seen the hatred in Jarred's eyes after she'd slapped him. "Sorry for what?" she asked.

I lifted my head and gave her a look, brief as it was, that told her how desperately ashamed I was. "The wedding, the scandal, the...the whole fucking mess."

She leaned in and wrapped her arms around my shoulders, pulling me into her embrace, and I folded like a towel. I fell over her. I collapsed. My head rested on her shoulder, arms limp by my side, and the growing pressure of all the despair I carried got closer to bursting out of me. "Don't be," Natalie said. "Christ, I have you two to thank for dodging that bullet."

I snorted, though it sounded half like sobbing.

When she finally released me, Natalie looked me straight in the eyes. "Jarred was a mistake," she said seriously. "A beautiful, passionate, attractive mistake."

I blinked. I knew a thing or two about such mistakes.

And Natalie squinted like she could read my thoughts. "It's not at all similar, Levi," she said. "I was blind to Jarred's flaws until I saw how happy he was to belittle someone. It wasn't even because you're my brothers, but because he enjoyed it so much. The drama, the heartbreak. It made him the happiest I'd ever seen him."

I opened my mouth, but there was virtually nothing I could have told her that would have made an iota of difference. So, I closed my lips and blinked in surprise.

"But you have something totally different," she said.

I stiffened my jaw when a tremor passed over my lips.

Natalie found my wrist and wrapped her fingers around it. She held it tight and leaned closer to me. "You've known him for half your lives," she said, lowering her tone and speaking quicker, like time was running out. "You knew his faults before you fell in love with him. It's different, Levi."

I squirmed. Facing the fact that Natalie knew there was more than just sex involved made me want to crawl out of my skin. I wasn't only the embarrassment of the family, but a pathetic loser, too.

"And I don't think you should give up just like that," she said flatly.

I pulled back and frowned. A million thoughts crossed my mind, synapses sparking with ideas all over my brain. "No," I muttered lamely, then sorted through my thoughts. "You heard him. It was just for fun."

"Bullshit," Natalie said. "And you can't convince me you believe that charade, either. You're stuck here living with them. You have your own battles to fight, college and all. Don't you get it?"

My frown deepened.

"If you really think Parrish didn't throw himself under the bus down there just to make it a little easier for you to live here, then I won't say another word. But think about it, Levi. Think hard." She spoke with such urgency that all my senses were on alert and the wave carried me to tense my muscles and be ready to jump. Jump where? My reality was all haze and confusion. I couldn't get my brain to work.

"He still left," I said dryly.

"Of course he did," Natalie said. "He knew how everyone was going to react. He played them. He played everyone and took the responsibility. Then he got the fuck out. What else was he gonna do?"

He could have taken me with him, I thought, but immediately scrapped that idea. I grudged him that he left *me* behind. But I also knew he had no fucking reason to consider anything else. Even if he had sacrificed himself down there, he had reached the end we'd both expected.

I nodded to what Natalie was saying and that seemed to encourage her. She sucked in a breath of air and went on. "I need a little time to sort this mess out. I need to visit Jarred, return the ring, look his parents in the eye, you know? He's a crybaby and enough of a sadist that I would rather not, but I know I have to close that door gently. No point in burning more bridges, right?"

DESTRUCTIVE RELATIONS 253

I wished I had a tenth of her wisdom, but here we were. Still, I lifted my eyebrows. She was telling me…something.

"When that's done, and when I break it to Harry and Mom, I'll…" She tightened her hand around my wrist. "I'm going to New York."

Countless things happened at once, too quickly for me to keep track of. My body hurt all over at the thought of New York City and Parrish living his best life there without me. But whatever was left of my heart now cracked at the idea of Natalie leaving, too. And finally, fearful expectation before she even said it.

"Come with me," the inevitable words rolled over her lips.

"No," I whispered right away.

Natalie ignored it and went on. "Parrish expects me. He doesn't expect you. He doesn't even know you would do it for him. He wouldn't ask you to come. You know him; he doesn't understand why anyone would ever love him back."

My chest shuddered. *Love him back?* That implied he loved me already. But he couldn't. Why would he?

"I swear, it's a bulletproof plan, Levi. It's the only way you can prove to him he's worth loving," Natalie said, eyes glimmering.

I opened my mouth and closed it right back again. Could he really not know? Could he really be so sure he was despicable that he never noticed? I have fucking loved him since I was fourteen. Loved and hated in equal parts for a goddamn decade until he gave me such a huge taste of life that nobody would ever come close to him. I would die a lonely man with one good memory of Parrish, but still happy that I'd had that much at all.

"You both deserve to be happy and..." She shrugged and let the silence linger. "I haven't seen either of you this happy in a long time."

I blinked at her.

"Think about it," she said, as she lifted her hand and scratched the back of my head like she used to. "I'm leaving tomorrow afternoon before I change my mind. I need to break free. And so do you."

She got up, walked away, and glanced at me from the door on her way out. She gave a half-smile, then closed the door and left me unable to fall asleep.

I couldn't just leave.

And to Parrish of all people. What if she was wrong? And she probably was. What if he saw me and made that disgusted expression again? I wouldn't be able to survive that. And even if he didn't. Even if he welcomed me with open arms, what then? What would I do, without a skill or a degree, in a place like New York City? Be his burden until he really got sick of me and wished he'd meant the things he'd said tonight?

No, no, no. It was silly to even consider these things.

I wasn't going to surprise him, be it bad or good. I wasn't going to do any more rash things than I had already. I was drowning in the cesspool of my own making and adding more trouble was the surest way to sink to the bottom.

I would miss Natalie.

And I would never get over Parrish. That much was guaranteed. I couldn't get over him before he'd even noticed me, though I hadn't seen him in five years. How could I hope to move on after finally feeling alive, guided by his hands. He was the spark I had needed to finally wake up from the fever dream these four years of college had been. He was the reason my heart beat for a purpose greater than simply pumping blood.

That was alright. I would cry and sometimes sketch and live a solitary life here in River Bend.

I barely slept that night. It was like I was returning to the state I'd been in before Parrish with determination. Just now, as I blinked at dawn, I realized how good it was to have his arms around me. I'd appreciated it at the time, but I hadn't had the faintest idea of how badly I would miss it once it was gone. I'd blocked out those thoughts, stupidly enough.

The day dragged on. I had no appetite for French toast or an elaborate omelet or whatever else Margaret was cooking that morning. Even less appetite I found for the drama that happened once she wailed in despair and Dad comforted her, all of it followed by Natalie walking out of the house and driving away to Jarred's place. Like she had said, she was going to close that chapter in her life for good, leaving heartbroken parents who could no longer hope to be related to a local politician.

When I did show up, not because the smell of food made me drool but because dizziness alerted me that I needed to refuel, the low murmurs on the back porch died down suddenly.

Lauren gave me a wary and pitiful look, blending two things I hated the most.

Dad looked down at his plate.

Margaret, who had been the one speaking, pursed her lips, then smiled. "Hungry?"

"Yeah," I breathed, then sat down opposite of Dad, with Lauren to my left and Margaret to my right. Margaret scurried to fill up my plate, even though I was perfectly capable of doing it myself. She made it a show of support, while Lauren was tilting her head and regarding me with something I couldn't quite put my finger on.

"Well, then," Margaret said airily, sitting back down and watching me. There was a trace of judgment in her look, though she did her best to conceal it. Oddly, it was missing in Lauren's eyes. And Dad wasn't looking at me because he was awkward, not because he was judging me exactly. Maybe he was deep down, but I couldn't see it.

"You gotta love family reunions," Lauren said, swirling red wine around in her glass.

Margaret choked, then hurried to have a sip of water.

Dad's knife scratched the plate.

I laughed. I hadn't realized I was doing it until the bark of laughter ricocheted off the wall of the house.

Lauren snorted, though I couldn't begin guessing at what precisely.

It was Margaret who spoke, at last. "It seems there won't be a wedding after all," she said, choking on a sob. "Maybe you heard already. Natalie's leaving this afternoon."

"She's already packed and all," Lauren supplied.

Margaret shot her sister a stern look of 'be quiet,' and turned her attention back to me. "She's taking Parrish's side, apparently."

The corners of my lips stiffened at the partition of the family. It was all my fault and I...fuck. I was on the wrong side. Never mind. I deserved it, if not worse.

"I'm sorry you came all this way for nothing, love," Margaret told me.

I sniffed out a laugh. For nothing? *Oh, but I got all my dreams to come true. For a moment.* I nodded. Having to tell them I won't be leaving seemed almost like nothing important at all. So much had happened. They could take one more disappointment, right? It wasn't going to snap something in them to send them on a murderous rampage. I hoped.

Dad looked up at my reaction and met my gaze. "Nobody blames you, Levi," he said nasally and directly. "Parrish." He looked at Margaret, who nodded her approval. "Parrish is a complicated person. He can be very convincing. We've had battles with him for years, Levi. We know what he's like. Really, we shouldn't be surprised. I only wish you learned your lesson."

"And what lesson is that?" I asked, unable to hold back the erupting anger. "That I should have listened to you that morning? When you isolated him? When you all but disowned him?"

Dad stuttered and wiped his mouth. "Now look here, Levi. That's not what I was saying. We're here to support you, son. You were...you were..." He looked down, struggling to get the words over his lips.

"...seduced by the devil," I supplied dryly.

"Enough," Margaret said.

But Dad seemed to get unstuck. "You mock, but it isn't far from it, Levi. That boy flirts with disaster wherever he goes. We never should have let him back under this roof. We're on your side, boy, so don't twist my words."

"I'm not so innocent," I said grimly. Why? The fuck if I knew. I was feeling particularly self-destructive right about now. And Dad and Margaret blaming Parrish for every rainy summer day and every bad harvest and every stubbing of the toe was getting on my nerves. I inhaled, feeling like I was just about able to scratch the itch I'd been carrying for longer than I cared to admit. "I seduced him just as much. And I loved it. Every goddamn moment of it, Dad. It's what I dreamed of since I knew how to dream of those things. It's what I'd do for the rest of my life if only I could. And if you gave me a chance to start from the beginning, I wouldn't change a thing." I smiled, blinking quickly to stave off the tears that welled in my eyes. "And that's not even half of it. He was the only friend I had. The only ally. The only person who had enough heart to give me a helping hand when I struggled the most. Because, here's the thing..." I sucked in a shallow breath of air. It almost felt like pulling a trigger. "I'm not going back to Portland. I dropped out four months ago. There aren't any flying colors and there won't be a degree. I've been lying."

Margaret nearly screamed, slapping her hands over her mouth and jumping away from the table like I'd released a venomous snake under it.

Dad's face darkened, his fork dropping from his fingers.

Lauren was pretty fucking chill.

Looking around, I couldn't help but laugh. My masterpiece. The absolute destruction of one's self. Of an entire life. And I shrugged guilelessly. "Yep. I've been lying to your faces for a good year now. The grades I sent back in February? Forged. I know a guy who knows a guy. I'd only passed two exams back then, both were just over sixty percent."

"Now hold on a goddamn minute," Dad rasped. "You can't be serious."

"As serious as my not so innocent feelings for Parrish," I spat.

Margaret sobbed and walked into the house, while Lauren barked out a hearty laugh.

"Marge," Dad called, then shot me a hateful look of disapproval. *How could you do this?* He asked silently. He jumped up, nearly pushing the heavy table forward, and ran after Margaret, blurting soothing words, concocting plans how I could make things right and still graduate. As if...

I sat still while Lauren sipped her red wine.

The burden was gone.

Heartbreak remained and it seared my insides, but the pressure had been lifted off my chest. Maybe I could grieve now. Maybe I could lick my wounds, get a job at the grocery store, and finally focus on what I was so goddamn good at; feeling sorry for myself.

Silence was thick on the porch. A gust of wind rustled the deep green leaves on the trees in the backyard and Lauren's long, red nails tapped against the half empty glass as she wrapped her fingers around it. "Your parents are wrong," she said bluntly, then sloshed the rest of the wine down her throat. She sighed, sniffed, and wiped something from her eyes with the back of her index finger before she directed her foggy blue gaze at me. "Hearts have no clue what modern-day family is. As they shouldn't. Stepbrothers or perfect strangers, Levi. Hearts don't discriminate." The corners of her lips dipped down. "Take it from me, my dear. If you truly love him, don't let ignorant people stand in your way. Even if it burns you up, love while you can." She sighed. "There's never been any love lost between Parrish and me, but he's no worse than Ned or Joel or any of the bunch. And I still regret nothing."

She stood up, swayed a little, then put a hand on my shoulder, both as comfort for me and to steady herself. She gave my shoulder a gentle rub, then made her way back to the house. There, she paused, and breathed for a moment.

"I can only hope you don't have my luck, Levi," she said and disappeared down the hall.

I sat there, stunned and so profoundly sad that tears were redundant. Did I have any luck at all? And what was I going to do with the rest of my life? And how was I ever going to crawl out of the pit of despair in which I was making myself so very comfortable?

I had no hope of answering any of these questions. Lauren's words echoed in my head as much as Dad's. Dad's were venomous, looking for someone to blame, just so he could keep me as the prize and justify my actions in his own head. Lauren's were pure, if fairly drenched in wine.

This was how Natalie found me.

I'd heard her enter the house and make her rounds. She loaded her luggage into the car before she said she would call from New York and visit in a couple of weeks. At the very end of it, she made her way to the back porch, and found me in my sleeping T-shirt and a stained pair of shorts.

She looked at me, smiled, and nodded that she understood.

We didn't say a word to each other. She could see I was neither ready nor in a hurry to get there. I wasn't moving. I wasn't budging. I couldn't even decide, let alone do the thing she was asking me to do.

So, Natalie hugged me, and whispered that she loved me, and I whispered it back to her. And it welled in me to tell her to take care of Parrish. To remind him once in a while that he's a decent guy and not the thing Dad and Margaret claimed him to be.

But she knew all that already, I hoped.

And I let her go.

Sitting quietly, gazing at the calm surface of the water in the pool, and remembering his professional sweeps of arms and the dripping water on the morning when I realized that getting him to touch me and kiss me was the only objective in my life, I listened to Natalie's footsteps retreat.

She opened the front door and murmured another goodbye to parents who decided to pretend they were deaf and she was a ghost of no importance at all if she could betray them like this.

And I grabbed the armrests of my chair. Everything I'd been holding in was starting to spill out of me. I couldn't stop myself. I didn't even want to try.

Chapter Seventeen
PARRISH

I left Bud to finish cleaning up the parlor after he insisted for the third time that I was just making more of a mess than actually helping. "You're not right today, boss," he'd said as he nudged me outside.

So I walked a couple streets away to my apartment building, a red brick and mortar structure with a rusty fire escape ladder in the alley my French balcony overlooked.

Instead of going to my apartment, I paced around the building, trying to burn excess energy. Though I had hardly slept, after a night of driving and despair, I couldn't sit still. I couldn't stay inside for too long, either.

That was why I'd showed up at the parlor in the first place.

Natalie had sent a message that she was on her way some hours ago. She hadn't told me how long she'd been on the road by then or where she was texting me from. She could be three hours away or just around the corner.

I paced up and down, back and forth, left and right. Walking, walking, walking. I needed to tire myself out like a parent tired out their young child to get a good night's sleep. I was burning up, but I was still restless as fuck.

And then, a familiar voice sounded from behind me. "You've got ants up your ass. Did you know that?"

I stopped dead in my tracks and turned around. "How long have you been watching me?"

Austin grinned. "You've passed me four times, Parrish," he said teasingly.

There were people coming and going down the street. I hadn't been paying attention to anyone but the one that was in my thoughts.

"If I didn't know better, I'd say you look..." Austin narrowed his eyes at me and pondered. "Hmm. Hungover or heartbroken? I'll go with heartbroken."

"Wrong," I muttered back, not ready to share whatever the hell it was that I felt. Heartbroken was only the beginning. I felt like I was grieving the loss of something integral in my life. Like something that made me face my own mortality, and impending doom, too. "Were you waiting for me?" I asked, trying to be casual as I stepped up and hugged him.

Austin snorted. "You wish."

I joined him when he laughed. "I couldn't afford you," I teased.

"You joke, but that's starting to be true," he said. He wore torn jeans and a T-shirt that wasn't exactly a crop top, but didn't cover him all the way, either. He knew how to advertise himself even if he was off the streets these days. A couple years back, Austin was literally waiting for some passerby to get curious and hire him. Now, though, he was in a far better place, with a roof over his head and a safer way of doing his business.

"It's not even a joke," I said. "Didn't I see you get picked up a couple blocks away in a black limo the other week?"

Austin gave a mischievous smile and zipped up his lips. "I don't kiss and tell."

"Mm. Smart," I said.

"But you should." The look he gave me now was piercing and intense. He had eyes as brown as mine, but a smooth face and a shade paler complexion. Well built and manicured for the utmost desirability, Austin was objectively beautiful, but he was the opposite of what I wanted. I wanted a slim blond, preferably off limits, and ideally carrying two tickets for Hell Express. I'd ride that train any day.

"A gentleman never would," I said quietly, bumping Austin with my shoulder.

"How exactly does that affect you?" he asked cheekily.

"You've got a mouth on you today," I growled, but couldn't resist smiling.

"Bingo," he whispered, his gaze on my stretching lips. "Go on. Tell me about him."

I looked at Austin, then noticed a car slow down in the periphery of my vision. "Your ride's here, I think."

Austin glanced, then nodded. He didn't seem to be in a hurry. "Are you okay, Parrish?" he asked me.

I clasped his shoulder. "I am. I promise. And one day soon, you, me, and Bud will get blind drunk at Erick's and I'll tell you all about it."

Austin gave me his handsomest smile, which I didn't think was practiced at all. He had that air of attraction and appeal that some people used so effortlessly. He winked, then jaywalked to the other side of the street and hopped inside the huge, expensive looking car. I was guessing that his client wasn't exactly going to leave him sore for days.

The thought made me chuckle. Austin charged a steep price, but I'd never asked him if there was a size discount or if a night of work was a night of work no matter what. He'd roll off the chair with laughter, bubbly fucker that he was.

I went upstairs to my apartment, rubbing my chest like that would soothe the pain that wasn't even physical. How could it hurt this fucking much? How could every second of silence feel like a year of solitude?

I couldn't wait for Natalie to show up. I was dying for her company. Aside from Levi, who would hate me for the rest of his life, I could only talk to her and know I was understood. Bud and Austin and the rest of the bunch were great, but Natalie understood me when I didn't understand myself sometimes. And Levi was the same for a few brief and glorious moments.

Levi *had been* the same.

Next time he saw me — if there ever was that time — he had more than plenty of reasons to look away.

I walked in and walked through life mechanically. I did what I needed to do. I ate. I showered. I flicked the lights on when the sun dipped below the horizon. I even turned the TV on and played the news in the background to create an appearance of chatter and conversation. But I enjoyed nothing. The food was ashen and the shower was just about getting wet then dry. The news was depressing and the world was going to hell and taking me with it. And I couldn't even be with the person I wanted the most.

The fact that I had just recently refurnished my apartment and swapped the second hand furniture with new stuff, painted the walls, and made this space something I loved, barely made any difference to me right now. You could have thrown me under a bridge to sleep with nothing more than a blanket and a pillow. I wouldn't feel any different.

I felt rotten somewhere deep inside. Broken in ways nothing could fix. Malfunctioning. Unlovable. Bitter and resentful and jealous of imaginary people. I wasn't someone he should be with anyway. And it was good that he was free of me.

Margaret and Harold were right. Where I went, trouble followed.

I ran my hands through my hair and wanted to shout at the voices that grew louder in my head. I was worthless. I was trouble. I was nothing. Hell, even Natalie was at risk of destruction if she stayed with me for too long.

I texted her as I couldn't keep myself sane any longer. I couldn't just sit here. If she was still hours away, I would go to Erick's and get blind drunk right away.

Me: Are you close?
Natalie: Very.

The reply came quickly. Too quickly. She must have parked the car somewhere around the block and was walking here already. I had minutes, maybe less, to pull myself together.

But when she rang my doorbell downstairs and I buzzed her in, I didn't feel dead anymore. Emotions, none very good, flared to life and overwhelmed me. I had been lonely and desperate for the last twenty-four hours. I had been lifeless. I had been helpless. But here was my little sister, still willing to love me, climbing the stairs to take all my pain away. She was coming to rescue me.

I felt so small in that moment, as I heard her footsteps on the stairs. I rested my forehead on the closed door and shut my eyes. My lashes were wet with tears and my lip was trembling. My sister was coming to me. And I didn't care if she found me a blubbering mess. I wanted to hug her and cry it all out.

I couldn't hold it in any longer. I loved him and I couldn't have him. It was the worst pain I'd endured in my life. Breaking three ribs after falling off a tree was a fucking walk in the park compared to this.

"Natalie," I whispered to myself, almost whimpering, my voice cracking as her footsteps reached my floor. She knocked on the door just as I released a long, shuddering breath of air and let the tears roll down my cheeks.

Everything's better now, I whispered to myself, reaching for the knob. *She's here. You can cry now. She'll help you through it.*

I pulled the door open and nearly collapsed on my knees. My mouth opened but no sound came out. A cry I'd been holding in choked me as my throat constricted.

But Levi looked no more put together than me. He managed to give a weak smile, though his red eyes shimmered with tears. "Natalie's not coming," he said.

My jaw trembled, still hanging open, and my eyebrows curved. *You came. You came to me.* My mind kept coming up blank. It ran in circles for these few moments of silence.

He licked his lips and shook his head. "She'll come around tomorrow. She, er, found a room above some bar and...uh..." He looked at me, tears rolling down his cheeks when he blinked. His voice wavered and he whispered. "Will you let me come in?"

Whatever had been blocking me, keeping me frozen in that spot, preventing me from thinking and acting, disappeared in an instant. A request from Levi was all it took. A request to be allowed inside. He was asking for help, for privacy and a safe place where he could cry. He was my frightened little stepbrother and my brave hero. He was here and he was asking.

I moved swiftly, my arms shooting up and wrapping around him. I hugged him tightly. "Of course I will," I whispered into his neck as I pulled him in. "Of course I'll let you in." As I murmured these things, I pulled us in and shut the door. "God, it's good to see you."

He sniffed and coiled his arms around me, hands on my back, fingers digging into my muscles almost like when I brought him to the highest ecstasy.

"Christ, it's so good to hold you," I whispered. "I'm sorry. I'm sorry I said those things. I didn't mean them. You know I didn't. Right? You know that, right?" Words poured out of me in a panic as everything returned to me. The blur that that day had been was clearing up, thoughts swirling in my head. "I needed to distract them, you know? I needed them to forget you were a part of it. Didn't have the time to plan...didn't think..." I held him tighter and tighter with each word I said. Explanations and thoughts were pouring out of me faster than I could form sentences. "I would never, ever say those things, Levi. I would never. These days with you...Christ, it's good to hold you." I hadn't realized I was crying until he began patting my back and rubbing it in circles.

Jesus...was I letting him comfort me? Was I making myself an even bigger burden to him? But holding him was all that kept me on my feet as I broke down and cried into his shoulder and his unruly, blond hair, inhaling the sweet and spicy scent of his cologne.

"I didn't mean to hurt you," I said. "I'd never hurt you. I'd die before I hurt you again, I swear."

"Parrish," he whispered, his voice still trembling. "Stop. Stop apologizing."

"No," I protested. "I have to." So much goddamn guilt...so much that I didn't know I could have held it in me all this time.

"Parrish, don't apologize. I already forgave you," he said, firmer, but there was a trill in his cracking voice at the end of the sentence. He pulled back from me and took my face in his hands just as I did his, at the same time, and looked into my eyes. His green eyes were redder now, but dimples appeared in his cheeks as he smiled. "I love you," he said.

My mouth worked, but no sounds came out. I sniffed, shook my head, and thought of all the ways I'd tormented him our entire lives together. "Why?" I whispered.

Levi smiled in a knowing way like he had anticipated this. "Because you're awesome." He shrugged innocently. "You make me feel amazing whenever you look at me. And for all the shit you gave me back in the day, you've still been the most caring guy I've ever met. And if you think I haven't loved you with every breath since the moment I realized I was gay, I've got a surprise for you." He shrugged the backpack off his shoulders and unzipped it. Inside was a couple T-shirts, a pair of pants, and two sketchbooks. "Sorry," he blurted. "I had no time to pack. If you keep me, you'll have to put up with a lot of nudity on laundry days."

I wanted to laugh and tell him how that wouldn't be a problem at all, but he moved on, pulling the sketchbook out and handing it to me.

As I examined its cover, Levi seemed to shrink into a tiny ball of self-consciousness and anxiety. But I flipped the notebook open and something punched me in the stomach. Every page, every bit of space on the quality cream paper, was filled with portraits. Some fantastically stylized, others oddly accurate, but all of them were of me. Me as I had been five, six, seven years ago. Every single one.

If there still existed any crack in my heart, I could feel it heal instantly. I could hear the scars form and I could feel my heartbeat return. I felt the blood pumping through my body and my life returning to the empty shell I had turned myself into. "I..." I breathed for a moment, vision blurring and clearing in erratic waves. "Levi, you have to understand, I've...I've never said this to anyone in..." I shrugged. "Who the hell knows how long. I.."

Silence. For a long moment, I gazed into his shimmering, mossy eyes as I bit my lip hard. When was the last time I'd said this? Hell, when was the last time I felt it? I loved Natalie; but that wasn't the same. The things I felt for Levi were explosive and they frightened me in ways I hadn't felt before. They frightened me of being alone and without him. They frightened me of losing him or hurting him. But they also made me infinitely happy when I even considered the possibility of touching him and hearing his voice. And he deserved to know that. He deserved to hear me say it.

Like immense water breaching a dam, the words burst out of me. "I love you, Levi. I love you so fucking much."

And as I fell apart in his arms, he swiftly put me back together. He had the healing touch of some mythological, magical being that nobody but me knew about. He was so goddamn special that I wanted to kick myself for not seeing it five years ago.

When I was finally patched together as much as a crying mess of a man could be, I looked into Levi's gorgeous, moss-like eyes. "How are you even here?" I whispered.

He smiled, not shying away from giving me a look at his deepest dimples. "Unprepared, but with a lot of help from Natalie."

"But...Margaret and Harold," I said, like that was an explanation of something. Like they were a factor.

Levi shook his head. "They know how I feel about you," he said softly. "And they know about college. I'm not sure how they feel about everything as a collective, but I am pretty sure it is not up to their standards."

I raised my eyebrows in surprise. He'd done it all by himself.

"And I don't care," Levi said firmly. "I'll figure it all out. It's not important. Not nearly as important as this." His hands clutched my T-shirt and tugged me a little closer. "I shouldn't have let you leave. I should have come after you immediately."

"You didn't know," I said. I refused to let him take any responsibility for this entire mess. Especially now that he was here. "What are you...?" I wanted to ask about his plans, but he read my mind before I said anything else.

"I don't know," he said, laughing. "I'm just happy. Fuck, I'm just so happy right now."

I wrapped my arms around him and closed the few inches of distance between us, pressed our bodies together, and kissed him deeply. Then, when he swayed and swooned, I looked into his eyes again. "I know what you're going to do," I said. "You're going to be mine. Here. With me. And we're going to figure it all out together."

He blinked. "Are you sure?"

"I love you," I said. That was enough of an argument. "I won't ever let you make another hard choice by yourself, Levi. Never."

He pushed himself up to the tips of his toes and pressed a kiss to my lips. It seared me and made me want him so much more. "I didn't want it to end like this," he said softly, an inch away from my face. "I didn't want the family in factions. But I realized, it was never you or me who made that divide. And I wasn't going to lose you because of it. Not now that I had you."

"You can't lose me, Levi," I whispered. "I'm yours. Now and forever."

"And I'm yours, Parrish," he promised. "I've been yours all this time. It'll never change."

I lifted him quickly and whirled him around, his legs coiling around my waist and his head leaning down. He kissed me and I kissed him back, hard and fast like we were running out of time. But we weren't. We had all the time in the world.

The love of my life and I.

EPILOGUE

***

ONE YEAR LATER

Parrish took his time. He either seriously loved watching the rolling, windswept hills, and cows out in the pastures, or he didn't want to reach our destination.

"Natalie just texted," I said.

"Oh yeah?" Parrish asked, knowing what the contents of the text must have been but pretending he didn't have a slightest idea. "How is she?"

I snorted. We'd seen her just this morning.

"She's there," I said. "She couldn't text sooner from all the fanfare."

Parrish gritted his teeth so hard it was audible. "Just watch the fanfare die an awkward death when we arrive," he muttered sourly.

I shrugged. It was going to be awkward. I expected no less. "They still might be happy to see us."

I wondered if he could tear the steering wheel off with the intensity of his grip. "I figured she'd be the first one they forgave. I told you so. Remember?"

I sucked my teeth. "Like I told you a million times, we're not begging for anyone's forgiveness. We've got nothing to apologize for." Parrish reached for my hand as soon as the words rolled over my lips. He found it in my lap and wrapped his fingers around it. He held me tightly, eyes on the road. "But I can't just let things stay as they are."

"I know, I know," he said with genuine empathy. "And we're going there. See?"

"Oh, we're moving? Feels like we've been stuck by that cow for an hour," I teased.

"It's a different cow, baby bro," Parrish said, his voice dropping at the last two words.

I shuddered. "Shush," I managed through my constricting throat, a sneaky smile pulling at the corners of my lips. "We don't have the time for that."

He gave me the briefest glance, then quickly locked his eyes to the empty road. "We have all the time in the world."

"The cows will see us," I said, laughter slowly bubbling within me.

"I've got nothing to hide," he purred.

I jerked my hand free, then closed it over his instead. We were quiet for a while, feeling one another's skin as a way of finding comfort in turbulent times, like today.

Returning to River Bend had been a project of mine for the entire year.

Not that I was aching with regrets. Far from it. For the entire year, every day was better than the one before it. Every day, waking up in his arms, starting the day with him across the dining table, and waiting eagerly to see him in the afternoon, gave me the sort of joy I hadn't experienced before. More than that, being with Parrish had given me a purpose. And a sense of safety I hadn't felt in years. Day by day by day, Parrish helped me; he supported my wild ideas of diving into art, not only in spoken words, but in actions. He'd helped me by finding me an instructor he trusted with his life, which transformed everything. Six months after that, I'd been asked to work as her assistant. Three months after that, I'd had a modest exhibition at Erick's pub, which drew in the alternative and artsy crowd. Now, the talk of actual art school was becoming common. And Parrish was my muse and my model. He didn't shy away from posing for hours, nude and seductive, beautiful in all the right ways, radiating the fire that he was made of, but also intense love underneath it.

He loved hard and fast.

And I loved him just as much.

But even so, with all we'd achieved, thinking of Dad and Margaret had never gotten any easier. It was me who'd made the first contact, though I was sure Natalie had been secretly working on it for longer. She'd always been the peacemaker. And she never would have told me if she really had covered the ground before I reached out.

And when I did, I found little resentment, and much more sadness. It was hard to work through it with either of them. Neither Dad nor Margaret knew what to say or how to say it. They were heartbroken, though they couldn't clearly say why.

Parrish had his theory. Negative as always. "They can't brag about us to anyone without admitting their sons are pervy." I'd snickered at the word he used to describe us. Being with him was so natural that I often forgot about the years we'd spent as stepbrothers. Except in those moments when Parrish called me his little bro and every cell in my body swelled with desire.

I had my ideas, too. I imagined that Margaret and Dad were heartbroken, no matter how the family ultimately fell apart. I wasn't so sure they were still hurting over their inability to understand the two of us. Hell, the whole bunch of us; Natalie had broken their hearts in another way, but she was living a life now that she couldn't have dreamed of a year ago. She was putting her business degree to good use and consulting up and coming firms all over the state. And I was fairly sure she was hiding a possible relationship, or at least a promise of one, that she wasn't ready to share yet. Either way, when I saw her, every week or so, she was smiling more every time. There was that look in her eye, subtly and only on occasion, where she would have her attention drift away and the dreamy sigh would escape her.

I hadn't called her out on it. She would tell us when she was ready.

"What are you doing?" I asked as the car slowed down. We were still an hour away.

"I really need to stretch my legs," Parrish said.

"Liar," I accused. He hadn't even bothered to make that sound true. Instead, he grinned and stopped the car by the road. There was another road forking to the right, though it was a dirt one leading between low slopes of hills.

I got out of the car after Parrish and rushed to catch up with him. He locked the car over his shoulder and kept smiling to himself. I didn't know what he found so amusing, but if he was planning on rolling in the grass, he was about to be sorely disappointed. Somehow, for once, he'd decided to trade comfy cotton shorts for a pair of well-fitted dark green pants and his sleeveless T-shirt for a fine, white shirt with a high collar and rolled up sleeves. And though he was always the handsomest man in the room, his good looks were sky high today. And he wasn't getting it stained for a quickie in the field. Not when I'd worked so hard on booking us a room at the inn. One with the most space and privacy for the extended weekend in River Bend. Or all the things I was already planning on begging him to do to me tonight.

Obviously, I didn't like the idea of staying in the house. It would be too much, too soon, to be a living, breathing reminder to Dad and Margaret. I didn't want them imagining things every night Parrish and I closed the doors. And I wanted even less to let them hear something, God forbid, because I'd stopped being quiet the moment I got to New York.

I followed Parrish, letting him have his little smirks and sneaky glances at me. I didn't say a word until we reached the peak of the dirt road, where the two hills met into one. Beyond it were vast fields and a forest in the distance, so clear on the breezy summer day that I felt like I could count the leaves on all the trees that kissed the sky on the horizon. "So?" I asked, tucking my hands in my pockets.

"I want us to have a moment," Parrish said. That was far more honest than the leg stretching story.

I smiled. It was too cute to resist. But, as the breeze came and moved the locks of my hair into my eyes, and I ran my fingers through them, I discovered a worried look in Parrish's eyes. It was gone as quickly as it had appeared. "You know it'll be okay, right?" I asked, reaching to caress his face. His beard was neatly trimmed, but still covering the lower half of his face, and just as coarse under my fingers. I loved feeling it all over my body as it emphasized his kisses.

He took my hand in his. "I'm not sure," he said.

I looked into his eyes and found that he really was worried. Not a lot, but it was there. "What's the worst that can happen?"

He shrugged. "You'll get your heart broken," he said, eyes gazing at me gently.

I clenched my jaw. In all of the planning, that hadn't crossed my mind. And, as I thought about it, I realized why that didn't worry me. "I won't. I have you to keep me safe."

He smiled his best smile. "That's true, my love."

It always made me grin when he called me that. "Besides," I said, trying to pull that goofy smile off my face. "We'll be subtle. We won't make out in front of them and flaunt it. It would be asking for trouble."

"We're not hiding, either," he said.

"Of course not," I assured him. "You know what I mean." I pulled a little back, then turned away from him, freeing my hand from his. I walked two paces down the hill, letting the sunlight kiss my face.

"It won't be easy to be subtle, Levi," Parrish called from behind me. "I won't hide how much you mean to me."

I stopped and stood still, ears perking up and a smile creeping to my face. I loved it when he talked dirty to me, but I absolutely adored when he got all soft.

"Because you do mean so much to me, you know," he said. "You're everything to me."

My heart tripped. Why was he saying this? I wasn't going to complain though.

"And whoever even thinks it's wrong can go fuck themselves," Parrish said joyfully. "Because I'm never going to apologize for loving you. Not ever. You're the best goddamn thing that ever happened to me."

I licked my lips. My vision blurred a little and my eyes stung. It was hard to keep all the emotions low when he was raw and passionate. I loved him to shreds. I loved every burning moment with him. And I lived to hear him say the same.

"And, if you agree to wear it, it won't be easy to miss the ring," Parrish said, far more quietly that I almost thought I'd misheard him.

I turned on my heels as my heart climbed into my throat and pounded there with fearful excitement. And there he was, on one knee, with an open black box. Inside a golden ring carved with a weaving, vine-like pattern, gleamed in the open sunshine. But the brightest of things in this image were his glimmering eyes.

I opened my mouth and gasped like someone had kicked air out of my lungs. "Parrish," I whispered, not sure what else to say. A million yeses wouldn't be enough.

Parrish licked his quivering lips. "I often wonder what I would be like if I knew sooner how much you loved me," he said. "Maybe I wouldn't have wandered through life for as long as I had, looking for purpose. Maybe we wouldn't have lost all the years we had. But I'm not going to regret anything, I swear. This one year with you wiped away every trace of bitterness and made up for all the lost time three times over. So, Levi Bartlet, I can only offer you all the years I've got left. Hopefully too many to count." He laughed, but it was a choked laughter as the tears shimmered in his eyes and rolled down his cheeks. "If you'll do me the honor of marrying me."

I discovered that the tickling sensation that was all over my face were the tears streaming from the corners of my eyes. Abruptly, I found myself tumbling down to my knees and whispering so many yeses that I couldn't count them. "I love you so much...love you so much...so much..." I was blurting out as he took my hand and clumsily slipped the ring on my finger. It was only with me that Parrish ever let himself be clumsy and vulnerable, and tears weren't strange to us when we were alone, either from joy or deep sadness or finishing a really good book. And now, as he cried and laughed, I found myself marveling at how absolutely gorgeous he was.

"You make me so happy all the time," he whispered, pulling me in and pressing his lips hard against mine. He kissed me, his hand on the back of my head, the other on my hip as the sunshine licked the back of my neck. And I kissed him back. I kissed my fiancé.

God, how lucky I was.

And how I loved him.

I wouldn't stop loving him so long as I breathed. Damn the whole world if it tried to stand in our way. But, another thought crossed my mind as our lips parted and I let my head rest on his shoulder, hugging him tightly. I thought, there couldn't be a soul on this planet who could stand in the way of the love we had for one another.

Nothing could be more right than what I felt for Parrish.

Now and forever.

The End

If you're curious about all the sweet and hot things Levi and Parrish did on their honeymoon, you should read the exclusive bonus chapter, which you can claim by visiting haydenhallwrites.com. Don't miss out on all that steam!

Acknowledgments

Let me preface this by thanking you for coming this far. My fingers are crossed that it wasn't the case of hate-reading every word of the book! In fact, I hope that, to some small extent, you were able to feel how proud I am of this story. It's the foundation of a great many things to come and it's thanks to you that those things will really happen. I appreciate your support immensely. It truly is *everything*.

But I can't let you close this book before I tell you this. *Destructive Relations* exists thanks to the many conversations, passing comments, and stubborn and relentless prodding done by my amazing friend, Sabrina Hutchinson. It must have been a full year since she floated the idea of me writing a story about stepbrothers. Really, you have her to thank for this, as well as for the fact that what you've read made any sense whatsoever. With the amount of changes I make in each book from the early drafts to the final story, Sabrina is the only person who can keep track of what's what and who's who. I sure as hell can't!

I'd also like to give the biggest shoutout to my partner, Xander, for keeping this show going from behind the scenes. His support is huge.

A million thanks to my ARC team. You are all wonderful. And to my small, dedicated street team. I will never be able to thank you enough for your help. And finally, thank you to everyone who's gotten in touch one way or another. Thanks for reading my stories, leaving reviews on Amazon (they are priceless), joining my mailing list, following me on Instagram, sending lovely messages, tagging me in your posts, recommending my books to other readers, and every other way in which you made my life better. Thank you.

Hayden

MORE STORIES FROM HAYDEN HALL

Rescued, a heartfelt standalone novel of emotional abuse and an unlikely HEA.

Frat Brats of Santa Barbara

The Fake Boyfriends Debacle

The Royal Roommate Disaster

The Wrong Twin Dilemma

The Bitter Rivals Fiasco

The Accidental Honeymoon Catastrophe

The Bedroom Coach Agreement

The Office Nemesis Calamity

About Hayden Hall

Gay. Sweet. Steamy.

Hayden Hall writes MM romance novels. He is a boyfriend, a globetrotter, and an avid romance reader.

Hayden's mission is to author a catalog of captivating and steamy MM romance novels which gather a devoted community around the Happily Ever Afters.

His stories are sweet with just the right amount of naughty. You can learn more about Hayden by visiting haydenhallwrites.com.

Printed in Great Britain
by Amazon